LETHAL GAME

Off The Grid: FBI Series #14

BARBARA FREETHY

Fog City Publishing

PRAISE FOR BARBARA FREETHY

"Grab a drink, find a comfortable reading nook, and get immersed in this fast paced, realistic, romantic thriller! 5 STARS!" *Perrin – Goodreads on Elusive Promise*

"Words cannot explain how phenomenal this book was. The characters are so believable and relatable. The twists and turns keep you on the edge of your seat and flying through the pages. This is one book you should be desperate to read." *Caroline - Goodreads on Ruthless Cross*

"Barbara Freethy is a master storyteller with a gift for spinning tales about ordinary people in extraordinary situations and drawing readers into their lives." — *Romance Reviews Today*

"Freethy (Silent Fall) has a gift for creating complex, appealing characters and emotionally involving, often suspenseful, sometimes magical stories." — *Library Journal on Suddenly One Summer*

Freethy hits the ground running as she kicks off another winning romantic suspense series...Freethy is at her prime with a superb combo of engaging characters and gripping plot." — *Publishers' Weekly on Silent Run*

"If you love nail-biting suspense and heartbreaking emotion, Silent Run belongs on the top of your to-be-bought list. I could not turn the pages fast enough." — *NYT Bestselling Author Mariah Stewart*

ALSO BY BARBARA FREETHY

OFF THE GRID: FBI SERIES

PERILOUS TRUST

RECKLESS WHISPER

DESPERATE PLAY

ELUSIVE PROMISE

DANGEROUS CHOICE

RUTHLESS CROSS

CRITICAL DOUBT

FEARLESS PURSUIT

DARING DECEPTION

RISKY BARGAIN

PERFECT TARGET

FATAL BETRAYAL

DEADLY TRAP

LETHAL GAME

SHATTERED TRUTH

Did you read the Lightning Strikes Series?

Lightning Strikes Trilogy

BEAUTIFUL STORM

LIGHTNING LINGERS

SUMMER RAIN

For a complete list of books, visit Barbara's Website!

LETHAL GAME

Alisa Hunt's quiet life takes a violent turn when she narrowly escapes a carjacking. But as the dust settles, she realizes she wasn't just a random target—someone wanted her dead, and the secrets she's uncovering may destroy everything she thought she knew about herself.

FBI agent Jason Colter is driven by revenge, relentlessly hunting the terrorist who shattered his life. When Alisa, a beautiful nurse, is caught in the crossfire, she may hold the key to bringing down the man he's been after. Together, they are drawn into a web of deception, danger, and a connection neither expected.

With a deadly conspiracy closing in and time running out, Alisa and Jason must confront not only their enemies, but also the explosive truths that bind them. Their survival depends on trusting each other—but with lives on the line and betrayals at every turn, will the truth save them or destroy them both?

LETHAL GAME

───────

For more information on Barbara Freethy's books, visit her website:
www.barbarafreethy.com

CHAPTER ONE

"This can't be about revenge, Jason," Flynn MacKenzie said as they met in the conference room before the briefing.

"It's about justice," Special Agent Jason Colter returned, meeting Flynn's gaze with an unapologetic look.

"Is it? Arseni Novikov killed your father."

"Along with thousands of other people."

"And he injured your partner."

"I don't need a recap," he said shortly. "What I need is a team to help me take Novikov down."

While he was officially assigned as a special agent to the LA Field Office of the FBI, because of security breaches the last time this particular Russian terrorist was on US soil, the director had moved the case to the elite task force run by Flynn, with Jason on temporary assignment.

He'd worked with Flynn several years earlier when he'd first joined the bureau. Flynn had been good then, and he was even better now with a top-notch team of experienced agents. He would need every one of them to catch one of the FBI's most wanted men. And despite Flynn's misgivings, he had no intention of sitting this one out.

He had been the one to receive the tip that Novikov was

back on U.S. soil. He was the one who knew more about Novikov than anyone. The only person who might have known more had been his father, who had spent thirty plus years chasing the terrorist—until he lost his life three years ago in an operation that was compromised by an internal leak. That leak was the reason this investigation now rested with Flynn's team.

"I just need to know where your head's at," Flynn pressed. "Emotion clouds judgement."

"I'm not known for my emotion," he said dryly. "Ask any woman I've dated in the last six years. My head is good. Now, can we get down to business? We don't have a minute to lose."

"My analysts have already been working since six a.m. I've briefed some of my senior-level agents. I'm going to bring them in now."

While Flynn called in members of his team, Jason turned on the monitor behind him and then clicked into his computer, bringing up several images, including one of Arseni Novikov's face. The silver-haired man with cold gray eyes and a mocking smile haunted his nightmares. Novikov was a man who believed himself to be invincible, and unfortunately, that had proved to be true. But that was going to change. Novikov was in LA, and he wasn't leaving this time—not alive, anyway.

Jason squared his shoulders as Flynn's team entered the conference room. Besides Flynn, he had also worked with Beck Murray, who was dark and unreadable, the perfect contrast to Flynn's blond and sunny look. The other two, a stunningly pretty blonde, who introduced herself as Savannah Kane, and a dark-haired, dark-eyed man named Nick Caruso, he didn't know.

After introductions, they sat down around the table, giving him their attention.

"As I'm sure you know by now," he said. "Arseni Novikov, who currently sits at number one on the FBI's most wanted list, arrived at LAX last night. The two pilots of the private plane who flew the nonstop flight from Warsaw to LAX were found dead in the cockpit. The plane's owner claims the plane was coming to LA to pick him up. There were no other passengers."

"Did anyone get off the plane alive?" Beck asked.

"There was no sign of anyone else in the security footage. Novikov vanished into the terminal. We're still piecing together where he went." Jason waved toward the monitor, which displayed an image of Novikov from three years ago, the last time he was in LA. "As a quick refresher: Born in Leningrad—now St. Petersburg—Novikov followed his father into the KGB. After the Soviet Union collapsed, he moved into the Bratva, the Russian Mafia. He later formed his own criminal enterprise, dabbling in mercenary and terrorist activities. He's known for aligning himself with extremist groups to destabilize governments, amass money, and gain power." Jason paused, ensuring their attention before continuing. "We need to find him fast. The only reason Novikov would risk coming back to US soil is for something big—something catastrophic."

"Have you identified potential targets?" Beck asked.

"The LA Book Festival on Saturday in Westwood. The global tech conference starts Monday in downtown LA, and the World Series is at Dodger Stadium on Monday as well. Those are all target-rich environments, but Novikov likes to be unpredictable."

"We'll be working with Homeland Security and local and state agencies to make the city as secure as possible," Flynn added. "But as Jason said, the sooner we find this guy, the better."

"Sounds like we have a lot of ground to cover," Nick commented.

"We do," he agreed. "We've been tracking previously known contacts. Last week, there was a message exchange between one of Novikov's top-level associates, Dominic Ilyin, and Novikov's former girlfriend, Tatiana Guseva, who runs a dance studio here in LA. Ilyin expressed concern about a rumor he'd heard that Tatiana had cancer. She confirmed the diagnosis and was afraid she wouldn't survive. Ilyin asked her if there was anything she needed, and she replied that hearing from an old friend was the best medicine. She could have been referring to Ilyin or suggesting Novikov should get in touch with her. It's a reach, but we'll need to get eyes on her."

"Would Novikov risk entering the US for an old girlfriend?" Savannah asked doubtfully.

He met her gaze. "I doubt she's the reason he came here, but he still might contact her. They haven't been together in at least ten years, but they grew up in the same town. They have a lot of shared history. We interrogated her after the courthouse explosion. She insisted she hadn't seen Novikov in years, and we couldn't find anything to negate her statement, but she's still someone to watch."

"Jason has provided us with a long list of Novikov's other contacts," Flynn added. "You'll find that information in the case file."

As Flynn gave further directions to the team about breaking down the workload, Jason glanced toward the glass door and saw a familiar figure standing outside. He wasn't surprised. Whenever Novikov showed up, Mick Hadley wasn't far behind.

Mick was of medium height, with a fit, muscular body, and a sharp, angular face. He was in his late fifties and had worked at the CIA for over thirty years. Mick and his father had spent many years trying to bring Novikov to justice. Since Mick was the one who had sent him the footage of Novikov getting off the plane, he was clearly still determined to take Novikov down.

When Flynn finished speaking, the team got up and headed out to the operations center to work while he and Flynn stayed behind to hear what Hadley had to say.

Mick entered the room, giving them both a brief smile. "Flynn, good to see you again."

"I hope it's good," Flynn said dryly. "But you and good don't always go together, Mick."

"We're on the same team," Mick said lightly, taking no offense. "Right, Jason?"

His father had never completely trusted Mick, and the few times he'd worked with the CIA agent, Jason had felt as if Mick had his own agenda. But in this circumstance, he felt like they were on the same team. "Right. Do you have additional information?"

"Novikov traveled to Belarus three times in the last two months. On one of those occasions, he met with Dominic Ilyin and Gregor Petron."

His gut tightened at that information. Ilyin was a notorious assassin, and Petron was an explosives expert and believed to be responsible for a bombing in France three months ago.

"There's been chatter that Novikov is assembling a team for a big project."

"Where are Ilyin and Petron now?"

"Petron has disappeared. He left his home a week ago. There's no evidence he's in the US, but we're looking for him. Dominic Ilyin was last seen in Zurich ten days ago, but he's also in the wind."

The conference door opened, and a young man asked to speak to Flynn. As Flynn stepped out of the room, he said, "Is there anything unofficial you want to share now that it's just the two of us, Mick?"

"I've told you everything I know, Jason. But I'm concerned about information getting compromised, as it did three years ago."

"None of the people who worked that case will be involved this time around," he assured Mick. "We're going to keep the information as tight as we can by using Flynn's team."

"But things have a way of leaking out, especially when the leaks are coming from the inside. I still wonder if your father had any idea who sold him out."

His lips tightened. That question had haunted him for three years, but he still had no answers. "I wonder the same thing, but it doesn't matter anymore. Leak or no leak, Novikov killed my father and many other people. He's not going to get away this time."

"You're going to finish what your father started," Mick said with a nod. "I think he'd like that. Drew was very proud of you for following in his footsteps. He told me you have his same dogged determination and willingness to put the job above everything else."

He didn't want to think about his father's legacy. Not now. Every time he did, the sense of unfinished business gnawed at him like a wound that refused to heal. "It's important work," he said, knowing he'd also used his work to keep himself too busy to think about the loss of his dad, about the fact that he was alone now, really alone...both parents gone, no siblings to remember the good old days. Not that they had all been good.

"I'm going to help you all I can," Mick said. "While I respect Flynn, I'd like to keep a private channel open with you because you're the one person I know I can trust."

"Of course."

"Good. I'll see you later."

He was almost to the door when Flynn returned. "You're leaving?" Flynn asked.

"Yes, but I'm sure we'll meet again soon," Mick replied as he slid past Flynn and left the room.

"Did he say anything else?" Flynn asked.

"Only that he was concerned about leaks."

"There won't be any from my team. I don't know how well you know Hadley, but it's wise to weigh anything he says against facts you already know. I'm not saying he's working against us, but in my experience, Hadley usually has his own agenda."

"I don't disagree, but so far, he's given us the biggest lead we have." Trust wasn't something he could afford to give freely—not to Flynn, not to Mick. But right now, they were his best shot at taking down Novikov.

The conference room door reopened, and Savannah entered with a gleam in her eyes. "Good news. We picked up Novikov leaving the airport in a rideshare. The driver dropped him off in front of a fast-food restaurant in Torrance, but he didn't enter the restaurant. Instead, he got into a car parked in the lot. There was another individual behind the wheel. We've been tracking the license plate through traffic cams, and it was picked up ten minutes ago at a light in West LA. We couldn't tell if Novikov was still in the car, but it's worth checking out. The vehicle turned into the parking lot at the Wexford University Medical Center."

His pulse jumped at the speed in which they'd gotten another clue. "That's great, Savannah. Well done."

"We caught a break. Shall I drive?" she asked.

"As long as you drive fast."

"I always do."

———

Wexford University Medical Center had been Alisa Hunt's second home since she'd started working there as a nurse three years ago, but today was different because the patient in front of her was her mother. Her mom had been plagued by a mysterious illness that had begun a week ago and had taken a turn for the worse on Monday when her father had brought her into the ER just after seven a.m. It was now Wednesday, and her mother was doing better after forty-eight hours of IV fluids. She was looking much more like her old self, albeit a tired, paler version of that self.

She sat down on the side of the bed, giving her mom a smile. "You're doing good today."

"I feel better, Alisa. I'm ready to go home."

"Probably tomorrow," she said, knowing Dr. Grayson was still concerned they hadn't found a diagnosis for her mother's condition. "Where's Dad?"

Her mother averted her gaze, picking at a loose thread on the blanket covering her legs.

"Mom?" she questioned in concern.

She hadn't seen her father since yesterday when he'd gone home for a break. His continued absence concerned her.

"Your father had to go somewhere for a day or two," her mother said finally, giving her a tired look. "His friend is ill, and now that I'm feeling better, I told him he should go and say his goodbyes. It might be his only chance."

"Who are you talking about?" she asked in surprise.

"Greg. Greg Palmer," she said. "He was a childhood friend of your father's."

"I've never heard that name."

"I'm sure you have at some point. He and your father grew up on the same block."

"Dad told me he doesn't talk to anyone from his childhood, and he surely hasn't seen this guy in years. Why would he leave now while you're in the hospital?"

"I told you. Greg is very sick, and your dad has something he needs to say to him. He'll be back soon."

"How soon? Tonight? Tomorrow?"

"I don't know," her mother said, irritation moving through her brown eyes. "Please, just let it be, Alisa. It doesn't bother me, so it shouldn't bother you. I'm doing well. Dr. Grayson said it's amazing how quickly I've recovered. You need to stop worrying about me."

Her mother had certainly gotten better in the two days she'd been in the hospital. There was more color in her cheeks, although her brown hair had thinned and grayed in the past week. She'd been feeling off for a while, before things had gotten bad enough for her to come to the hospital. She should be grateful her mom was getting back to normal, but the lack of a clear diagnosis troubled her.

"Why don't you go home, Alisa? You must be tired after

working all day. Or better yet, why don't you call Tim and go to dinner with him, take a break from all this?"

"Tim is obsessed with his fantasy football league." She felt disheartened that the guy she'd been seeing for the past month hadn't been able to come to the hospital the last two days. If the situation were reversed, she would have made time for him. "I'll just sit with you for a while."

Her mother shook her head. "You've been with me every minute you can spare since I got here, and for a week before that. I don't need you by my bedside anymore. I'm okay."

"I am glad you're better. I just wish Dad was here to stay with you. I don't want to leave you alone. I'm going to call him."

"No," her mother said with more force in her voice than she'd shown in days. "Your father will be back as soon as he can. I don't want you to pressure him."

"I don't understand."

"You don't have to understand, because I do."

As their gazes clung together, Alisa was reminded of other moments when she'd questioned something and had been met with the same stubborn glint in her mother's eyes. But she didn't need to add stress by arguing with her. If she was okay with it, then she'd have to get on board. But she still might give her father a call. She'd see how her mother did tonight. Glancing at her watch, she realized it was almost six. "You should get your dinner soon," she said. "I can help you with that."

"I feel strong enough to eat on my own, not that I'm at all hungry."

"That's why you need someone to encourage you."

Her mother gave her a small smile. "All your nursing friends have taken excellent care of me. Go home. And don't worry about me being alone. Henry is going to stop by to visit. It's all good. I wish you could believe that."

"I'm trying. You just gave me a big scare."

"I know. And you're a wonderful daughter. But I'm all right."

She got up from the bed. "I'll call you later tonight."

"I'll probably be asleep, so don't worry if I don't answer. Now, give me a kiss, and I'll see you in the morning."

She leaned over and pressed a light kiss on her mother's cool cheek, which thankfully wasn't as cold as it had once been. Maybe this nightmare would be over soon.

As she turned to leave, Henry Cavendish, a longtime friend of her parents, entered the room. Henry was the director of the oncology research center at Wexford University, and his lab was in the building next to the hospital. Henry was one of the first people to encourage her to go into nursing when she'd been trying to figure out what to do with her life. After she'd graduated, he'd helped her get her current job. Since her mom had gotten ill, both she and her father had leaned on him for advice. But Henry had not been able to offer an explanation, either.

A tall, thin man with dark hair, graying at his temples and also his sideburns, Henry wore glasses and always seemed like someone who needed to get out in the sun more. His skin was extremely pale. But then, he spent a lot of time overseeing the groundbreaking research being done in his lab.

In one hand, he held a vase of flowers, while in the other hand was a small white bag.

"Hello, Alisa," he said, giving her a smile before he turned to her mother. "Pamela, I hear you're doing better."

"I'm on the road to recovery," her mother said.

"That's excellent news. I brought flowers to brighten your room." He paused, his gaze coming to rest on the vase next to her bed. "I guess I wasn't the only one who had that idea."

"I don't know who those are from," her mother said. "I woke up and there they were. I think Dan might have sent them."

"I'll put yours on the dresser," Alisa told Henry, taking the vase out of his hand and setting it on the dresser by the window.

"I also brought you something to tempt your appetite, Pamela." Henry handed her mother the bag. "Chocolates from your favorite place."

"I can't believe you went all the way to Claire's to get these," her mother said as she peeked into the bag. She gave him a big smile. "This is so thoughtful, Henry. I'm going to love them later, but I haven't had much of an appetite today."

"Hopefully, it will be back soon." He put his hand on her shoulder as he finished talking. "We've all been anxious about you, Pamela."

"I appreciate the concern," her mother replied.

"You must be happy to see your mother so improved, Alisa."

"I am. I just wish we knew what caused her symptoms," she replied.

"We're not getting into that discussion right now," her mother said. "I don't want to think about it anymore tonight. I want to just chat, and you can tell me about your work, Henry. Alisa is going home now." Her mother gave her a pointed look. "Right?"

"I guess," she muttered as Henry pulled a chair closer to the bed and sat down. At least her mother wouldn't be alone, and she was pretty exhausted and ready to go home.

"By the way, Alisa," Henry said as she turned to go. "Do you know what's happening downstairs? I saw a lot of security gathered in the lobby. Is there a patient of importance?"

"Not that I'm aware of. Maybe they just came in. I'll call you later, Mom. And Henry, make sure she eats something when dinner comes."

"I will," he said with a reassuring smile. "Don't worry. Your mother is in good hands."

Her mother should have been in her father's good hands, but Henry wasn't a bad backup.

After leaving the room, Alisa went downstairs to the nurse's lounge and opened her locker, putting a sweater on over her blue scrubs and then grabbing her large tote bag. She set it down on a table in the center of the room and took out her phone.

She hadn't heard from Tim since last night, and she was more than a little annoyed. His absence during this crisis in her life had definitely made her question their relationship, if she could even call it that. She sent him a text with a quick update on her mom's condition and then stuck her phone back in her bag and headed out of the lounge.

When she got to the lobby, she saw a security guard talking to her friend Robin, who was working at the information desk. As he left, she walked up to the counter, wanting to make sure she wasn't leaving her mother alone in the hospital with some situation going on. "What was that about, Robin?" she asked. "There seems to be a lot of security in the hospital tonight."

"They're looking for some guy," Robin said. "But I haven't seen him walk past my desk, not that I see everyone, but I'm usually pretty observant."

"Did they say why they're looking for him?"

"No, they did not, and I asked—twice. Security told me there was no reason for concern. It was just someone they wanted to speak to."

She felt uneasy about Robin's answer, but the guard was no longer in sight, and everything seemed to be normal in the lobby, with visitors coming in and out, heading for the bank of elevators behind her or to the cafeteria or gift shop. "Okay," she said, stepping away from the desk.

It had been a long couple of days, and she didn't need to manufacture more problems to worry about. She had enough to deal with. If there was any kind of security breach, the hospital would be on lockdown. Whatever was going on had to be fairly minor.

When she left the building, she felt immediately better, the crisp, cool air of mid-October making it easier to breathe. Fall was one of her favorite times of the year in Southern California. The chillier fall evenings were a pleasant respite from the unrelenting heat of summer, but today, the dark shadows seemed stressful, the turbulence in her life exacerbated by a sense of foreboding she couldn't explain. Her mother's mysterious illness and her father's unexplained trip felt like the tip of an iceberg, and she had no idea what kind of devastation lay ahead.

Or maybe she was letting her imagination get the best of her.

But she couldn't shake her dark thoughts as she entered the parking structure and went down the stairs to the bottom level where the employees parked.

There was no one around, and as she walked down the row of vehicles, she opened her bag and fished inside for her car keys. Her fingers brushed against everything—her phone, her wallet, a packet of tissues—but not her keys. She felt an odd sense of desperation. She just needed to get home, make some dinner, pour herself a glass of wine, and take a deep breath. Everything would be fine.

A chill ran down her spine as she heard footsteps behind her.

As she turned her head, she saw a tall man running toward her. He wore a black sweatshirt with a hood pulled up over his head and dark glasses covering his eyes, despite the dim light in the parking garage.

Her keys—where were her damn keys? She frantically searched her bag, but her fingers were trembling now.

If she couldn't find her keys, she couldn't get in her car.

She was out of time.

In one quick motion, he grabbed her arm and shoved her against her car. The metal was cold and unforgiving against her back as she tried to push him off, but he was too strong. She screamed with terror, her mind racing as adrenaline pumped through her veins. She had to think. She had to do something...

CHAPTER TWO

Alisa screamed as she struggled to get free.

"Keys," the man ordered in a low, gruff voice.

"I—I can't find them." She dug into her purse again.

He yanked the bag out of her hand, dumped everything on the ground, then grabbed her keys and flipped the locks.

Her breath caught in her throat. Her car didn't matter—nothing did—except getting away. The moment he took his eyes off her, she bolted.

She didn't care about her car. He could have it.

She had barely taken two steps when he grabbed her arm and dragged her back to her car. If she got into the car, she was dead. This was her only chance to survive. She had to escape now, so she kicked and screamed as hard as she could until he put a gun to her head, and she froze.

"Get in the car," he commanded.

There was something foreign to his voice. He didn't sound like he was from LA.

"Why? Just take the car and go. You don't need me."

"Shut up."

Despite his order, she screamed again and used all her energy to push him away from her. But as she turned away, his gun came down on the back of her head, knocking her to the ground.

Her world exploded, her vision blurring, her knees buckling under her. Her thoughts scattered as pain ricocheted behind her eyes. Her knees took the brunt of her fall, but all too soon, he was hauling her to her feet.

She could barely focus, but her instinct was to fight. As he pulled her toward the car, she used her one free hand to grab for the bumper. She had just wrapped her fingers around the metal when he yanked her away so hard, that the metal cut her hand. More pain rocketed through her body.

He had the car door open now, and in another minute, he was going to shove her into the backseat.

"Please, just take the car and leave me here," she begged.

"Shut up," he repeated.

"Let her go!" someone yelled.

To her amazement, she saw a man running toward them. He was young and athletic, wearing black pants and a dark wind-breaker...and he had a gun.

She gasped at that fact, and her lack of focus allowed her attacker to pull her to her feet, using her as a shield in front of him. He had one arm wrapped around her neck, the other holding a gun pressed against her throbbing temple.

"Stop. I'll kill her," her attacker warned.

The man stopped, but he didn't lower his weapon. She had no idea who he was. He wasn't wearing a uniform. He wasn't hospital security. But he was here, and that was all that mattered.

"I said let her go," the man repeated. "You're not getting out of here."

The arm around her neck tightened as her attacker debated his options.

There were more footsteps coming from the other direction. A woman appeared. She was blonde and wearing gray slacks and a black jacket. She also pulled out a weapon.

"Drop the gun," she ordered. "There's nowhere for you to go."

"Do it," the other man said forcefully. "Now."

She wasn't sure her attacker was going to let her go. If he killed her, they'd kill him. That wouldn't be good for him, but it also wouldn't be good for her. She couldn't just stand by and let him decide for both of them.

His uncertainty allowed his grip on her to ease, and she saw her opening.

She jammed her elbow into his midsection and spun free of his grip.

His gun went off.

Then another blast rocked the air as she dropped to the ground, the glass from the car window next to her shattering all over her.

She covered her head with her hands.

Someone else was yelling in pain, someone besides her.

And then the man who had come to her rescue squatted down in front of her. "You're safe," he told her, putting his hand on her arm.

Alisa blinked, still in shock. Her head pounded, her body ached, and her mind struggled to catch up with what had just happened. She stared at him in confusion. His eyes were so blue, they were almost shocking. "Who—who are you?"

"Jason Colter, FBI."

"FBI?" she stuttered. "Why are you here?"

"We heard you scream."

She licked her lips, looking over her shoulder to see the blonde woman standing over her attacker, who was now face-down on the ground, his hands tied behind his back, blood coming from his shoulder. "Did you shoot him?"

"Yes. But he'll live." As he finished speaking, security guards and police flooded the garage.

"Your hand is bleeding," he said, his sharp blue gaze sweeping across her face and body.

"I cut it on the bumper," she said dully.

"Are you hurt anywhere else?"

"My head. He hit me with his gun. He was trying to get me in the car. He got my keys. I don't understand why he didn't just take the car and go."

The same question moved through the agent's eyes as he glanced away from her toward her assailant. "We'll figure it out. Can you stand up?"

"I think so." He got to his feet, then held out his hand.

She put her uninjured hand in his as he helped her to her feet. She winced as more pain ran through her head, and she couldn't seem to let go of his hand. "Sorry, I'm a little shaky."

"We're going to get you to the hospital so you can be examined and treated. Did the man say anything to you?"

"He just told me to get in the car. He had an accent." She paused, looking at her attacker, who was being loaded onto a gurney. "Do you know who he is? Is he the person security was looking for earlier?"

"How do you know about that?"

"I'm a nurse. I heard they were looking for someone."

"He's not who we were looking for, but hopefully, he'll lead us to that person."

"I don't understand." She felt suddenly dizzy and tightened her grip on his hand. But the garage was spinning in front of her, and as she lost her balance, she stumbled against him.

He wrapped his arms around her. "You're okay," he said.

"I don't think I am." Her eyes closed, and the world faded away.

———

Alisa woke up in the ER to bright lights and the sound of her heartbeat on the monitor next to her. She squinted as she looked into the concerned face of ER nurse Georgia Fulton, who was also one of her friends and someone she'd worked alongside during her stint in the ER. Georgia had sandy brown hair and brown eyes that were filled with concern.

"It's about time, Alisa," Georgia told her, relief flooding her gaze.

"What happened?"

"Apparently, someone tried to carjack you in the garage. After you were rescued, you passed out."

Her memories came flooding back. "I hoped that was a nightmare."

"I'm sure it was a nightmare," Georgia said tersely as she checked her pulse. "Your hand needs stitches, by the way. I've cleaned the cut, but Dr. Lawson will be in shortly to take care of that. You also have a large bump on the back of your head, so I need to ask you a few questions. Do you know your name?"

"Alisa Hunt."

"How old are you?"

"Twenty-eight," she said with a sigh. "I'm fine, Georgia."

Her friend ignored her. "Where do you live?"

"Santa Monica."

She squinted again as Georgia checked her eyes with a bright light. "Can you follow my finger with your eyes?" Georgia asked.

"Yes," she said as she completed the test. "I just have a terrible headache."

"You were out for about ten minutes, according to the orderly who brought you in. That's long enough for Dr. Lawson to order a CT scan."

She hated all the fuss. She was a much better nurse than patient. But her head was throbbing, and despite her desire for this to all be over, she didn't have the energy to get to her feet. She also knew the protocol for a concussion, and she would have to follow it.

"There's an FBI agent outside who wants to talk to you," Georgia added. "I told him he'd have to wait."

"Does he have gorgeous blue eyes and dark hair?" she asked,

still trying to remember what was real and what was a dream. Her reality seemed very muddled at the moment.

"Yes," Georgia said, smiling for the first time. "And a very attractive face."

"He saved my life."

Georgia's expression grew more serious as she put a comforting hand on her shoulder. "I'm so glad he did."

"Me, too."

Georgia cleared her throat as they shared an emotional look. "I need to get you to radiology. Do you want me to call anyone while you're having your test? I know your mom is upstairs."

"I don't want her to know anything about this. The last thing she needs is stress."

"What about your dad? Or Tim?"

She hesitated, then shook her head. Tim had been distant, unreliable, and more obsessed with his fantasy football league than with showing up when she needed him most.

And her dad...She wanted to speak to her father, but not now, and not about herself.

"I don't need you to call anyone," she said.

"All right. Then let's get you checked out."

It was almost two hours later before she was finished with tests and treatment. The CT scan had shown no signs of a concussion. The cut on her hand hadn't required too many stitches, and while still painful, it would eventually be fine. She was instructed to rest for the next forty-eight hours, hydrate, and call if she became nauseous or disoriented.

She slid off the exam table and put her sweater back on, seeing the blood on her sleeve that had come from the cut on her hand. The sight of that blood made her a little shaky, and she sat down in the chair to wait for Georgia to get a wheelchair to take her out to the lobby.

A moment later, the door opened. It wasn't Georgia; it was the man who'd rescued her, his eyes just as blue and compelling as she remembered. But now she noticed more details about his very handsome face, from his firm jaw to his beautifully sculpted features, tan skin, and sexy mouth. His brown hair was thick and wavy and a little mussed. He was tall and exuded power and confidence. She was more than a little grateful he was the one who'd heard her scream because he hadn't hesitated to jump into action, to put his own life on the line for a total stranger.

She got to her feet. "I forget your name."

"Jason Colter. And you're Alisa Hunt. How are you feeling?"

"Like someone hit me in the head with the butt of a gun; a sentence I never thought would come out of my mouth."

A small smile parted his lips. "That sounds about right. Concussion?"

"Just a nasty headache. Thank you for saving me. I don't know what would have happened if you hadn't come when you did—if you hadn't shot him." As she thought about those moments in the garage, a knot grew in her throat and moisture filled her eyes. She bit down on her lip, and his gaze softened.

"Don't think about what might have happened," he said. "You're safe now. That's all that matters."

"I almost wasn't safe." She drew in a strangled breath. "I could have died tonight." She blinked back a tear. "Sorry, I suddenly feel emotional."

"That's not surprising. The adrenaline is wearing off."

"I guess." As she looked at him, she remembered being in his arms, feeling safe in his embrace. She kind of wished she was there now, feeling protected, rather than chilled and alone.

"Why don't you sit down?" he suggested, tipping his head to the chair behind her. "You look a little shaky."

She couldn't say no, because if she didn't sit, she was probably going to either throw herself into his arms or pass out again. She took a seat as he sat down in the chair next to her.

"Do you mind if I ask you a few questions?" he asked.

"No. Go ahead."

"Can you tell me what happened when you got to the garage, Alisa?"

"I didn't see anyone around when I came down the stairs. As I got close to my car, I started looking in my bag for my keys, and I got a bad feeling. Then I heard footsteps. I turned around, and the man rushed toward me. He shoved me against the car and demanded my keys. He got impatient when I couldn't locate them, and he dumped everything from my purse on the ground." She realized she had no idea where her bag was. "Where are my things?"

"Your belongings were given to the nurse at the ER desk. She said she would get your bag to you."

"Oh, okay."

"Why were you struggling with him if he just wanted your keys?"

"He didn't just want the keys. He tried to shove me into the car. I told him to take the car and go. But he insisted I get in, and I knew if I went with him, I probably wasn't going to be found alive, so I tried everything I could to stop him from putting me in the car."

His gaze filled with respect. "Good for you."

"But if you hadn't come when you did..." She shuddered again as she thought of all the horrific things that could have happened to her.

"You were very courageous to fight the way you did, Alisa."

She was touched by his words, by the admiration in his blue eyes. Another odd shiver ran down her spine as their gazes held. "I think you're giving me too much credit," she said.

"I'm not. Did he say anything to you?"

"He just told me to get in the car and shut up. It sounded like he had an accent. You must know who he is by now. Where is he? Is he in jail?"

"He's in surgery. His name is Victor Kashin. Does that name ring a bell to you?"

"No, but I don't know why it would. I've never seen him before. Is he a...criminal?" she finished, not wanting to say predator or rapist because that just made the memories worse.

"I haven't had time to find out everything about him, but I will."

"Why do you think he was trying to take me with him?"

"I don't know. It's possible he wanted to use you as a cover. We were looking for the vehicle he drove into the parking lot earlier in the day. We didn't know who the driver was until now. He must have seen the increased security and decided to switch cars and grab someone else to make him look like part of a couple."

She thought about his answer. "Would he have let me go after he got away? If I had gotten in the car?"

Jason shrugged. "It's better not to speculate."

He was probably right, but she couldn't help herself. "If he was driving the vehicle you were looking for, then he must be connected to your person of interest?"

"Possibly."

"Can you tell me more?"

"I can't."

"You can't or you won't?" she asked.

"Both," he said bluntly. "Sorry."

She frowned. "Well, can you tell me if this other person is going to be a threat to me?"

"I believe you were in the wrong place at the wrong time. He needed a vehicle, and you crossed his path."

"So, I was just unlucky."

"But lucky in the end," he reminded her.

"This man you're looking for must be dangerous if the FBI is involved. Is it possible he's still in the hospital? My mother is a patient upstairs, and if something is going on in the building, I need to get up there as soon as possible."

"There's nothing going on. The building was cleared."

"Then why are you still here?"

"I wanted to talk to you, to make sure you were all right."

She knew he was only talking to her as an FBI agent to a

victim, but it still felt nice to have someone who wanted to make sure she was okay.

He reached into his pocket and handed her a business card with a handwritten phone number on it. "This is my personal cell phone, Alisa. If you remember anything else about the attack, please call me."

"I've told you everything I know."

"Sometimes minor details come back later when you've recovered." He stood up. "Take care."

"I'll try."

As Jason left, she stared down at his card, at his phone number. Of course, she'd never use it...but it was still nice to know she could. She was feeling attached to him, probably because he'd saved her life.

The door opened again, and her pulse leapt, but it was Georgia bringing in a wheelchair along with her bag.

"You got my purse. Thank you."

"No problem. I called Carrie to come and get you. She's waiting in the lobby. You can get your car tomorrow. I don't think you should drive tonight."

"I agree." She didn't want to go into the garage again or drive home with a sharp pain in her head. "I'm just sorry Carrie had to come back to get me." Carrie was a pediatric nurse and lived in her apartment building. They had been friends since they'd both started working at Wexford three years ago.

She felt strange getting into the wheelchair. She was used to being the nurse and not the patient, but it was hospital protocol.

Georgia wheeled her out to the ER lobby. Carrie, a fair-skinned, freckled redhead, was standing by the front desk, wearing jeans and a sweatshirt, her hair pulled up in a ponytail. They'd worked the day shift together, and it was now after nine. But Carrie had jumped into her car as soon as Georgia called. Carrie was a good friend.

"I heard what happened," Carrie said with concern in her gaze. "Are you all right?"

"I will be. I just want to go home. Thanks for coming to get me."

"Of course. I was happy to do it. I'm parked right outside the door."

"Great." As she got up, she smiled at Georgia. "Thanks for taking care of me."

"Rest and hydrate."

"I will. I know the drill."

Carrie stayed close as they walked out of the hospital. As she got into the car, she couldn't help looking at the big, shadowy parking structure in the distance and thinking about how close she'd come to losing her life.

"Are you really okay?" Carrie asked, shooting her a worried look.

She was happy to have her dark thoughts interrupted. "I will be."

"Do you want to talk about what happened?"

"I don't. Is that okay?"

"Of course. I'm sure you just want to forget it."

"That's exactly what I want to do."

"How about food? I'd offer to feed you, but my refrigerator is bare. Should we pick something up?"

"I'm not hungry. And I have food in my fridge, if that changes."

"All right."

The ride to their apartment building in Santa Monica took only ten minutes. She'd picked the location based on the easy commute. Traffic in LA could be bad at any time of the day.

Carrie lived with her boyfriend, Ray, in a two-bedroom apartment on the second floor, while she was on the third floor in a studio. After being with people all day, every day, she enjoyed having her own space, even if it was small. One day, she'd get a one-bedroom, but she had student loans to pay off first.

After parking in the garage, they walked to the elevator together, and she was grateful for Carrie's presence, fighting the urge to grab her friend's hand. She didn't think she was disguising her fear very well because Carrie gave her a sharp look when they got in the elevator.

"You're really spooked, aren't you?" she asked as the doors closed. "I should have parked in front of the building."

"No. I'm going to have to get over my fear at some point. I have to park at the hospital. I have to park here. I can't avoid garages forever."

"Maybe not forever, but for now. I'm going to go with you to your apartment and get you settled, and then I'll go down to my place," Carrie said. "Don't argue. Otherwise, I'll stay all night."

She gave her a weak smile. "I wasn't going to argue. Thank you."

A moment later, the doors opened. There were four apartments on her floor, and everything was quiet, as it usually was. A lot of nurses and medical students lived in the building and when they weren't working long shifts, they were often sleeping.

As she reached into her bag for her keys, her hand shook once more. And the keys slipped from her grasp again. "Dammit," she swore, feeling the taste of metal in her mouth as her panic increased.

"Do you want help?" Carrie asked.

"No," she said through tight lips. She finally pulled the keys out of her bag and inserted her apartment key into the door. As she did so, she couldn't help thinking about the man whose hand had held these keys just a few hours ago.

Her fingers were shaking so badly she could barely turn the key, but finally, the lock clicked. She turned the knob and practically fell into her apartment. She took several deep breaths and then set her keys and bag on the small table by her kitchenette.

As she turned around, she saw the look on Carrie's face. "He wanted my keys," she said, drawing in another hard breath. "I couldn't find them fast enough. He grabbed the bag and dumped everything on the ground and then he put his hands on the keys."

"I'm so sorry, Alisa. You must have been terrified."

"I was, but it's over. And it feels good to be home."

She'd been thinking her apartment was way too small, but now it felt comforting to have no other rooms to wonder if someone was hiding somewhere. She could see everything, including inside her bathroom and closet because both doors were open. She needed to relax. Her attacker hadn't gotten her keys or her ID, and he was in the hospital in surgery. He wasn't coming after her. He didn't need her or her car anymore.

"Why don't you sit down, and I'll make you some tea?" Carrie suggested.

"I don't need tea. I just want to watch some mindless television. Go home, Carrie. You have to get up early for work, and I'm fine."

"Are you sure?"

"Positive."

"Okay, but I'll keep my phone on. If you need anything, even if it's just someone to watch a stupid movie with, call me."

She gave Carrie a hug. "You're a good friend. Thank you." She walked her to the door, and after Carrie left, she turned the dead bolt.

Then she grabbed her phone out of her bag, trying not to look at her keys, which somehow were still disturbing to her. Taking her phone to the bed, she sat down, comforted by the pillowy softness surrounding her. Her apartment wasn't much, but her bed was a comfortable haven, and she could finally let go of her stress.

She checked her messages. There was nothing from her mother or father or anyone at the hospital regarding her mother's condition, which was good. But she still felt very much alone. She wanted to call her mother and tell her what had happened, but she couldn't do that. Her dad, however...

She impulsively punched in his number and waited for the ring, but it never came. Nor was there an option to leave a voicemail. She tried again. Same result. Her body tightened once more. She sent a text message to her dad's number. A moment later, it came back as undeliverable.

What the hell was going on? Had her father changed his number? Had his phone been disconnected?

She tried calling several more times, but nothing changed. Something was wrong, and she didn't know what to do about it.

Debating her options, she punched in Tim's number. It rang several times and went to voicemail. Instead of leaving a message, she sent him a text: *Terrible night tonight. Someone tried to kidnap me from the parking garage. I'm okay but I cut my hand, and I'm really upset. Please call me. I need to talk to you.*

She set her phone on the bed, waiting for him to text her back.

As the minutes ticked by, her mind turned to the man who'd saved her life. She wished he was still around. The only time she'd felt safe tonight had been with him.

But she'd probably never see him again. He was an FBI agent, and it was crazy that their paths had crossed at all. It was doubtful they'd cross again. They already had her attacker in custody, and they didn't need her to ID him. Although, she might have to talk to the FBI again when they charged him. Hopefully, he'd go to jail. And she wouldn't have to worry about him ever coming back into her life.

She picked up her phone again, wondering why Tim hadn't replied. But was it really a surprise? Things had been off with him since her mom got sick. Tim was a fun-loving guy who wasn't worth much in a crisis. She really didn't need any more information than that to know he wasn't the guy for her. But dealing with a breakup conversation was more than she could handle. Setting down the phone, she laid back and closed her eyes.

But with her eyes closed, the feeling of terror came back, and she immediately opened her eyes again. It was going to be a long night.

CHAPTER THREE

Alisa barely slept. And when the sun rose on Thursday morning, she was relieved she'd made it through the night.

Reaching for her phone, she saw a message from Tim: *I can't believe what happened to you! Glad you're okay. Will check in later.*

Seriously? She texted back. *Can't believe that's all you have to say. Don't bother checking in. We're done.*

There was no reply. He'd probably been done days ago.

As she scrolled through her messages, she saw concerned texts from nursing friends, which made her feel better. Rolling out of bed, she walked to the window to open the blinds. It was a sunny day, and it almost made her feel like last night had just been a nightmare, but her aching head and stinging hand were impossible to ignore. She could have been killed last night, and that thought made her shudder again. But she'd survived, and today was a new day. She needed to stop looking back and move forward.

She put a baggie over the bandage on her hand so she could take a shower. After that, she got dressed and called for a rideshare.

When her ride pulled up in front of the hospital, she couldn't bring herself to look at the parking garage. Entering the hospital, however, felt like going into her second home, and she tried to hang on to that positive feeling as she made her way upstairs to her mother's room.

She opened the door with a smile on her face, which immediately faded when she saw her mother was asleep. As she neared the bed, she was stunned by her mother's pallor. Her face was white, and when she touched her hand, it was cold again.

Checking her vitals, she saw her mother's respirations and heart rate were quite low. She felt a rush of fear. She'd seen patients who looked like this before, and it was never good.

The door opened and Dr. Mitchell Grayson walked in. He was in his early sixties with gray hair and kind brown eyes. He was accompanied by a nurse she didn't know, except that her name was Shannon, and she'd started working at the hospital a few days earlier.

"I'm glad you're here, Alisa," Dr. Grayson said, a somber tone in his voice. "Your mother's condition has deteriorated. She's having trouble staying awake. She can't keep food down, and her respiration is shallow."

"What happened? She was doing so well last night."

"I don't know, but I've ordered more tests. Shannon will take some blood now. Hopefully, it will give us insight into what's changed in the past twelve hours."

"I don't understand. She was practically back to her old self last night. When did things change? Why didn't someone call me?"

"Her vitals were stable until about an hour ago," the doctor replied. "We're going to figure this out, Alisa."

"Are we? Do you think we should bring in some other doctors to consult?" She didn't care if her question offended him. She needed answers.

"I already put in a call to someone I think can help. He'll get back to me soon. He's in surgery this morning." He gave her an empathetic look. "I know you're frustrated, but I want you to know that I'm not going to stop looking for a diagnosis or a treatment plan. In fact, I'd like to send her for an MRI scan of the brain. I don't want to leave any stones unturned."

She felt somewhat comforted by his words, but she needed results more than comfort. As Shannon finished taking her mother's blood, her mom stirred and grimaced. She moved back to the bed and placed her hand over her mother's.

"Mom," she said gently, but loud enough to rouse her. "Mom," she repeated.

"It's okay if she rests," Dr. Grayson said. "We'll get the blood work to the lab, and then Shannon will take your mom downstairs for the MRI."

"All right. I'll stay with her until then."

As they left the room, she looked back at her mom, whose eyes were still closed. "You're going to be okay, Mom. The doctor just wants to run a few more tests. Hang in there for a while longer."

Her mother's eyelids flickered and then slowly opened. There was confusion in her gaze.

"Alisa?" she said, her voice weak and raspy.

"I'm here. You aren't feeling too good, are you?"

Fear and worry entered her mother's gaze. "No. Something is wrong. I think you should go somewhere, Alisa. I don't want you to stand by my bedside and watch me—"

"I'm not going anywhere," she said fiercely, refusing to let her mother finish that sentence. "And I am not giving up, Mom. We will figure this out."

"I still want you to leave. I want to be alone. I don't want you here."

There was a somewhat desperate note to her voice now that Alisa didn't understand.

"I'm not leaving. You're my mother. You've always been there for me, and I'll be there for you." She paused. "Especially since Dad isn't here. I tried calling him. His phone isn't working. Don't you think that's odd?"

"He said his phone was breaking. Don't worry, Alisa. He'll be in touch."

"I don't want to wait for him to get in touch," she said with annoyance. "He should be here with you. I don't understand why he's not."

"I know you don't. I wish I could explain."

She was even more confused by her mother's words. "What do you mean? Why can't you explain?"

"Because I can't. But he's a good man, and I love him."

She wanted to believe her father was a good man because she loved him, too. But she was also angry with him.

Her mother drew in a ragged breath. "I'm so tired. Sometimes when I close my eyes, I'm not sure I'll have the energy to open them again. And then I get a sharp pain in my stomach. It takes my breath away."

"The nurse will take you down to radiology in a few minutes for an MRI scan. I'm going to wait with you until then, and I'll be here when you're done."

Her mother's fingers curled around hers. "I love you, Alisa. I want you to be safe. And that means you need to go. Take a vacation. Go to Fiji. Remember our vacation there? What did you say to me?"

"That it felt like we were at the other end of the world, very far from our lives."

"That's where I want you to be, sitting on a sandy beach, the sun warm on your face, a cold drink by your side, the blue sea stretching out in front of you. Maybe Tim can go with you. I haven't seen him lately, have I? Sometimes I can't remember who has been here and what day it is."

"Tim and I aren't together anymore."

"Why not?"

She shrugged. "He's not for me."

"Maybe he's not, since he hasn't been here for you since I got sick. I want you to be someone's priority, Alisa. Your father always made me feel that way."

"Even now?" She couldn't help asking.

But her mother's eyes were already closing. Either she hadn't heard what she'd said, or she hadn't wanted to hear.

She let out a breath, thinking a trip to Fiji sounded good right now. Her mother had painted a beautiful picture, but that wasn't their reality. When this was over, they'd go there together, she promised herself. They'd sit on that beach, looking at the beautiful sea, feeling like there was nothing but possibility in front of them. As soon as her mom got well, she'd make that trip happen. She didn't want to think about the alternative. She didn't want to lose her mom, especially when it felt like she'd already lost her dad.

When had her life gotten so messed up? Everything had been so normal before this. They'd had no family drama. Just a happy life. Maybe she should have been more grateful for that instead of sometimes thinking they were a little boring. She'd trade everything she had for boring right now.

Her gaze moved toward the door. The man who'd tried to carjack her was probably in a room on the floor. She wondered what he'd have to say for himself. If he'd told the FBI why he'd been in the garage, why he'd gone after her, why he'd wanted to get her in the car.

A shiver ran down her spine as the memories ran through her head. She told herself to calm down. It was over. That man was going to jail. And eventually, she would have answers to all her questions.

Her gaze returned to her mom, hoping she'd also get answers to her mother's condition soon. She felt so helpless, but for now, all she could do was sit and wait for the doctor to find a diagnosis and a treatment plan to save her mother's life.

———

Jason stood over the hospital bed, his gaze locked on the man who had terrorized Alisa just hours before. Victor Kashin's thick beard did nothing to hide the hard set of his jaw, nor the calculating look in his dark, soulless eyes. Originally from Chechnya, Kashin had built a life on violence and fear, and now he lay silent, his hands cuffed to the bed, scowling at the ceiling like a man who had already accepted his fate.

Kashin had been in trouble many times over the years and had a record of theft, burglary, and multiple assaults. He was in his early forties and had worked as an auto mechanic, but his employment history was so spotty it was doubtful that was how he made his money. His last known residence was an abandoned apartment building. Since then, Victor's address and employment had been nonexistent.

Victor had not said a word to either him or Savannah, even though they'd asked him multiple questions. He'd simply stared straight ahead with a scowl on his face, his lips tight, even when asked the most basic questions: *What's your name? Where do you live? Why were you in the garage? Who are you working for?*

He hadn't mentioned Novikov because he didn't want to tip his hand that they knew Kashin and Novikov had, at some point, been in the same vehicle yesterday. Not that Victor could communicate with anyone, but he still wanted to keep the information to himself.

"Look, we're going to find out everything about you," he told Kashin. "We already know your name, where you're from, where you've lived, who your relatives are. Someone will talk. Someone will tell us more than you want us to know." He paused, then added, "I believe you're working for someone else, and that person might be of more interest to us than you are. You could trade that information to help yourself because right now you're facing attempted murder, kidnapping, and many other charges. You're looking at serious prison time."

Kashin's gaze remained fixed on the wall.

"If you have information we can use," Savannah interjected, "you can make a deal."

Finally, Victor turned his head to look at them. "Lawyer," he said. Then he returned his gaze to the wall.

He wasn't surprised at the request but still frustrated. "You don't have to talk, Victor, but you can listen. You screwed up. You failed. Now you're a loose end. I doubt you'll last long in jail."

Victor's profile hardened. His dark eyes burned with anger as he looked at Jason. "If I tell you anything, I won't survive long enough to get to jail."

"We can protect you," Savannah put in.

He gave them both a derisive look. "Neither of you have any idea what you're talking about."

"Well, without our protection, you'll be even less likely to stay alive," he said.

"Lawyer," Victor repeated.

"Do you have someone you want us to call? Or do you want a public defender?" Savannah asked.

It was a good question. If Victor gave them an attorney's name, they might be able to tie the lawyer to Novikov.

But Victor wasn't falling into that trap. "Call whoever you want. I'm done talking."

"You have a small window of time in which you can change your mind," he told him. "But it's closing fast."

"Lawyer."

He let out a sigh and motioned Savannah toward the door. When they left the room, one of the two security guards on duty entered the room to stand guard, while the other remained outside, blocking the door.

"We're not getting anything from him," he said in frustration.

"No," Savannah agreed. "The doctor said he won't be released until tomorrow, so I'll make a call and get an attorney down here."

"Thanks."

As Savannah moved down the hall and stepped into the

LETHAL GAME   35

waiting room to make her calls, he turned back to the glass window that showed the guard standing just inside the door while Victor had laid back and closed his eyes. He might be asleep or just resigned to whatever consequence he would have to suffer because of his botched carjacking.

Clearly, he was more worried about his employer than about going to jail. If that employer was Novikov, he could certainly understand Victor's fear. Novikov was a cold-blooded assassin. All he cared about was money, power, and terror, not necessarily in that order. And he suspected that Victor Kashin was expendable.

"Is that him?" a woman asked.

He turned his head, surprised to see Alisa Hunt. She looked much better than she had last night. She'd exchanged her scrubs for dark jeans and a coral-colored sweater over a white top. Her dark-brown hair was no longer in a ponytail but falling halfway down her back in pretty waves. Her eyes were brown but flecked with gold, her cheeks holding far more color than the night before. Her left hand was wrapped in a bandage, reminding him of the cut she'd suffered on her palm, and while there wasn't any sign of a concussion, he suspected she still had a big headache. But apparently, she wasn't one to stay home and sit on the couch.

"Is that the man who tried to kidnap me?" she asked, her gaze moving to the window behind him.

"Yes."

"Do you know any more about him? Or why he wanted me to get in the car?"

"We know he's originally from Chechnya."

She looked at him in surprise. "Really? Isn't that in Russia?"

"It was part of the Soviet Union at one time. Victor has been in the US since he was a teenager. He hasn't said anything except to ask for a lawyer, so I don't know why he grabbed you and tried to put you in your car."

"Can I talk to him?"

"Why would you want to?" he asked, surprised by her request.

"Maybe he would tell me because I'm not FBI. I'm just the woman he tried to kidnap."

"I don't think so."

"Please? I couldn't sleep all night. I kept hearing his voice, feeling his grip on my arm, shaking with terror at every memory. He grew into a gigantic monster in my head, and maybe if I spoke to him, he would stop being a monster and just be a criminal. Perhaps he just needed a car, and he didn't have any money."

"Don't make excuses for him," he said sharply. "Some people are just bad."

"I know that's true, but I'm trying to vanquish the monster in my head."

He couldn't help but admire her spirit and her determination to not let what happened control her. But he could also see the fear in her eyes. She was an intriguing and very attractive mix of bravery and fear. She had a soft girl-next-door look about her, but he knew she was also a fighter. However, he couldn't let her go into the room. She wouldn't get the result she was hoping for, and he didn't want her anywhere near Victor. She'd already had one unfortunate encounter, and that was one too many.

"The monster is cuffed to the bed," he told her. "He's going to prison. You're safe. And the less contact you have with him, the better. You're just a random woman who got in the way of whatever he wanted to do. Let's keep it that way. He doesn't need to know your name or see you again, at least not until the trial."

"Trial?" she echoed.

"You'll probably have to testify to what happened."

"Oh. I hadn't thought about that." She wrapped her arms around herself as if she were suddenly cold, and the color in her cheeks that he'd been admiring earlier faded away.

"Are you all right, Alisa?"

"I don't think so."

He felt another wave of compassion at her honest words. "It will take time to get past what you went through. But talking to him won't help. Trust me on that."

She let out a sigh. "I feel like I can't control anything in my life right now. Everyone wants me to trust them. It's not that I don't want to, I just feel helpless. I'm not good at waiting."

He smiled as their gazes met. "I'm not a patient person, either, but sometimes you don't have a choice."

"Like now," she murmured.

"You should feel good about what you did last night. You were incredibly brave. Be proud of that. You saved yourself."

"You saved me," she corrected.

"Only because you fought him long enough to give me the opportunity to get there."

"I am glad I didn't freeze. My instincts screamed at me to fight."

"Your instincts were good."

"I just wish it hadn't happened. I have so much to deal with right now."

"Maybe you should get some rest. You can't be planning to work today. I hope you didn't come all the way down here just to see this guy. He's not worth your time."

"I'm not working, and I didn't come here to see him. My mother is sick with an illness that no one has been able to diagnose. Last night she was doing better, but this morning, she's worse again."

"I'm sorry to hear that."

"They just took her to radiology to get another test. I was sitting alone in her room, and I started thinking about what happened last night, and I couldn't stop myself from coming down here. I thought vanquishing one monster would help, but he's not the monster I'm most worried about." She drew in a shaky breath. "My mother is in terrible shape. I don't want to think about what might happen. But I can't help it. I'm a nurse. I can see the signs."

He saw the stress and fear in her eyes and could relate. He had known nothing about medicine when his mother had died, but he could still remember the odd look in her eyes the day before she passed, the way she'd slumped in her chair, staring into space in a way that had made him feel she was already gone.

Clearing his throat, he pushed that unexpected memory from his head. It had been seventeen years. But he still couldn't get that image out of his head. But this wasn't about him. "I understand a little of how you might feel. I lost my mom when I was fifteen. It's the worst thing that ever happened to me."

She met his gaze. "I can't lose her. I just can't."

"I hope you won't," he said, feeling oddly protective toward her. He didn't know her. He shouldn't feel anything but compassion for a stranger going through a difficult time, but there was something about Alisa that made it difficult to keep a distance between them.

Knowing what she'd gone through in the garage and what was happening now with her mother, he could understand her need to put one of her fears out of her head.

"I shouldn't be telling you all this." She gave him an apologetic look. "It's not your problem, so I shouldn't be taking up your time."

"Right now, I'm just waiting for this guy's attorney to arrive, so it's not a problem. It sounds like you need someone to talk to. What about your family? Or a boyfriend?" he ventured, not sure why he'd felt the need to put that question out there.

Her frown deepened. "No boyfriend. As for family, my father seems to have disappeared."

He straightened at that unexpected piece of information. "What do you mean?"

"My mom said my dad went to see an ill friend, and it's no big deal, but considering my mother is in seriously bad health, it's hugely concerning. When I called my dad last night, his phone was disconnected. I tried again this morning and it still wasn't working. It's so strange. He never goes anywhere. And he adores my mother. I don't understand why he would leave."

"It sounds odd," he said, his always curious brain already trying to put the puzzle together. "Your mother isn't concerned?"

"No. She said he'll be back when he can, and I don't need to worry about it. In fact, she told me I should take a trip, get out of town. Like I'm going to leave her alone now."

Every word that came out of her mouth gave him a bad feeling. "What about the old friend he went to visit? Can you reach out to that person?"

"I don't know him. I never heard his name before last night."

"What exactly is wrong with your mother?"

"No one knows. She has a lot of odd symptoms. She's sleeping all the time. She's nauseous. She can't keep food down. She passed out at home before we brought her in on Monday. She also says her feet and her hands hurt, and she has a weird taste in her mouth. Oh, and her hair started falling out. Everything got better yesterday. She was almost back to normal. But when I came to see her this morning, she was in such a deep sleep I could barely rouse her. I'm really worried. And I'm driving myself crazy waiting for answers." She paused. "Are you sure I can't go in there and just yell at him? He doesn't have to talk. I can just tell him what a horrible person he is."

He smiled at the fierce look in her eyes. "Sorry. But no."

She blew out a breath. "Fine." She paused as her phone buzzed. Reaching into her bag, she pulled it out to read a text.

Her expression went from one of anger and frustration to shock.

"What's wrong?" he asked. "Is that about your mother?"

"No, it's about my parents' house. It's on fire."

"What?" he asked, shocked by her words.

Ignoring his question, she punched in a number on her phone, then said, "Jerry? What's going on?" She listened for a moment, putting a hand to her mouth in horror at whatever she was hearing. "Oh, my God! I'm coming right now." She ended the call and looked at him. "That was my parents' neighbor. The fire is huge. I don't know how a fire could even start. My mom has been here the last couple of days. And my father left Tuesday night or maybe yesterday morning. But no one has been in the house today."

His investigative instincts kicked into high gear. It seemed unlikely that all the events she'd just told him about were unrelated: her mother's mysterious illness, her father's sudden disappearance, and her parents' house fire.

He couldn't leave out the fact she'd almost been kidnapped last night. He'd assumed it was random. That she was just going to be used as a cover for Victor to get away from the hospital. Maybe that wasn't it at all.

"I have to go. I have to see what's happening at my parents' house," Alisa said, then suddenly frowned. "But my car is still in the garage, and I don't think I can go in there and get it. I still feel traumatized. I'll take a cab. But then I won't have a way to get back. I should really just go get the car."

She was talking more to herself than to him, but Jason jumped in, anyway. "Take a breath, Alisa. I'll go to the garage with you."

She stared at him with hope in her beautiful golden-brown eyes that made his stomach clench.

"Really?" she asked. "You don't mind?"

"Let me just tell my partner I'll be back in a few minutes. She's in the waiting room."

She nodded, then followed him down the hall. Savannah was just getting off her phone when they entered the room. She gave Alisa a questioning look.

"Ms. Hunt," Savannah said. "How are you today?"

"Not good," Alisa replied. "It's a long story."

"Alisa has an issue at her parents' house," he told Savannah. "I'm going to walk her to the garage so she can get her car."

"Okay," Savannah replied. "The attorney is on his way. He

should be here in about twenty minutes, so I'll wait here for him."

"Great. I'll be back soon."

He could feel Savannah's speculative gaze on them as they walked to the elevator. She probably thought his behavior was odd, but he didn't have time to explain everything he'd just learned, and his gut told him that Alisa's unfortunate series of events might lead to a clue he had never expected to get from her.

CHAPTER FOUR

"I feel ridiculous," Alisa muttered as the elevator descended to the lobby. "I should be able to walk into that garage and get my car. I work here, for God's sake. How am I going to keep avoiding it?"

"It will feel easier after the first time. And it's not a problem."

"Well, I appreciate it." She let out another sigh. "I can't believe my parents' house is on fire. And I have to take care of this. My mom can't do it. My dad isn't around. It's just me."

"I'm assuming you don't have siblings."

"No, I'm an only child."

Another thing they had in common. He knew very well the pressure that came from being the only child.

"Every day some new bad thing happens," she murmured as they exited the elevator on the lobby level and then walked through the front doors of the hospital, taking the path to the parking garage. "My life used to be calm and kind of boring, to be honest, but everything changed about a week ago when my mother started feeling sick. The problems have snowballed since then. Now, everything feels like it's upside down and backward."

Were Alisa's problems all just coincidence? A rough patch in her life?

Had she just been in the wrong place at the wrong time last night? Or was there something else going on?

He couldn't shake the feeling there was something else happening, and if her attack by Kashin was not random, then Novikov had orchestrated it.

Was it possible this very ordinary American nurse was tied to a Russian terrorist?

He wanted to pepper her with questions, but they had reached the stairwell leading down to the employee level, and even though they weren't touching, he could feel her shaking. He offered her his hand, and after a momentary hesitation, she took it.

As he wrapped his fingers around hers, he was struck by the heat between them. He reminded himself he was just taking care of a victim of a crime. This wasn't personal.

But it felt a little more personal than it should have, and that surprised him.

He never had a problem compartmentalizing while on the job, but there was something about Alisa that made that difficult.

As they entered the bottom level, she moved even closer to him.

"It's okay," he reassured her. "I won't let anything happen to you."

"I know," she said, but she didn't sound confident.

As they neared her vehicle, Alisa's foot crunched down on a piece of glass left over from the shooting the night before, and she paused, staring down at a few pieces of glass still next to her car. "It really happened, didn't it?" she murmured. "A part of me still wants to believe it was a nightmare." She turned her gaze to his, her eyes pleading for reassuring words.

He was more of a man of action than words, but he had to try. "It happened, but it's over," he said. "Kashin will never get close to you again. You're safe."

She nodded. "Thank you for saying that. I guess I should be

grateful it wasn't my window that got shot out. What happened to the other car?"

"I don't know. Security was going to find the owner and help them get their window fixed." As she made no move to open her car, he said, "Do you have your keys?"

"They're in my bag, but the keys seem to freak me out. I keep remembering how I couldn't pull them out in time to get in the car before he reached me. My damn bag is too big. They keep falling in between things, and it takes me too long to get them out."

"There's no rush now. Take your time." He could have offered to go through her bag and find her keys, but he thought she needed to meet that goal in order to feel like she was getting her life back.

She put her hand in her bag, and a moment later, she pulled out her keys. She gave him a triumphant look, even though her hand was visibly shaking as she tried to hit the button to open the lock. Eventually, the lock clicked as the keys slid from her hand and fell to the ground.

Alisa bit down on her lip. "Damn," she muttered.

"I've got them." He quickly grabbed her keys and opened the driver's side door. Then he hesitated. "I don't think you should drive, Alisa. You're trembling."

"I'll be okay. I have to be. The house is on fire. I have to get there. And I have to go now before my mom is done with her test."

He debated for a split second. Victor's lawyer wouldn't be there for another twenty minutes. "How far away is your mother's house?"

"About ten minutes," she said. "They only live a few miles from here. I can make it."

"I'll drive you," he said, making a quick decision. "We'll check out the situation at the house, and then I'll bring you back."

"Really?" She gave him a hopeful look that twisted something inside his gut. She was a beautiful woman, and he had a hard time looking away from her.

Clearing his throat, he said, "I have a little time. I have to wait for the lawyer, anyway."

"Thank you, Jason. Is it okay if I call you that?"

He probably should have told her to call him Agent Colter to keep some barrier between them, but he couldn't bring himself to do that. "It's fine. Let's do this."

He slid behind the wheel as she moved around the car and got into the passenger seat. Before starting the car, he sent Savannah a quick text of explanation and told her to start without him if the attorney got there before he returned.

Alisa fastened her seat belt, and he pulled out of the parking spot. Her Toyota was at least ten years old and not a car someone would steal if they had other options. Since she'd been the only one in the garage at the time of the carjacking, he had to assume she had been the target and not the car.

He drove up the ramp to the main level and then exited the garage. The medical center and several adjacent buildings were on the top of a hill next to the 405 Freeway, and the only way in and out of the area was a two-lane road that wound down the hillside for about two miles before reaching a busy intersection where the Wexford University campus was located. From there, one could head in a variety of directions: Westwood, Santa Monica, or Culver City.

He'd lived in Los Angeles for four years now, but he still wasn't used to the urban sprawl and the variety of cities and neighborhoods that ran into each other.

Alisa cracked her window, taking several deep breaths. She was clearly happy to be out of the parking garage.

As he started down the hill, he tapped the brakes, but they didn't immediately respond. He tried again, pressing the pedal to the floor. *Nothing!*

His heart sped up as his brain computed the problem.

"You're going too fast," Alisa said, giving him a frightened look. "Please, slow down, Jason."

"I can't." His voice tightened as he pressed the brake pedal again. Nothing. His pulse spiked. "The brakes aren't working." He downshifted, his hands gripping the wheel tighter, but the car surged forward.

"Oh, my God!" Alisa gasped, her eyes wide with fear. "Jason, we're not going to stop, are we?"

He didn't have time to answer her. He couldn't deal with her fear and the problem at hand. In about five minutes, this road was going to take them straight into an intersection filled with cars and people. He had to make a move before then, but there was nothing on either side of the road but rocky hillsides filled with trees and brush. He was going to have to find something to soften their landing.

"Hang on," he told her.

"I can't die in this car, Jason. I have to be there for my mom."

"We're not going to die," he vowed. But he had no idea how he was going to keep that promise.

As they flew down the steep road, Jason searched for a place to turn off, something that might provide a slowdown but not kill them. There weren't any good choices and as their speed increased, he no longer worried about the intersection down below because he wasn't sure they could make the next turn. They'd only passed one car coming up, but that could change at any moment.

This was his opportunity. It wasn't good, but he had run out of options.

He swung the wheel to the left, crossing the lane next to him and flying through a wood barrier that barely slowed their speed. The car bounced off rocks and bushes, the windows shattering, dirt spattering the windows.

Alisa cried out in terror. But he couldn't look at her or comfort her. He was trying to steer the vehicle away from a patch of trees coming up, but his vision was almost gone.

A lot of things ran through his head, his thoughts going as fast as the car. But only one jumped out at him. *He didn't want to die, either.*

He clung to the wheel, trying to keep them upright. But his control was just an illusion, and suddenly they were both thrown forward, the airbags deploying as the car slammed into what felt like a brick wall but were probably the trees he'd been trying to avoid. The car screamed as loudly as Alisa as it crumpled and broke apart.

He hit the airbag hard, feeling the wheel behind it as his head crashed forward, and everything went black.

———

Alisa's heart was beating out of her chest, her screams finally ending as she realized that they'd come to a stop, and she was still alive. She was still breathing. She could hardly believe it.

She shoved at the airbag, her breath coming in sharp gasps as she struggled to sit up. Her seat was crushed forward, but when she wiggled her toes, relief coursed through her—she could still feel her legs. The pain was there, dull and throbbing, but not debilitating. She was alive.

As she turned her head toward the left, her heart jumped at the sight of Jason slumped over the wheel. There was blood dripping down his face, and his eyes were closed.

Oh, God!

"Jason," she said, her voice hoarse from the screaming.

He didn't move.

She shifted in her seat as best she could, putting her hand on his shoulder. She was afraid to shake him in case he had a neck or back injury. She moved a little closer and put her fingers on his neck, praying for a pulse.

There was a heartbeat. Faint, but steady. Relief hit her like a tidal wave. *He was alive!*

"Jason," she repeated. "We made it."

Even as she said the words, she wondered where exactly they'd made it to. She couldn't see anything because tree branches were coming through the broken glass, and the windows were covered in dirt. But there were small slivers of light that she clung to. They weren't dead, and that was an enormous victory in itself. But she didn't know how badly Jason was hurt. Nor did she know if she could get out of the car. Even if she could get out, should she try? What if the car slid further down the hill? The wild ride could start up again, only this time there wouldn't be any airbags blowing up to protect them from a fatal injury.

She looked over at Jason again, knowing he was the real reason she was alive. And she would hate herself forever if he didn't survive along with her. It was her fault he was here. If she hadn't been scared to go into the garage, he wouldn't have offered to go with her. If she hadn't been shaky, he wouldn't have offered to drive her to her parents' house.

Her parents' house!

Had it burned to the ground?

What the hell was happening? Why was her life falling apart in such a spectacular fashion?

But that wasn't the most important question.

She shuddered as reality smacked her as hard as the airbag had done. This wasn't an accident. Her brakes had been fine yesterday. She'd had her car checked out six weeks ago. They'd told her she wouldn't have to replace the brakes for at least another year.

Why would they suddenly fail? Had someone tampered with her car while it had sat in the garage overnight? But why? Why would anyone want to hurt her?

Was this tied to what had happened last night?

Jason had told her she'd been a random target. Maybe that wasn't true. Her breath was coming fast as anxiety and panic ripped through her. She had to get out of this car. She had to get

Jason out. That was what she needed to think about right now. The rest would have to wait.

"Jason," she said again. "Please wake up." She could hear the desperation in her voice and maybe he could, too, because he started to stir.

"Easy," she said, putting her hand on his shoulder again. "Don't move too fast."

He lifted his head with a groan, squinting as he opened his eyes, and his stunning blue gaze almost made her want to cry.

"You have blood on your face," she told him. "I don't know where else you're hurt. Do you have any pain anywhere? Can you feel your legs?" She was worried that the way the car had crumpled, his legs might have gotten crushed.

He blinked a few times and then sat up straighter, his gaze focusing on her. He pulled his hand out from under the airbag and touched the blood on his face. As he took his fingers away, he stared at the blood for a second and then glanced back at her.

"Are you all right?" he asked.

"I think so. I feel better now that you're awake. I'm so sorry, Jason. This is my fault. I shouldn't have let you drive me."

"This isn't your fault."

"I had my car checked out six weeks ago. The brakes were fine."

"I'm sure they were fine until someone messed with them," he said soberly. "This wasn't an accident, Alisa."

"It doesn't look that way. We need to get out of here, but I'm afraid to move. What if opening the doors makes the car slide farther down the hill?"

He looked around, assessing the situation. "I think we were pretty close to the bottom when we stopped."

"You mean when we crashed?" she asked dryly.

He gave her a faint smile. "I prefer to think of it as a hard landing. But we're alive, and things can only get better from here."

"Are you sure? Because every minute of my day seems to get worse. And while I am ecstatic to be alive, I'm worried about my mom and her house and how we're going to get out of this car and back to the hospital. Do you think someone saw us go off the road?"

"I didn't see any other cars. I had to make the turn, Alisa. It was our only chance."

"You were amazing. Saving my life is getting to be a habit— bad for you, good for me."

"Well, I had a vested interest in saving your life this time." He shifted in his seat. "I don't believe I've broken anything."

"Which seems like a miracle."

"You had good airbags."

"I never ever thought I'd use them," she said. "Nothing like this has ever happened to me. And I still don't know why it's happening."

"We'll figure it out. In the meantime..." He put his hand on the door handle. As he moved it, the door gave a loud creak, swung open, and then fell to the ground, making the car rock and sending a wave of new terror through her.

She held her breath, praying the car would settle back into place. Eventually, it did.

"We're good," Jason said.

"No. We're definitely not good. We're barely okay."

"I know I'm a pessimist. But you're giving me a run for my money," he said lightly.

"I always thought I was an optimist until the last week, but I don't feel that way now. Everything around me is dark."

He put a hand on her arm as he gave her a reassuring smile that seemed incongruous with the blood on his face. "You're doing great, Alisa. We'll put one foot in front of the other until we're out of here, and then we'll keep doing that until we figure out what's going on."

"Are you confident we will figure it out?"

"Yes," he said with a certainty that gave her hope. "Because I don't give up—ever."

She believed him. He certainly hadn't given up on getting them down the hill as safely as humanly possible. His confidence was contagious. They'd made it this far. She had to keep believing. "Okay. I won't give up, either."

"Good. Now I'm going to slowly get out of the car. Once I see where we are, I'll come around to your side."

"I'd rather get out at the same time as you, just in case the car moves when you do," she said, putting her hand on the door and giving the handle a yank. Nothing happened. She looked over at him, feeling panic again. "I don't think my side will open. It feels like there's a weight against it."

"That's okay. That means the car isn't going anywhere."

He slowly eased his body out of the car until he was standing on the ground.

"What do you see?" she asked.

"We hit a couple of trees. But the good news is that we're at the bottom of the hill, in what appears to be a gully. The car isn't going to slide any further. There's nowhere for it to go."

She blew out a breath of relief.

"I'm going to come around to your side," he said.

She felt another rush of anxiety as he disappeared from view, but she told herself to get a grip. The worst was over. Now, it was just about getting out of the car.

A moment later, she heard his voice behind the tree branches that were sticking through her window. "I can't open the door," he said. "It's crushed against a tree."

He came back around to his side and gave her a questioning look. "You're going to have to crawl out this way. Can you get the seat belt off?"

It took her a moment to wrestle with the belt, but she eventually got it off. It took another few minutes to crawl out from under the airbags, over the console, and then through the open door.

Jason helped her out of the car, wrapping his arms around her as her feet slipped on the rocky ground. They were still on a slight incline, but as she looked around, she could see that he'd been telling the truth. They were at the bottom of the hill, and far above them was the road that wound its way up to the medical center. Hopefully, someone would notice the broken guardrail and stop to question if something had happened.

"How are you feeling now that you're on your feet?" Jason asked.

She looked into his face, suddenly realizing he was holding her very close, and she wasn't making any attempt to get out of his embrace because it felt really, really good.

"Anything hurting?" he questioned.

"My head, my wrist, my knee..." She was slowly noticing the pain points in her body. She looked down at her left wrist, which was the same hand she'd cut against the car last night. Her wrist didn't look broken, but there was another long cut on the back of her hand that went up her arm. She glanced down at her leg. Her jeans were ripped at the knee, and there was blood on the denim. "Nothing is broken, but I'm cut in a few places." Her gaze moved to Jason, and she saw similar cuts and bloody spots on his clothes. "You are, too."

"Cuts will heal," he said, giving her a smile.

She shook her head in wonder. "You don't let anything get you down, do you?"

"I'm happy we're alive. No cuts are getting me down."

"I'm happy, too. You...are something else, Jason."

He inclined his head. "As much as I'd like to take the credit, luck was on our side."

She needed to let go of him, and he needed to let go of her, but neither of them seemed inclined to move. It was probably just the joy of being alive after their shared terrifying experience. But she felt a connection to him that she hadn't ever felt with anyone.

Jason's gaze darkened as he looked at her. "I should let you go," he muttered. "You know what this feeling is, right? It's just amazing relief and gratitude that we're alive."

"That's what I was thinking, too," she agreed. "But I have this crazy urge to kiss you right now. That would be really inappropriate—"

Before she could finish, Jason closed the distance between them, his lips pressing against hers in a kiss that silenced everything else. It was exactly what she needed—more than words, more than comfort. In that moment, it wasn't just about surviving. It was about feeling alive. About connection. And maybe it was something more...

CHAPTER FIVE

He shouldn't be kissing Alisa, but every time Jason thought about stopping, her mouth invited him back in. It took several minutes before he could finally put an end to the impulsive desire that had ripped through him when she'd looked at him the way she had, when she'd put into words what he was feeling, too.

Her face was flushed, the breeze lifting her dark-brown hair as the surrounding trees rustled, bringing him back to reality, to the situation they'd found themselves in.

"I'm sorry," he muttered as he stepped back, fully breaking the contact between them.

"Don't apologize. I wanted to kiss you, too," Alisa said, her voice soft. "I know it's crazy—we barely know each other."

"We just went through something intense," he said.

"That's probably why," she agreed, though her eyes still held a lingering question, daring him to admit it might be more.

But he wasn't going to admit that. He knew the high that came with a close call. And that was why they'd ended up sharing one of the best kisses he'd had in a long time.

Clearing his throat, he said, "We need to get out of here."

"Right." Her gaze moved up the steep hillside. "I still can't believe we didn't flip over on the way down."

That surprised him, too. He was also astonished they'd missed other trees on their way down the hill. Thankfully, the brush had slowed the car down enough that by the time they'd reached the last set of trees that the impact hadn't been as destructive as it could have been.

There had definitely been luck or someone watching out for them because it was a miracle they were not just alive but also not seriously injured.

He pulled his phone from his pocket. "I've got a weak signal. But hopefully, that will get us some help."

"Oh." She looked back toward the car. "My bag is still in there. I need to get it. I need to check my phone, too."

"Hang on," he said. "I'll get it." He moved away from her, leaned into the car, and grabbed not only her purse from under the airbag but also pulled her keys out of the ignition. He handed everything back to her, then used his phone to call Savannah.

"Jason, where are you?" Savannah asked. "The lawyer came and went."

"I was in an accident. I was driving Alisa to her parents' house, but we'd barely started down the hill when I realized the brakes on her car didn't work. I'm sure someone cut the line."

"Seriously? Are you both all right?"

"We're okay, but we were in an accident. We're stuck at the bottom of the hill leading up to the hospital. I don't think anyone can see us from the road, but we went through a guardrail, so that should identify where we are. Can you call the fire department?"

"Of course. What about an ambulance?"

"We don't need an ambulance. Just help to get out of here."

"I'm on it."

As he ended the call, he saw Alisa on her phone. "The test was negative?" she asked, then listened for a moment. "Okay, thanks."

"How's your mom?" he asked.

"Her brain scan was normal. But she's sleeping again, and her vitals are still weak. Dr. Grayson will stop by my mother's room in about an hour. Do you think we'll be out of here by then?"

"I think so. Help should be here shortly. It's good that her scan was normal."

"It is. But we still don't know what's wrong with her." She blew out a breath. "At least we've ruled out one more thing. I guess that's something." She looked back at her phone. "I should call Jerry, too, my mom's neighbor." She punched in another number on her phone. "Hello? Jerry? Can you hear me?" She frowned. "Jerry, are you there?" Then she swore. "Damn. The phone just dropped the call."

"You can call him later. There's nothing you can do about the fire now. I'll talk to the fire department and find out what happened. I'm guessing it was arson."

She met his gaze. "Arson? Why? Because...someone just tried to kill me?"

Her shaky voice made him want to give her another hug, but he dug his hands into his pockets to stop that from happening. He didn't need to confuse the situation any further. "Yes, that's why. Someone must have tampered with your car last night, assuming at some point you'd be back to get it. The good news is there are probably cameras in the garage, so maybe we'll be able to see who did it."

"I just don't understand why someone would want to kill me. I'm nobody. I'm just a nurse. I don't have money. I'm not tied to anyone important. I've never broken the law or hurt anyone that I know of. I'm an ordinary, rather boring person." She gave him a baffled look. "Why would someone hate me this much?"

"It's not about hate, Alisa. And there's something about your life that is not as ordinary as you think it is. I suspect your missing father might be in the middle of it all."

"Why?"

"Because of your mother's undiagnosed illness and the two attempts on your life."

"Two?" she echoed. "Right. It wasn't just a carjacking or a kidnapping. They were probably going to kill me. I was right when I thought I might not survive getting in that car."

"Considering what just happened here, I think you made the smart decision last night to fight like your life depended on it, because it did." He felt a wave of anger on her behalf because Alisa seemed like an incredibly nice person, a loyal daughter, a woman who worked at a job caring for others. She didn't deserve any of this.

But a small voice in his head cautioned him not to let his admiration for her cloud his judgment. Maybe she wasn't as innocent as she appeared to be. Perhaps she knew more than she was saying.

But that seemed doubtful. She had very expressive eyes. He didn't think she'd be a good liar. Every emotion she had was revealed in her gaze. He'd seen that firsthand a few minutes ago when her sparks of desire had lit the fire inside him.

The sound of sirens sent both their gazes to the hillside.

"We'll be out of here soon," he said, then paused. "Alisa—"

"Don't," she said quickly. "We don't need to talk about it."

"Okay, but if that changes..."

"It won't." She smiled at him. "I do want to say, however, that I'm sorry I got you into this. When you were unconscious..." Her smile faded. "I felt a lot of guilt that I might have been responsible for you dying, and I couldn't stand that idea. You were just being kind to me by dealing with my fears and look at what happened."

"I wasn't just being kind. Your series of problems intrigued me, and I started wondering if the kidnapping attempt wasn't as random as I thought it was. I didn't think you should drive because you were shaky, but a part of me also wanted to go with you to see what was going on with the fire at your parents' house. We're going to figure it out, Alisa."

"The FBI will get involved in this?" she asked.

"Yes. We'll see where the investigation leads us."

"Do you think it will lead to the man you were looking for yesterday?"

Her question sent a chill through him. "I hope not because he's a terrible person."

She shivered at his words. "Now I'm sorry I asked."

"I don't want to lie to you, Alisa."

"You shouldn't lie because, clearly, I need to know what's going on before someone tries to do this again. I do not want the third time to be the charm."

Her valiant attempt at dark humor impressed him. She might not think of herself as brave, but she had a deep well of courage inside her. He had a feeling she might need every ounce of that courage before this was over.

———

Getting back up the hill was almost as harrowing as the trip down, Alisa thought, as she was strapped into a metal basket and hoisted up the hill on a shaky ride that made her nauseous and dizzy. Finally, she reached the top and was helped out of the cage and into the back of an ambulance, which had come despite Jason's claims they didn't need one. While Jason was being brought up to the road, the paramedic gave her water and assessed her condition.

She knew she needed some treatment, cuts that should be cleaned to prevent infection, and a better look at the pain she was now feeling to make sure the adrenaline rush hadn't covered up anything more serious.

Jason joined her a moment later, speaking to his blonde female partner for a moment before joining her in the back of the ambulance. They were whisked away to the hospital on a short ride, reminding her just how quickly everything had gone wrong.

Once in the ER, they were taken into separate exam rooms and treated for their injuries.

Georgia, the nurse who had been on duty the night before, came in just as another nurse finished cleaning her wounds.

"What on earth happened to you now?" Georgia asked.

"My car brakes didn't work. I went off the side of the road."

"Oh, my God! You are living under a dark cloud."

"Tell me about it." She slid off the exam table. "I need to go upstairs and check on my mom. I'll see you later."

When she reached the lobby, she saw Jason talking to his partner.

His concerned gaze immediately flew to her. "Everything check out?" he asked.

"Just some cuts. You?"

"Same."

"You were both extremely lucky," the woman said. "We haven't officially met, Ms. Hunt. I'm Savannah Kane."

"Thanks for your help today and last night," she said.

"No problem. I'm just sorry you needed help."

"Me, too. I need to go upstairs."

"I'll meet you up there," Jason said.

"Okay." It felt strange to walk away from him. He'd become her anchor in a very stormy sea. This latest storm had passed, and while she hoped there wouldn't be another one, that was probably wishful thinking.

———

Jason led Savannah into the hospital cafeteria. He needed coffee, and she needed to catch up.

"How are you really feeling?" she asked, giving him a speculative look as they sat down at a table.

He sipped his coffee, happy for the hit of caffeine that might help drive some of the fog from his brain. "I'm okay."

"Why were you in the car with Alisa Hunt? I thought you were just walking her into the garage?"

"I was going to leave it at that, but she was too shaky to

drive. Look, there's a lot going on with her, and I don't know how it fits with Novikov's appearance in LA, but I believe there's a connection."

"Seriously?" she asked in surprise.

"Yes. I no longer think the attack last night was random. Kashin went there to kidnap her. When that didn't work, someone sabotaged the brakes on her car. If she'd been driving, there's a good chance she wouldn't have survived."

"Having seen the crash site, I would believe that. What else are you thinking?"

"Her mother is upstairs, sick from a mysterious ailment that the doctors have not been able to diagnose. Her father, who allegedly adores her mother, has disappeared and his phone number no longer works. Her mother's health issues are very serious. So why would he disappear?"

"Okay," Savannah said. "I see where you're going. Is there more?"

"The reason Alisa had to leave the hospital was because her parents' house was on fire. Obviously, we never made it there, so I don't know if it was arson or an accident. Considering everything else, I'm going to assume it was arson."

"Does Alisa live with her parents?"

He thought about that. "She didn't say. She talked about it like it was their house, so I don't think so. But that's a good question." He paused. "Putting all that aside, Kashin is the connector. He was in the car that we saw Novikov get into at LAX. Then he shows up here at the hospital and tries to kidnap Alisa. It has to fit together. We need to know more about her father, her family, anything that might tie them to Novikov."

"Agreed," Savannah said, quick to jump on his train of thought. "I'll stop in at security before I leave and look at the camera footage from the garage last night to see who might have tampered with the car. That will give us someone else to track. I don't believe we'll get anywhere with Kashin. He's not afraid of us. He'd rather go to prison than talk." She paused, taking a sip of her coffee. "Has Alisa told you anything about herself? Her family?"

"We haven't really had time. I know she's a nurse here. She claims her family is super normal and on the boring side. She can't imagine why a Russian terrorist would be after her. And it's difficult to believe she's lying because she has a very open face."

"A very pretty and open face," Savannah said with a small, knowing smile. "And she looks at you like you're her personal action hero."

"Well, I saved her life twice. You know how it goes," he said, trying to avoid her gaze as his mind flashed back to the kiss they'd shared. "At any rate, I'm focused on finding Novikov, and Alisa is an unexpected clue. I also think she's probably still in danger. They tried to take her out twice. There will be another attempt. And the mother is a target, too."

"We can get her mother protection and move Alisa into a safe house."

"I don't think she's going to a safe house while her mother is fighting for her life."

"She won't be able to help her mother if she's not alive," Savannah said pragmatically.

"No, she won't." He took another long sip of his coffee. "I need to go upstairs and find out what's happening with the mother. I'll talk to her more about her parents. What they do for a living, where they're from, all that..."

"Okay. After I check with security, I'll go back to the office and check in with the team. In the absence of any other good tips, Alisa's family seems to be the best lead."

He was happy to hear her say that because he didn't want to make the mistake of getting too caught up in Alisa's situation just because they'd almost died together. And definitely not because he'd kissed her.

"Nick is going to pick me up," Savannah added as she passed him the car keys. "The car is under the direct eye of the valet. No one will tamper with it."

"Thanks."

"On our way back to the office, Nick and I will check out the fast-food restaurant where Novikov first went after leaving LAX. He didn't go inside, but maybe we can get better camera footage from the restaurant or some other buildings in the area. There are a lot of small, local businesses whose cameras we can't access online." She paused. "Andi also called me while you were driving off a cliff to tell me she's doing a deep dive into Tatiana's life, and we have an agent watching her moves. She's been at her dance studio all day, but he'll follow her home and anywhere else she might go."

He didn't know who Andi was, but he was impressed with the way Flynn's team had jumped into the investigation. "Your team is good."

"Your team for now," she reminded him with a smile.

"Right. Well, thank you." He finished his coffee, and then got to his feet. "I'll check in with you later. If anything comes up in the meantime, let me know."

"I will," she promised.

They walked out of the cafeteria and parted ways in the lobby. He headed upstairs, feeling like it had been hours since he'd seen Alisa when it had only been about twenty minutes. But judging by how much had happened in the last twenty-four hours, a lot could have happened in those twenty minutes.

———

Alisa couldn't believe how much better her mother looked since she'd returned from her MRI. She wasn't a hundred percent back to normal. She was still extremely pale, but she was able to say hello, to confirm her nausea was improved, and to ask for water.

As her mother sipped water through a straw, Alisa didn't know how to feel about the change in her condition. She was happy, of course, but it was also odd how her symptoms came and went. Maybe everything was going to be all right. She desperately wanted to believe that because the rest of her world was spinning out of control.

"What happened to you?" her mother asked suddenly, her gaze narrowing. "You have dirt in your hair and on your clothes. Your jeans are ripped, and you have bandages on your hand. What's going on, Alisa?"

"I don't want to get into it now. I'm fine. That's all that matters, and I want to concentrate on you."

"And I want to concentrate on you," her mother returned. "I'm still your mother."

The simple statement made her tear up. She was hurting, but she couldn't tell her mother why. She couldn't put any stress on her fragile condition. She had to solve her own problems and stand on her own two feet. "I'm okay."

Before her mother could argue about that, a knock came at the door, and Jason stepped into the room, giving her a questioning look.

"Hello? Who are you?" her mother asked curiously.

"He's my...friend," she said.

"Well, tell your friend to come in."

She didn't have to do that because Jason was already approaching the bed.

He offered her a smile, then turned to her mother. "It's nice to meet you, Mrs. Hunt. I'm Jason Colter. I hope you're feeling better."

"I am." Her mother frowned again. "You look like you've been in a fight. In fact, you look like Alisa does. What happened?"

"We were in a car accident," she told her mother. "We both got some cuts, but we're okay."

"She's right," Jason agreed. "By the way, you have an amazing daughter."

Her mother found the energy to smile at that comment, even

though it was a tired smile. But it was something Alisa had seen little of in the last ten days.

"She is amazing," her mother said. "I'm so proud of her. Her father and I both are."

"Speaking of Dad. Do you know how I can reach him? I have a problem I need to talk to him about. My car is totaled. He'll know what I should do about it."

"He'll be back as soon as he can. Trust me on that, Alisa."

Her mother had never given her a reason not to trust her. Nor had her dad, for that matter. But something was off.

Before she could say more, Dr. Grayson entered the room.

"Well, this is a much better sight than I saw this morning," he said as he moved to the bed to look at her mother. "How are you feeling, Pamela?"

"Not nearly as bad as I was," her mother said. "I could hardly keep my eyes open this morning."

The doctor checked her chart and looked at the monitors. "You're definitely doing better than you were. How's the nausea?"

"It seems to be gone."

"And your breathing?"

"My chest doesn't feel so tight or heavy," she admitted.

"Good. Very good," Dr. Grayson said with an approving nod.

"Do you know what's wrong with me?" her mother asked.

"I'm getting closer to figuring that out," he replied. "Why don't you rest now? We'll talk more later today."

"I am feeling tired again. I wish I could find some energy."

"You will," he promised. "Rest."

"I'll walk you out," Alisa said, sensing the doctor wanted to speak to her alone. "I'll be back shortly, Mom."

"Don't hurry. I'm going to nap." Her mother gave her a sleepy smile, then turned to Jason. "I hope you'll come back, too. I like getting to know Alisa's friends."

"I will definitely be back," Jason replied.

"Make sure my daughter eats something. She's burning the candle at both ends, trying to work and take care of me."

"I will do that," he promised.

With that, Jason followed her and the doctor into the hallway. When her mother's door had closed, she said, "What do you think is going on?"

Dr. Grayson glanced at Jason. "Perhaps we should have this conversation in private."

"It's okay," she said quickly. "He's my friend. You can speak freely."

"Very well. Your mother's blood work came back with several anomalies. Her liver enzymes are elevated, and so is her white blood cell count. We saw increases in these numbers when she was first admitted, and then they went down, only to reappear today."

She stared at him in bewilderment as he continued talking about her mother's blood work, none of the lab results making sense. "I don't understand. Why would her numbers be jumping around so much?"

He gave her a long look. "I have a theory. That's all it is right now, a theory. I need to do more research."

"What's your theory?" she asked, her body tensing.

The doctor glanced at Jason, then back at her. "I think your mother is being poisoned."

CHAPTER SIX

Alisa gasped, his words echoing around her head in a confusing blur. "Are you serious?"

"I'm afraid so," Dr. Grayson replied gravely.

"Her condition has been going on for ten days," she said, trying to make sense of what he'd just said.

"And it gets better, then worse, as if she's being repeatedly dosed."

"That's true. When she first came into the hospital, she was in terrible shape, but with IV fluids and rest, she got better. You're saying she didn't get better because of those things..."

"The fluids may have helped, but perhaps it was also because of a lack of exposure to the toxin."

"What kind of poison are you talking about?" Jason asked. "I'm not just Alisa's friend; I'm also an FBI agent. If her mother is being poisoned, we need to find out who's doing it and how."

"It could be something she inhaled or ingested," Dr. Grayson said, his tone cautious. "Given how her symptoms have fluctuated, I'd suspect it's something introduced into her environment —food, drink, maybe even something in the air. I'd like to move her out of this room, restrict visitor access, and ensure that anything she's consuming has been kept in sterile conditions."

"Oh, my God," she murmured. She turned away from the doctor and opened her mother's door. Her mother was asleep in her bed, so she stepped quietly into the room, searching for contaminants.

Dr. Grayson and Jason came in behind her.

"The flowers," Jason said sharply. "Who brought those?"

"Henry brought the vase on the dresser. I don't know who brought the other one next to the bed. My mother said it was there when she woke up yesterday. We both assumed it was from my father." She started forward, but Jason called her back.

"Don't touch anything," he said. "What about food? Has she eaten anything from outside the hospital?"

"I don't know. She hasn't been hungry. I brought her cookies yesterday, but she only took one bite. Henry brought her the chocolates last night, but I'm not sure if she ate one."

"Let's go into the hall," Jason said.

When the door closed behind them, she turned to the doctor. "What do we do in terms of treatment?"

"I'll get more insight into that after we get the results of her next blood work. In the meantime, I want to flush her system out and hydrate her to get rid of the toxins as soon as possible. I think some have already left her system, which is why her numbers have improved. Whatever she was given was not enough to..." His voice faded away.

"Kill her?" she finished, feeling shocked that someone could want to kill her mother, to kill her.

"Yes," he replied grimly.

"So, if we make sure she doesn't eat anything or breathe anything that could be toxic, she should recover."

"I believe so, but I have to caution you not to get too far ahead, Alisa. I'll run another blood panel later today and see where her numbers are. In the meantime, I think we should take steps to isolate her and control her environment. I want to move her to the sixth floor, where we have more stringent protocols in place."

The sixth floor was where they treated highly infectious patients and also VIPs who needed more security. All rooms were cleaned to a higher level of standards, and the nursing staff worked under a stricter protocol for food delivery and visitor access. "That's a good idea," she said. "How soon can we do that?"

"It will probably take about twenty minutes to ready the room, but I'll make it happen as soon as possible," he said.

"Thank you. I don't want her to stay in this room a minute longer than necessary."

"She's doing better, so whatever it was, it's no longer having a strong effect on her. However, I don't want her to eat or drink anything in the room. If you can make sure that happens, that would be helpful."

"I'd like to take things a step further and get security during the transfer and stationed outside her room upstairs," Jason said. "I'll talk to hospital security and my team as well."

"Whatever you feel is necessary," the doctor replied, glancing at his watch. "We'll do her next blood work at five and should have the results around seven. That will tell us if her numbers are going in the right direction. I hope to consult with another physician later today. In the meantime, it's fine if your mother sleeps. Her body needs rest to recover."

"Thank you so much," she said. As Dr. Grayson left, she looked at Jason. "What do you think?"

He gave her a sober look. "You and your family are caught in the middle of something, and we need to figure it out fast. Which brings me to your father..."

"I know. We need to find him."

"You're not going to like this next question, Alisa."

"Then maybe don't ask it," she said quickly, feeling overwhelmed.

He gave her a sympathetic look, but he pressed on. "Is there any chance your father could have been involved? The poison had to start somewhere—before she got to the hospital. How long was she sick before you brought her in?"

"About a week. Her symptoms fluctuated. She'd feel sick, then better. It was a strange pattern, but now it makes more sense. My father is the one who brought her in on Monday, so he couldn't have been the one who was poisoning her."

"When was the last time you saw your father or that he was with your mother?"

"I saw him Tuesday evening. When I went to her room after my shift on Wednesday, she told me he'd gone out of town. I don't know when she last saw him, but it might have been Tuesday as well. As I mentioned before, she made light of his absence. Since she was doing much better, I wasn't that concerned until everything else happened."

"Got it. Do you live with your parents?"

"No. I have an apartment a few miles from here. It's just the two of them in the house." She paused, realizing another disturbing fact. "We can't go to her house and look for poison because the house caught fire. Do you think that's why?"

"Possibly. It would make sense to destroy the evidence. The way the toxin is being used—it's calculated," Jason said, his voice hardening. "Whoever's behind this is keeping her on the edge, making sure she's sick but not killing her outright. It's deliberate, and that makes it even more dangerous."

She could see the wheels turning in his head, but she didn't know where he was going. "What does that mean to you?"

"It feels like someone is threatening her life, holding her hostage in a way, and I think that ties to the one person who isn't here."

"My dad," she said with a sigh. "It's not like him to be gone. He and my mother are so in love with each other, it's almost unbelievable. After thirty years together, they still have all the passion, the fire, and the trust. They never go anywhere without the other. Which is why I don't understand where my father is, why he would let her suffer without being here to comfort her. Do you think you could use your FBI resources to find him?"

"Yes. I'm also going to get a forensics team over here to go through your mother's room after she's moved upstairs. Have you felt ill while you've been with her?"

"No...I've been tired, but the past few days have been stressful."

"What about the man you mentioned—Henry? Who is he?"

"Dr. Henry Cavendish. He's a good friend of my parents. He runs a medical research lab in the building next door. His team's focus is oncology."

"When did he meet your parents?"

"It was about ten years ago at a high school science fair. Henry's son was in my father's class."

"Your father is a teacher?"

"Yes. He's been teaching high school biology forever. And when he met Henry, he found a friend who also loved science. Henry's wife, Jill, and my mother got along well, too. They were a foursome until Jill died several months ago. Anyway, Henry wouldn't do anything to hurt my mother." She frowned. "There were two vases of flowers in her room, though. I assumed my father had given her the other, but maybe it was someone else."

"We'll check out the flowers and everything else. Let me make some calls, get things going, and we'll talk after that. I'd rather you wait out here than in your mother's room."

"I can't leave her alone in there."

"Alisa, you need to stay as healthy as you can. Otherwise, you won't be able to help her or your father. She's improved. It's most probable that whatever she was exposed to has dissipated or hasn't yet been consumed again. But you need to be careful."

"I won't touch anything, but I'm going to stay with her until she's moved. If there's no danger to her, there's none to me."

He didn't look happy at her response, but he gave a quick nod of resignation and walked away. She opened the door and walked into her mother's room.

The first thing she did was open the window. It would only open a few inches for security reasons, but the small crack allowed some air to flow into the room.

Then she moved to her mother's bed and checked her monitor. Her pulse, heart rate, and oxygen saturation were stable. Her mother was sleeping peacefully.

She was careful not to touch anything. She didn't even want to sit back down in the chair. So, she stood watch over her mother, wondering what the hell her family was mixed up in and what fresh horror might come next.

———

Two hours later, Jason had his team working in a half-dozen different directions. Alisa's mother had been moved into a new room upstairs, where the air had been tested for toxins and every surface had been wiped down and sterilized. In the room that Pamela had left, a forensic team was still conducting tests to determine where she might have been exposed to a toxin.

Flynn had volunteered to speak to the fire investigator about the fire at the Hunts' home and would send an agent there to see if there was anything salvageable.

Savannah and Nick were still trying to trace Novikov's route after leaving the fast-food restaurant. And Beck was looking into Dan Hunt.

Victor Kashin still wasn't talking, but he would be transferred from the hospital to a holding cell later this afternoon.

There were a lot of balls in the air, and Jason was happy to see his new team jumping in wherever he needed them. But they were still a long way from figuring out why Novikov was in LA, what he planned to do, and how they could stop him.

When he walked down the hall to Pamela's new room, he saw a security guard outside her door. After showing his badge, he entered the room and found Alisa with her mother. Pamela seemed to be confused by the move, but she was more alert than she had been previously, which would hopefully give him a chance to ask her some questions.

Alisa gave him a tired smile. She looked as ragged as he felt. Neither one of them had showered or changed out of their dusty clothes, and he didn't know about her, but he had some aches and pains that were getting worse as the day went on.

But there was no time to rest or think about any of that. It was now almost four o'clock in the afternoon on Thursday, and Novikov had arrived in town on Tuesday night. That was almost forty-eight hours, an amount of time in which he could have done many things and met with many people. Unfortunately, there had been no sightings of him and no chatter in any of the underground networks. But he was somewhere, and he was planning something, and hopefully finding out more about the Hunt family would provide vital clues.

"What have you learned?" Alisa asked as she stood up.

"An orderly wearing a mask delivered the vase of flowers next to the bed," he replied. "No one on the hospital staff could identify him, and the security footage of him didn't reveal his face. He was in the room no more than two minutes and left about fifteen minutes before you arrived yesterday."

"So, the flowers were poisonous?" she asked.

"Wait—what?" her mother interjected, surprise in her gaze. "What are you talking about?"

"You haven't filled her in yet?" he asked.

"I was just about to," Alisa said.

"Fill me in on what?" Pamela asked as she pushed herself up into a sitting position, but she was still so weak, she immediately slid back against the pillows. She struggled again to sit up.

"Mom, just rest," Alisa said.

"No. I need you to talk to me, Alisa," she said firmly, getting herself upright again. "What's going on?"

"Dr. Grayson believes your symptoms are because of some type of toxic exposure or poison," she said.

Pamela's eyes widened. "What on earth? Are you serious? Someone has been poisoning me? How is that possible?"

"That's what we're trying to find out, Mom. That's why we moved you to this room. It's been cleaned and sterilized. There's a guard outside the door. And no one will come in or out without us knowing. We're going to limit outside food as well until we know what's going on."

"I can't believe this." Pamela's gaze moved to him. "You said you were Alisa's friend, but I can't remember your name."

"Jason Colter. I'm not just Alisa's friend; I'm an FBI agent."

"Oh," she said, her gaze turning wary. "I see. Did you make my daughter eat something?"

"Not yet, but I will," he said, giving her a smile. "First, I have some questions for you."

"I don't think I have any answers. I can't believe someone would poison me. And I got sick at home, so..."

"It would have had to start there," he said. "Were there any visitors to the house before you started feeling ill?"

"I don't know. I can't remember. The last week is fuzzy in my mind."

"Let's start with your husband then," he said. "Where is he?"

"He went to see a friend."

"The name of the friend?"

"Greg Palmer," Pamela said. "I don't have his address or phone number."

"How about a city or state?"

"Um. I think it was Florida, maybe Miami. I don't know. I wasn't thinking clearly when Dan left, but he assured me he'd be back as soon as he could. And I shouldn't worry about anything."

"Unfortunately, you have a lot to worry about," he told her.

Her gaze darkened. "Not about my husband. If you're suggesting he poisoned me, you're completely off base. He loves me, and I love him. He would never hurt me."

"But he's not here, and Alisa says his phone is off. He's

completely unreachable when you are very ill. Surely, you can see why that raises doubts about his disappearance."

"He didn't disappear; he left," Pamela said stubbornly, showing the same fighting determination he'd seen in her daughter's eyes.

"Mom," Alisa interrupted. "Jason is right. Dad is missing. And unless you can give us more details or a way to reach him, the FBI is going to look for him."

"There has to be a mistake. I couldn't have been poisoned. I don't want the FBI to get involved in this because of me."

"It's not just you, it's also me," Alisa told her mother.

Pamela's eyes filled with worry as she looked at Alisa. "What do you mean?"

"The cuts on my hand and arm, the dirt on my clothes—I was in an accident, Mom. Someone tampered with the brakes on my car. If Jason hadn't been driving, I wouldn't have survived."

"Oh, my God," Pamela whispered, her hand going to her mouth in horror. "When?"

"Today." Alisa drew in a deep breath. "I don't want to stress you out even more, but you need to know what's going on because then you'll understand why we need to find Dad. Last night, after I left your room, someone attacked me in the parking garage."

"Oh, no," Pamela said, shaking her head. "This can't be. What happened?"

"I thought he wanted my car, but he was trying to get me into the vehicle. Jason caught him and arrested him. He can't hurt me anymore, but obviously, he has friends who can. He was under arrest when someone did something to my brakes."

"This is unbelievable. You should have told me sooner, Alisa."

"I was going to tell you this morning, but you weren't doing well." She paused and drew in another breath. "There's one more thing, Mom. Jerry called me earlier."

"Jerry, my neighbor?"

"Someone set fire to your house. I haven't seen the damage, but he said it's significant."

Her mother's skin turned so white that Alisa gave the monitor a quick look, then said, "Do you want some water?"

"I—I don't know," her mother said somewhat breathlessly. "I can't believe what you're telling me. It feels like a horrible dream."

"I wish it was, Mom. The last thing I wanted to do was dump all this on you now, but your life is in danger, and so is mine. Maybe Dad's, too. We have to find him. Do you know where he is?"

"I don't," she said, her gaze moving from Alisa to him. "I'm sorry, but I don't. He didn't give me any more information. He said he'd be in touch soon, and I believe him. I don't know what else to tell you."

There was a sincerity and a fear in Pamela's eyes that suggested she was telling the truth. "Okay," he said. "I believe you, Mrs. Hunt. Let's talk about the week before you got sick. You said you don't remember visitors, but did your husband get any phone calls he seemed concerned about? Did his behavior change in any way? Was he worried? Was he home or away at unusual times? Did he take any money out of the bank?"

He could see her demeanor stiffen with every question.

"Please," she said, putting up a hand. "I'm so tired and confused. Can we do this later?"

"Maybe we should do this later," Alisa said, giving him a worried look.

"Just think for a minute," he told Pamela. "I'm sorry to press you, but I want to protect you and Alisa, and I don't know how much time we have."

"Okay. You're right," Pamela said. "Let's see. Dan got worried when I became ill. I heard him on the phone with Henry once, and he seemed upset about something. I didn't know if he was just worried about me or if there was another matter. I remember hearing him raise his voice, and he rarely did that. He's normally very soft-spoken."

"Did you ask Henry about it?"

"No. But Henry asked me where Dan was last night, and he seemed concerned, too, that he was out of touch." Pamela paused, her gaze troubled. "I feel like he said something else, but I can't remember what it was. Anyway, I told Henry the same thing I told you, that Dan was confident he'd be back soon, and everything would be fine."

"If only we could tell him we were in trouble, so he'd come back now," Alisa said, with a hint of anger in her voice.

"I'm sure he would come if he knew," Pamela said. "How are you going to be safe tonight, Alisa? Maybe you should stay here with me."

"We'll put Alisa in a safe house," he said. "She'll be more comfortable there, and I'll make sure she's protected."

"Will you make sure? Didn't you promise me you'd make her eat today? Has that happened?" her mother asked with a tart note in her voice.

"Mom, he's not responsible for me eating. I can take care of myself," Alisa said.

"But I will make sure she eats tonight," he assured Pamela, needing to get this woman to trust him.

"You better take care of my girl," Pamela said. "I'd do it myself if I could."

"I believe you would."

"I'll think about your questions," Pamela added. "Maybe I'll remember more after I take a nap. I'd like to rest before the nurse comes back to stab me with more needles. And you need to get something to eat, Alisa."

"All right. I'll check in with you later," Alisa said, leaning over to kiss her mom on the cheek. "I love you, and I'm going to make sure you get better."

"I love you, too. Please be careful. I don't want anything to happen to you, Alisa."

"Don't worry about me. Just rest. We'll talk again later."

"It's all going to work out, Alisa. Your dad will return, and everything will go back to normal. You'll see."

Alisa didn't look like she believed her mother any more than he did, but she just nodded and followed him out of the room and into the hallway.

As they stood outside her mother's door, Jason clenched his fists, resisting the urge to pull Alisa into his arms. She looked exhausted, fragile—everything in him screamed to comfort her, but he knew he couldn't cross that line. He could, however, keep his promise to her mother.

"Let's get you something to eat," he said.

CHAPTER SEVEN

Alisa doubted food would help her feel better, but as she went through the cafeteria line, her stomach growled, and she ended up filling her tray with spaghetti, salad, and garlic bread. Jason picked up the same items as she did, throwing in a couple of giant chocolate chip cookies at the end. She used her hospital keycard to get them a discount, and then they sat down at a table in the atrium, surrounded by lush plants and calming water features—a tranquil setting that Alisa desperately needed.

It was only five, but the yogurt and banana she'd grabbed before coming to the hospital this morning seemed like a very long time ago. So much had happened in one day. She could barely process it all, and she'd lived through it. She could certainly understand why her mother had trouble comprehending the magnitude of their problems.

"One of these cookies is for you," Jason told her. "Save room."

"I should say no, but they look good. And I didn't have lunch."

"You also survived a very traumatic car crash. If that doesn't deserve a little sugar, I don't know what does."

"Good point," she said as she twirled her spaghetti around

her fork and popped the bite into her mouth. It tasted delicious, and Jason was happily digging into his plate of pasta as well.

For several minutes, they just ate, and it felt good to not talk or think or speculate. Her body was aching from the knock on the head she'd taken last night to the cuts and bruises she'd sustained today. Besides food, what she really needed was a hot shower. But that would have to wait.

"Do you eat here a lot?" Jason asked.

"Not really. I usually bring a lunch and eat in the lounge or on the rooftop deck. I go home for dinner. I'm ready to get out of here at the end of my shift."

"Do you live alone?"

"I do, but I have nursing friends in the building, so it never feels lonely." She paused. "What about you? Where do you live?"

"Hermosa Beach."

"That's a nice town. Do you have a view of the beach?"

"As a matter of fact, I do. I bought a third-floor condo with an ocean view last year."

"That sounds great. I don't live by the beach. But I love going there. I've always found the ocean to be relaxing."

"I love sleeping with the windows open," he said. "Hearing actual waves crash on a beach is much better than a sound machine. Although, I have to admit I don't spend a lot of time there. I work a lot, and sometimes my job requires me to go undercover and establish a housing situation somewhere else for weeks at a time."

"That sounds interesting and dangerous."

"It's often both."

"You never told me the name of the person you came to the hospital to look for last night. Maybe I would recognize the person."

"His name is Arseni Novikov. Does that ring a bell?"

She shook her head. "I'm sure I've never heard that name before. Is he from Chechnya like Victor Kashin?"

"No. He was born in Leningrad, Russia, which is now St.

Petersburg. He's a very dangerous man. He's been on the FBI's most wanted list for three decades."

Her eyes widened. "Really? That long? Why can't anyone catch him?"

"He doesn't come to the States very often. That he's here now is disturbing. The last time he showed up three years ago, a bomb went off in a courthouse, killing six people and injuring dozens more."

"Oh, my God!" she said. "I remember that explosion. I'd just started working in the ER. It was madness that night. We were one of three hospitals getting victims, and no one knew what was going on."

His jaw tightened. "It was a terrible scene."

"Were you there?" she asked, seeing a disturbing darkness in his eyes.

"I got there too late to stop him."

There was raw emotion in his voice, which surprised her, because he wasn't a man who appeared to show much emotion. "I'm sorry. Did you know someone who died? There was a lot of pain in your voice just now."

"I didn't know anyone who was injured at the courthouse, but my partner and my father were trying to get to Novikov before he could set off the bombs, and they were both gunned down. My father died at the scene, and my partner was seriously hurt. It has taken her a long time to recover, and she's still not completely back to normal."

"Oh, my God! Jason, I'm so sorry." She reached across the table to put her hand on his arm. "I had no idea."

He shrugged, his lips tight, his profile hard. He really wasn't a man who liked to show his feelings. She probably should have let it go, but she was curious to know more.

"Why was your father there? Was he also in the FBI?"

"Yes. He was an FBI agent. He spent most of his career trying to stop Novikov and his reign of terror. Now it's my turn,"

Jason said, his voice hardening. "This time, I won't let him slip through my fingers."

There was no trace of doubt in his voice, just hard-edged determination. "So, this is not just your job; it's personal."

"Yes. It's very personal. But it's also my job. Both things can be true. And you should keep eating."

She let go of his arm as she sat back in her seat, thinking about what he'd told her. "This terrorist you're after...I can't believe he's targeting me or my mom. We've never even been to Russia. We've barely left California. As a family, our biggest trip was to the Grand Canyon. My dad is a teacher. My mom is a librarian. Do they sound like people with terrorist connections?"

"No, but there is a connection."

"Maybe not," she argued. "Whatever is happening to my family could be completely unrelated." Even as she made that case, she wondered if that would be better or worse. Right now, she had Jason and the FBI's attention and protection because they thought she was connected to their case. *If she wasn't, would she and her parents be on their own?*

"Kashin and Novikov shared the same vehicle at some point on Tuesday evening after Novikov arrived in the US," Jason told her. "Kashin went after you. He's what links you to Novikov."

She tried to eat a few more bites, but she no longer felt hungry. She wiped her mouth and set down her fork. "Okay, so what happens now?"

"We finish eating and then check on your mother. You're going to tell me you can sleep in the chair next to your mother's bed, but that's not good enough. You have to be exhausted and probably in pain. I know my aches are getting worse as the day goes on. So, after we check on your mom, I'll take you to a safe house."

"I would like to take a shower and change my clothes at some point," she admitted. "But I also want to see how my mother's labs turn out. Her blood work should be back around seven thirty or eight. I don't want to leave before then."

He thought about that, then said, "That's fine. I need to go into my office. I'll walk you to her room, and then I'll come back in a couple of hours."

"You must be getting bored babysitting me."

He smiled. "Not at all. Life has been anything but boring since I met you."

"Well, that's true."

"I'm sure you'll want to take some clothes to the safe house. Why don't you give me your keys and I'll go by your apartment and pack you a bag?"

She looked at him in surprise. "You could just take me to my apartment on the way to the safe house, and I can run in and grab some things."

"I don't want you near your apartment. I don't know what we'll find there. I'd rather check it out on my own. If you don't feel comfortable with me going through your clothes, I can take Savannah with me."

She didn't like the idea of either of them going through her clothes. "Are you using this to get into my apartment and look around? Do you not believe me when I say I don't know what's going on?"

He met her gaze. "I believe you, Alisa. This is standard protocol. I'm doing everything I can to keep you safe. After what happened at your parents' house, I'd rather not expose you to anything at your apartment."

"I was there last night. It was fine."

"That was last night."

"Okay," she said, too tired to argue. And it wasn't like she was hiding anything, except maybe a messy underwear drawer. The idea of Jason going through her underwear drawer made her more than a little uncomfortable. It felt too intimate, although it probably wasn't as intimate as the kiss they'd exchanged earlier, and making a big deal out of it would make it too big of a deal. She reached into her bag and pulled out her keys. As she handed them to him, she said, "Do you know what happened to my car?"

"It was towed to a police yard, where it will be inspected by a forensics expert. But it's not salvageable. You'll have to get a new vehicle."

"I know. That's a problem for another day. I should get back upstairs."

"Do you want to eat your cookie?"

"I'd like to save it for later."

"Me, too." He wrapped both cookies in a napkin. "We'll take them to go."

They left the cafeteria and walked through the lobby, taking the elevator to the sixth floor. The security guard gave them both a nod and said everything was quiet. The nurse had been in to take some blood, but no one else had come near the room.

She was about to open the door when Jason got a text. His expression stiffened as he swore under his breath."

"What is it?" she asked, her stomach knotting. It couldn't be more bad news...could it?

His gaze was hard and unhappy. "The vehicle transporting Victor Kashin to jail was in an accident. Kashin is dead. So is the guard who was in the back of the van with him. The driver is in critical condition."

Her stomach turned over. "Was it an accident?"

"I doubt it. Someone wanted to make sure Victor didn't talk."

"So, he's dead." She didn't know how to feel about that. She had no compassion for the man who had tried to kidnap her and probably would have killed her if he'd had the chance. But it still seemed surreal that he was dead.

"Yes. Which means Kashin can't tie Novikov to anything that happened to you. But his death won't stop us from finding Novikov. We just have to keep digging. Let's check on your mom, and then I'm going to take off."

"All right." She opened the door and entered the room, which still had the powerful scent of bleach in the air. She checked the monitors. Her mother's vitals were good. She was asleep, but she didn't seem in any distress.

"Everything okay?" Jason asked.

She nodded. "It looks like it."

"Then I'll take off. Don't leave this room until I come back. It's important that you don't."

"I'll stay here," she promised, feeling touched that he cared so much about her safety. "I'll see you soon."

When Jason left the room, she felt a chill, a void created by his absence and also by the shocking news that Victor Kashin had been killed. She didn't care that he was dead, but she worried any clues they might have gotten about who had hired him to kidnap her had died along with him. And if someone could take him out so ruthlessly and so easily, then she could never really think she was safe.

As she glanced down at her sleeping mother, she couldn't help wondering if her mom knew more than she was saying, because something was very wrong in their family. Her parents had always been like two peas in a pod, so close to each other, so loving, so honest. Their relationship had set the bar for what she wanted in a relationship.

Now she was terribly afraid it was all a sham. She just really hoped that it wasn't her father who had poisoned her mother. That was unfathomable.

But even if he hadn't done that, he'd left them alone while their lives were in danger, and what kind of man did that?

She had a feeling she wasn't going to like the answer.

———

Jason got into his office at seven, and despite the hour, there were several people still at their desks. Seeing Savannah, Nick, and Flynn in the conference room, he headed there, eager to find out the latest information on Kashin's accident.

"We just got back the results on the items taken from Mrs.

Hunt's hospital room," Savannah told him. "There was a slow-release capsule planted in the flowers that were delivered by the orderly, who we have now identified as Victor Kashin."

He blew out a breath at that piece of information. "That makes sense. He hit the hospital room before he went to the garage."

"It appears so," Savannah agreed. "The capsule probably released a toxin in the air over a gradual period that didn't appear to be a dose strong enough to kill her. Just make her sick."

"Which means her condition is being controlled by someone who wants her incapacitated but not yet dead. That sounds very much like Novikov. Poison is one of his specialties."

"But why Mrs. Hunt?" Savannah asked.

"That's the question. What happened to Kashin?"

"A truck hit the transport van. Kashin and a guard were deceased at the scene. The truck was abandoned four blocks from the accident site. We're coordinating with local police to search the area for the driver of the truck and to look for potential witnesses." She pointed to the monitor. "We have two shots of the driver running away, but we can't get facial recognition."

Dressed in baggy track pants and a sweatshirt, the driver had long brown hair that was pulled back in a ponytail. He was shorter, slighter, and younger than Novikov. "That's not Novikov, which isn't surprising. He would have hired someone to do the hit-and-run. Someone who may not even know who they're working for." He blew out a frustrated breath. "We should have seen this coming. Novikov wasn't going to leave Kashin alive to talk to us."

"It was impossible to predict he'd take out the transport van," Flynn said.

He knew that, but the result still bothered him.

"We also checked into the fire at the Hunt residence," Savannah continued. "A doorbell camera across the street caught some interesting action."

"When was this video taken?" he asked, seeing a suburban house on a dark street.

"Today at five o'clock in the morning. Watch."

A man came out of the house carrying two suitcases. He was also wearing a baseball cap, a jacket, and loose-fitting pants. He put them in the back of a car parked on the street, then went back into the house. A few minutes later, he brought out another suitcase and a large box, putting them in the trunk. Then he returned inside.

"He's in the house for eleven minutes," Savannah said as she fast-forwarded the video. "Then he comes back out with a shopping bag."

He frowned as the man put the bag next to his other belongings and then got into the vehicle. The camera never got a clear look at the man's face, but he appeared to be older, which made him wonder if it wasn't Alisa's missing father.

Savannah paused the video. "That was it. There's no evidence of anyone else entering the home. But at approximately ten a.m., smoke starts coming out of the house. A few minutes later, a woman walking her dog notices the smoke, runs up to the front door, and starts ringing the bell, but no one answers. She goes back to the sidewalk and gets on her phone." Savannah fast-forwarded the video. Then she said, "As you can see, the fire takes off very quickly. The 911 caller said she heard several pops and then the windows blew out and there were flames everywhere."

He watched the fire for several minutes. "So, the person who took things out of the house earlier in the day might have set some timed explosives to go off later in the day."

"But why wait?" Flynn asked. "Why not just set it when he left?"

"Maybe he wanted some time to get away before the fire started," Savannah suggested.

"Can you send me a copy of the video?" he asked. "I want to show it to Alisa Hunt. I think that man is her father, the one who's allegedly out of town. I don't know why he'd burn down his own house, unless it was to erase traces of the toxin that was slowly killing his wife. Although, I have to believe the poison in the house was something Mrs. Hunt ingested. If it was in the air, Dan Hunt would have had the same symptoms as his wife."

"That's true," Savannah said.

"I've been digging into Dan Hunt," Nick interjected. "His background prior to thirty years ago is fictitious."

His pulse jumped at that piece of information. "Seriously?"

"Yes," Nick said, meeting his gaze. "I found a photo of Mr. Hunt in his college yearbook and compared that to one taken for his teaching position last year." Nick tapped on the computer keys in front of him and put two photos on the monitor. "As you can see, the two men look similar: brown hair, brown eyes, similar build. But the young Mr. Hunt has a significant scar on his face and the older Mr. Hunt does not."

Nick was right. The scar that ran across the younger man's chin was definitely not visible in the second photo. The two men could pass for each other on an ID, but there were definite differences between their bone structure and features.

"I called an associate at the U.S. Marshals Service," Flynn interjected. "I thought Mr. Hunt might be in witness protection, but there's no record of him."

"When did he marry his wife?" he asked.

"Twenty-nine years ago," Nick answered. "Which leads to the question, does Pamela Hunt know who her husband really is? Or did he lie to her, too?"

"I don't know," he admitted. "She's difficult to read, and she has also been very ill, so I'm not sure how clear her head is. I'll talk to Alisa and her mother about all this."

"Anything else?" Flynn asked. "If not, it's been a long day. Let's regroup tomorrow and pick it all up again. Jason, why don't you hang back?"

He stood up as the others left the conference room. Flynn handed him keys and a piece of paper with an address on it. "You can take Miss Hunt here tonight. Do you want to stay with her? I'm short on other resources, but I can get someone else there tomorrow."

"I'll stay with her tonight. I need to find out more about her family, and she'll feel safer with someone she knows."

"Someone who saved her life twice," Flynn commented.

"Hopefully, there won't be a third opportunity to do that."

"What do you think about her? Is she innocent in all this? Is she holding anything back?"

"She has no idea what's going on," he replied. "She thinks her family is the most normal, most boring family on the planet."

"Sometimes, families that appear to be that normal are anything but."

"I agree. And knowing that Kashin poisoned her mother gives me no doubt that Alisa and her family are tied to Novikov. We need to find how they're connected."

Flynn nodded. "I agree. Be careful, Jason. Watch her back, but also watch your own. I don't want to lose the newest member of the team. You need to find Novikov before he finds you. I'm sure after what happened to your father, he knows who you are, and that might give him more motivation."

"I won't let him get away, not this time, not—"

Flynn held up his hand. "Please don't finish that statement with the words if it's the last thing I do."

CHAPTER EIGHT

Alisa found her eyes getting heavy as she sat in a chair next to her mother's bed. The events of last night and today were catching up to her. It was only eight-thirty, but she felt emotionally and physically exhausted, too tired to even worry about what was coming next. She'd spent the past hour trying to figure out things that made no sense, like where her dad was, why her mother was being poisoned, who had wanted to kidnap her and then kill her.

With no answers to any of those questions, her mind moved to Jason, to the very attractive FBI agent who had suddenly become her protector and maybe the only person she could trust. Her father had deserted her, and her mother was lying about something. She had no one else she could talk to, except Jason.

He wanted answers as much as she did, although his interests were much broader than hers. She wanted to know who was trying to kill her mother and herself. He wanted to know that, too, but he also wanted to find a terrorist.

It still blew her mind to think she had somehow become the target of a Russian terrorist. She lived such a normal life. She went to work every day to a job she mostly liked. She had friends to spend time with, although her big nights out usually involved a movie or dinner, maybe the occasional concert. She dated, although they'd all been duds, including Tim, her latest so-called boyfriend, who had never even responded to her breakup text. But other than that, she did nothing all that exciting.

And her parents didn't, either. They had friends over for barbecues. They went to events at the school where her dad taught or at the library where her mother worked. And they were both book people. They loved to read, especially on Sundays, when she'd often find them on the couch, each curled up with a book.

That image in her head was followed by other images just as happy and so ordinary: her dad making pancakes on Sundays because that was his day to cook and eat a big breakfast; her mom planting flowers in the garden she loved; her father taking care of his mountain bike, the one he'd ride on the weekends, getting in his miles on Saturdays when he didn't have to work.

He'd always come back tired and sweaty but looking happy. And the first thing he did when he came in the house was to kiss his wife. Then he'd look for her to ask what she was doing, if she had any problems, if anyone was bothering her. He'd always been very interested in her life. He'd wanted to know all the details. Even when she'd grown up and moved out and started working at the hospital, he always checked in at least two to three times a week to catch up, sometimes more.

That wasn't the kind of man who would get involved with a terrorist. There was not a hint of violence in his personality. He was quiet and kind.

But the man she'd known would be here now, and he wasn't.

She was jolted back to reality by the vibration of her phone in her lap. She glanced at the screen, expecting spam since she didn't recognize the unfamiliar number. But as she read the message, her heart pounded in her chest.

The text was from her dad.

I'm sorry, Alisa. I know you must have questions, that you probably think I've abandoned you and your mother, but I'm doing what I have to do to keep you both safe. I can't explain. I wish I could, but I need you to trust me, and I need you to help me out. I think your mother is being poisoned. Ask the doctor to check her blood and get her protection.

As for you, don't go back to your apartment. In fact, it would be better if you left town. I know you won't want to leave your mother, but you'll both be safer if you're apart.

Lastly, please don't tell anyone you've heard from me. Your life and your mother's life might depend on that. I promise to tell you everything as soon as I can. But please know that I love you. Whatever happens, know that.

Anger flared inside her as she read his words. *Whatever happens?* Too much had already happened. And how exactly was he keeping them safe from afar? They both could have been dead by now. Whatever he was doing to protect them wasn't worth much.

At least she knew he was alive. He still cared. He hadn't just dropped off the face of the earth. But she didn't know where he was or why he'd left. Clearly, he'd guessed her mother was being poisoned, but what would have made him think that? And if he believed that, why wasn't he here? Why hadn't he called the doctor and told him what he thought?

She also didn't understand his demand for her silence. He had no right to demand anything, to ask for her trust. He wasn't here. She was in charge of keeping her mother and herself safe.

As the door opened, she jumped, instinctively clicking off her phone as she got to her feet.

Jason gave her a questioning look as he entered the room. "How's it going?"

"Same," she muttered, walking over to him so as not to disturb her mother. "Her lab results showed slight improvement, which is good. She was up for a little while, but she didn't want to talk to me about anything. She said her head was too foggy, and she couldn't make sense. Then she fell asleep. She'll probably be out until morning."

"Then why don't I get you out of here?"

"I don't really want to go somewhere and be alone. I'd probably feel safer staying here."

He gazed back at her with reassuring blue eyes. "You won't be alone, Alisa. I'll stay with you."

She swallowed hard at that piece of information. She felt safe with him, but she also felt other emotions that were probably a little dangerous. And judging by the way he'd kissed her, he had some of the same feelings. "Are you sure?"

"Yes. We'll talk to your mother in the morning. She'll be safe. I promise you that. We found a time-release capsule in the flowers. They were delivered by the orderly—who we've now confirmed was Victor Kashin. My guess is he went to your mother's room before he clashed with you in the garage."

She thought about what he'd said. "So, he just dropped off flowers with a toxin that would be released over time? Why would he do that? If he wanted to hurt her, she was probably pretty vulnerable when he went into her room with the flowers. She was asleep. Weak. He could have smothered her with a pillow." She shuddered at that thought.

"He wasn't there to kill her, just to poison her. And don't ask me why, because I don't know. All I can say is that someone did not want your mother dead, just incapacitated."

"But they were fine to kill me in my car."

He met her gaze. "Yes."

She let out a breath. "You don't like to make things seem better than they are, do you?"

"Not when it's important that you stay on high alert."

"Oh, I'm on high alert. I jump at every noise, every shadow. It seems unimaginable I'll ever feel safe again."

"You will," he said. "Are you ready to go?"

"Yes." She grabbed her bag and followed him out of the room and downstairs to the lobby.

As they walked through the front door of the hospital, her steps slowed. "Where is the car parked?"

"Right in front. And the valet has had his eye on it since I parked." He gave her a knowing look. "You don't have to worry about the car."

She didn't think she was going to stop worrying about the car or anything else. And as much as she wanted a break from the hospital, she was also afraid to leave. The world seemed like a very scary place right now.

When they got to the black SUV, he paused. "Before we get in the car, I want you to turn off your phone. I don't want anyone tracking you."

"What if the hospital needs to reach me? If my mom's condition changes, I'll have to come back."

"I've given the nurse new contact information for you. Any calls will be relayed to an encrypted phone at the safe house. You won't miss a call about your mother. I've made sure of that."

"Well, it seems like you've thought of everything," she said, although she wasn't just thinking about the hospital not being able to reach her. She would be cut off from her father, too. But she doubted he'd be getting in touch again soon. And she'd be back here tomorrow and be able to use her phone again.

When Jason started the car, she felt a wave of panic.

"It's going to be fine," he told her, clearly reading her mind. He let the car roll a few feet, then tapped the brakes, even though it wasn't needed. "See...We can stop if we have to."

Despite Jason's calm, Alisa's hands clenched in her lap as they descended the hill. Her breath quickened, dread curling in her stomach. It was only a five-minute drive to the intersection below, and she'd made this drive a thousand times without a second thought, but it was dark, the road was empty, and all she could think about was the terror she'd felt earlier in the day. Her breath started coming fast, her heart pounding against her chest so hard she felt a little lightheaded. She was also sweating, a full-blown panic attack taking over her body.

Jason put a hand on her leg, but she pushed it away. "Please keep your hands on the wheel," she said tersely.

"No problem," he said, quickly putting both hands on the wheel. "The intersection is right up ahead, and I'm slowing down."

She could feel the car slowing and that helped ease some of her anxiety. When they finally stopped at the light, and traffic was moving normally through the intersection, she took her first full breath. "How long will it take before I'll be able to go up and down that hill without a panic attack?"

"Probably longer than a few hours," he said, giving her a smile. "But you're a strong woman, Alisa. You'll get past it."

She gave him a bewildered look. "I don't know why you'd think I'm strong."

"You fought for your life against Kashin. You came back to the hospital the next day to take care of your mother. You jumped into action when you heard about the fire, and even after we took that crazy ride down the hill earlier, you went straight back to the hospital to make sure your mother was all right. Through it all, I haven't seen a single tear."

"I've never been one to cry a lot. My nose gets red, and my eyes get puffy. I'm a really ugly crier."

Amusement ran through his gaze. "So, vanity is the reason you hold it all in?"

"Partly. Plus, my dad always told me crying was a waste of time. The best way to feel better was to come up with a plan of action against whatever or whoever was making me want to cry."

"Taking action is usually the best solution for any problem."

"Speaking of action, what else did you find out when you went to your office?"

"I'll fill you in when we get settled," he replied.

"Okay. I assume you went to my apartment. How did it look?"

"Perfectly normal. Nothing appeared out of place, as far as I could tell. I packed you a bag. I grabbed some clothes out of your closet and drawers. They should get you through a day or two. Hopefully, this will all be over soon."

"Hopefully," she echoed as she sat back in her seat, feeling a little less anxious now that they were driving city streets.

She noticed Jason checking the rearview mirror every other block. She assumed he was making sure that no one was following them. He seemed to be very good at his job, and he was so different from anyone she knew. He was a man of action. He ran toward danger instead of away from it. In the last few days, she'd realized she only needed people in her life she could count on.

Not that she knew who she could count on anymore. Her mother, yes, but she was sick. Her father was a big question mark. But Jason was solid. And if she had to go into hiding with anyone, she was really glad it was him.

About twenty minutes later, he drove down a residential street near the Santa Monica beach, eventually pulling into the driveway of a duplex. He used a remote to open the garage and then pulled the car inside. Once the garage door had closed, he got out and walked to the back of the car to open the trunk. She got out of the vehicle and waited for him as he retrieved her small suitcase. When he reached the door leading into the house, he put in a code and opened the door.

They stepped into a mudroom that led past a laundry and into a kitchen. The townhouse was very nice, she thought with surprise. Everything was clean, modern, and beautifully furnished. It was a two-story unit with a living room, dining room, kitchen half-bath and study downstairs and two bedrooms upstairs. She wandered through the house with Jason. She would have taken the smaller bedroom, but he put her suitcase in the primary bedroom with an attached bath.

When they went back downstairs, they moved into the study, where there were several monitors revealing camera angles from around the townhouse. After Jason checked the cameras, he put a code into a door at the far end of the room and opened it, revealing what she thought could be classified as a panic room. The door leading into it was fortified with steel. There were more monitors, as well as an array of weapons in a glass case. There was also a refrigerator stocked with water and other emergency supplies.

As he told her about the safeguards in place, which included a tunnel that led to a park a half mile away and could be accessed through the flooring in the panic room, she felt her tension increase as she became very aware again of the fact that someone wanted to kill her.

"I—I have to get out of here," she said, running out of the panic room and the study and into the kitchen. She grabbed a glass out of the cupboard and filled it with water. Then she took a long drink.

Jason came into the room and gave her an apologetic smile. "Sorry. I thought the safety measures would make you feel protected."

"They just reminded me that someone wants me dead."

"Well, it's not going to happen here."

"I wish you would have said it's not going to happen at all."

"Sorry," he said with a shrug.

She looked around the well-stocked and beautifully designed kitchen. "This is a nice home for a safe house, isn't it? I thought we'd be in a motel room or a small apartment."

"My boss, Flynn MacKenzie, owns this unit. His second-in-command, Beck Murray, has the one next door. They both lived here when they first started the special task force that I'm now on. They were single then. Now they're both married and live elsewhere, but they kept these units to be used as needed for safe houses."

"So you're on a special task force?" she asked. "What does that mean?"

"Normally, I work for the LA field office, but we needed the circle on this case to be tight, so I'm temporarily assigned to this smaller, more agile unit."

She slid onto a stool at the island. After a moment, Jason sat down across from her.

"We could go into the living room where it's more comfortable," he suggested.

"I'm okay here."

"Are you hungry?" he asked, then frowned. "Damn. I left the cookies at my office."

"It's fine. I don't want anything. This water is fine."

"Are you sure you don't want something stronger? There's wine and a full bar in the dining room. Whiskey, bourbon, tequila..."

"I need to keep a clear head." She took another sip of her water. "Why did the circle have to be small on this case?"

His lips tightened. "Before the courthouse explosion, we were close to catching Novikov. But someone in the FBI tipped him off. That's how my father and partner ended up walking into an ambush. I got to the scene about five minutes too late."

"Did you find your father?" she asked in horror.

"Yes."

"I can't imagine."

"It was the worst day of my life," he said darkly. "I knew my dad was gone the second I saw him. Luckily, Stephanie survived. I was waiting for an ambulance with her when the courthouse blew up. We were so close to stopping Novikov..." He shook his head, pain etched in every line of his face.

"I'm so sorry, Jason."

"That's why I'm working with a different team now. I can't change what happened, but I can stop Novikov from putting more people through hell."

She could understand why he was so motivated to capture the man. He carried a heavy personal loss. "I wish I could help you make the connection between my family and this Novikov person. I don't see one, but there's obviously something I'm missing. Do you have any idea what he's planning to do? Is it going to be another bomb, like the one at the courthouse?"

"Possibly. There are, unfortunately, too many possibilities. Several large events are taking place next week that could be targeted. We're focused on three of them, but we need to narrow it down, or better yet, catch Novikov before then."

"Next week is like three days away."

"Exactly. And whatever he is planning will be big and deadly. That much, I know."

Her stomach churned. "What on earth could this man want with me?" she asked in bemusement.

"He has to be connected to your father."

She shook her head. "Just because my dad isn't here doesn't mean he's working with a terrorist."

"Hang on a second."

She frowned when he left the room. He came back a moment later with a laptop computer and set it on the island. "What are you doing?"

"I'm pulling up my email. The devices in this house go through an encrypted server. I want to show you something." He hit a few more keys, then turned the computer around to face her.

It took her a second to realize she was looking at a video taken across the street from her parents' house.

"This is footage from a doorbell camera on your parents' block."

"When was this taken?"

"A few hours before the fire started. Do you recognize the man coming out of the house with suitcases?"

With each passing frame, unease churned in her stomach, tightening into a knot.

"Alisa," Jason said, forcing her gaze to meet his. "Who is that man?"

"That's my father." She took a deep breath as anxiety ran through her. "I think I'm going to need a drink."

CHAPTER NINE

Seeing the distress in Alisa's big brown eyes, Jason turned the computer back around and closed the lid. "I could use a drink, too. Let's go to the other room."

Alisa nodded and followed him into the other room. As she sat down on the big comfortable couch in the living room, he set the computer on the dining room table and then moved over to the bar. "What would you like? Wine, whiskey, tequila?"

"I'll take red wine if it's there."

He opened a bottle of wine, poured two glasses, and then took them into the living room. He sat down on the couch next to her and handed her a glass.

She took a long sip, then set her glass on the coffee table and slipped off her shoes. Getting more comfortable, she tucked her legs up under her and picked up her glass again.

"So, what do you think your father was doing at the house?" he asked.

"It looked like he was taking suitcases and putting them in his car for his trip."

"You said he left Tuesday. The video is from early this morning. He was still in town last night when you were attacked."

She stared back at him with a troubled gaze. "Maybe he left, came back, then left again."

"Why would he do that? And he didn't just take out one suit-case, he took several other items. I think he knew the house was going up in flames."

Her brows raised in surprise. "What? Why would you think that? The fire happened hours later."

"The fire started in two places. The initial report from the fire department was that there were probably at least two incen-diary devices that triggered the fire. It's possible your father started the fire by either setting the devices before he left or triggering them with a remote."

"Why would he burn down his own house? That doesn't make sense, Jason."

"If he was responsible for the toxins that made your mother sick, he might have wanted to hide his tracks."

She started shaking her head before he could finish his sentence. "No. He would never hurt my mother. Never. He adores her."

"I understand you want your father to be a good guy."

"He is a good guy," she said fiercely. "You're making assump-tions, but you don't have evidence that he did anything except take some things out of the house. You don't know him, but I do. He's been in my life for twenty-eight years, and he's been an amazing father. I don't have any reason not to believe in him. He's always been a great person. You can ask anyone who knows him. Every year, he's voted the most popular teacher in the school. He's not evil. He's not a killer."

"Whoever poisoned your mother had access to the house."

"That doesn't mean it was my dad. My father is not an explo-sives expert, nor does he know how to poison someone. This is crazy. He's a teacher. He's a dad and a husband. He coached my soccer team for three years. He ran an after-school club for kids who had nowhere to go. He used to take me and my friends to the mall and wait for us so we wouldn't have to walk home after dark. He was there with ice cream when someone was mean to me, or I broke up with a boyfriend. He's not the person you're describing."

"He sounds a little too good to be true," he said dryly, thinking she'd described a father who had been nothing like the man he grew up with. He'd loved his father, but his dad had never spent a lot of time with him. He'd been too devoted to his job.

"Everything I just said is true, Jason. I'm not lying to you."

"Okay. Then where is this super father of yours now?"

She hesitated, then said, "I wish I knew."

There was something about her slight hesitation that made him wary. "What *do* you know, Alisa? Because it feels like you know something you haven't told me."

She averted her gaze, staring down at her wineglass.

"Alisa," he prodded. "I can't protect you if I don't know everything."

"I don't know where he is," she said quickly.

"But?" He gave her a hard look. "Haven't I proved that I have your best interests at heart, Alisa? You can trust me."

"I do trust you, but I'm worried you're so set on my father being a bad guy you won't give him a chance to explain."

She definitely knew something.

"I'm your best bet at making sure nothing happens to him until he can explain what he's involved in. But make no mistake, he is involved." He paused, letting that sink in, then added, "My team has been looking into your father's life. It appears that he took someone else's identity about thirty years ago, shortly before he married your mother."

Her eyes widened. "What?" she asked. "That can't be true."

"It is. His educational background is tied to a man named Daniel Hunt, but your father is not the man who attended the college on his résumé."

"No. You're wrong."

"I'm not wrong," he said forcefully. "At some point, your

father reinvented himself."

"Why would he do that?"

"I can only assume he needed to escape his past. What did he tell you about his childhood and his family? Have you met any of his relatives? Grandparents? Aunts and uncles? Cousins?"

"My father was an only child, and his parents died when he was twenty. He said there wasn't anyone left on his side of the family after that, or at least no one he talked to."

"That aligns with someone wanting to start over. With no relatives, he could be whoever he wanted to be. What about your mother's relatives?"

"They were around. Her dad died when I was six, so I don't remember much about him. Her mother passed away seven years ago, and we saw a lot of my grandmother when I was growing up. She lived down the street. My dad always said she was a great blessing to him because he missed his mother so much. She was his second mom." She shook her head, her brown eyes troubled. "This is all so unbelievable, Jason. How could my dad teach science if he never got a degree? I know he's smart, but how could he fake it all these years?"

"I don't know. Did he mention traveling in his youth? Was he ever in Russia or any of the other Eastern European countries?"

"He told me he has never gone anywhere. His parents didn't have money to travel. He was born in Nebraska and lived there until his parents died, and then he moved to California to go to school."

"Do you know what ethnic background he is?"

"He said he has some Greek blood in him. He has dark hair and olive skin. He told me he'd like to go there sometime, but he never has. And like I told you before, I haven't even been out of the country, so..." Her words trailed away. "I just can't see a connection. It's like you're trying to take my very normal dad and make him into a spy or something. You're telling me a story about my life that doesn't feel true."

"I think the story of *your* life is true, Alisa. But I don't believe the story of your father's life prior to your birth is anything close to what he told you."

She gave him a wounded look.

"I'm sorry," he added. "I'm not trying to hurt you, but you have to see what's right in front of you. Your father is the reason your life is upside down. Now, I'm going to ask you again. Do you know something you haven't told me, Alisa?"

She let out a sigh. "Yes. He sent me a text right before you picked me up tonight."

His pulse leapt. "What did it say?"

"I could show you his exact words, but I'd have to turn on my phone."

"Why don't you tell me what he said, and I'll decide if I need to read it for myself?"

"He said he was sorry for not being with us, that he was trying to keep us safe. That he would explain at some point what was happening. He did mention that he thought my mother was being poisoned, and I should tell the doctors to test her blood."

"He thinks his wife is being poisoned, but he doesn't come running to her side?"

"I don't understand it, either. But he asked me to trust him, to know that he loves me and my mother. He also told me not to tell anyone he'd been in touch, that I'd be risking all our lives if I did." She bit down on her lip. "I hope I didn't make the wrong choice by telling you now."

"You didn't." He met her gaze. "Did he say anything else?"

"He told me to get out of town, to stay away from my apartment, to get my mother security—but he didn't say where he was, what he was doing, or when I would see him again. He didn't say anything about a terrorist or his past. It was not a long text." She took a breath. "I know it looks bad. And as much as I love him, I am angry with him. I feel like he abandoned us. But it's also impossible to ignore the faith my mother has in him and her absolute certainty that he is doing what he needs to do."

As she rationalized her father's absence, he had to ask, "Are you sure he didn't set up a meeting with you somewhere? Maybe tomorrow?"

"No. He didn't do that," she snapped, a bit of her rage toward her father turning toward him.

"I had to ask."

"You didn't have to ask." Her brown eyes flashed with fire. "You want me to trust you, then you have to trust me."

"You held on to the information about that text for a while, and I'm not sure you would have told me if I hadn't pressed you. I want to trust you, Alisa, but I can see how conflicted you are."

"I love my parents."

"I understand that, but this isn't just about your family. Thousands of people could lose their lives or could be injured for life. I'm trying to stop a catastrophically bad event, and I don't want to scare you, but you cannot bury your head in the sand."

"I'm not doing that."

"I hope not, because this isn't over. You and your mother are still in danger because of something your father did. We can sort all that out later, but we have to focus on what is going on now and getting your dad to talk to me is the best possible scenario."

"I understand. If he contacts me again, you'll be the first to know," she said with a heavy sigh.

"Maybe you should try to get some rest. You must be exhausted."

"After that lovely bedtime story you just told me about the end of the world coming?" she asked dryly. "I think we need to talk about something else for a few minutes. Otherwise, I don't think I'm going to sleep at all."

"How about some more wine?" he said with a smile "Would that help?"

"It couldn't hurt."

He got up from the couch and brought the wine bottle back to the table. He poured them both half a glass and sat back down. "How are you feeling physically?"

"Battered and bruised," she said. "What about you?"

"Same."

"We've talked enough about my family. Tell me about yours, Jason. You said your father was an FBI agent, so you followed in his footsteps?"

"Yes. I went into the family business," he said as he drank his wine. " My grandparents were both FBI agents—my grandfather even made deputy director before he retired."

"That's impressive. You're like FBI royalty."

He gave her a dry smile. "I have had big shoes to fill. My father was also quite the hero in his day. He had some big wins."

"What did your grandmother do in the FBI?"

"She was a profiler, and she loved it. She was great at reading people. Sharp as a tack and her insights were always right. But when she had children, she quit the bureau and became a stay-at-home mother." He smiled to himself. "Although her skills were still in evidence when I tried to lie to her as a teenager. She could see right through me."

"Is she still alive?"

"She is. She lives in a senior housing development in Encino. She moved there after my grandfather died eight years ago. That's how both my father and I ended up out here. We didn't want her to be alone."

"What about your mother? Was she also in the FBI?"

"No. She hated the bureau."

"Why?"

"Because it was my father's obsession, his mistress, she used to say. She thought he was more in love with his job than he was with her. They divorced when I was twelve, and three years later, she passed away from cancer."

"I'm sorry. You've had a lot of loss in your life."

"Too much," he agreed. "But that's life. We don't get to choose the path we walk."

"We get to choose some things," she said. "It's not all preordained."

"I didn't mean it that way. I just meant that when nasty shit happens, there's nothing you can do about it, except to keep going."

"That's true. Were you and your dad close after your mom died?"

"No. He was still burying himself in work. During the school year, we had a housekeeper who made sure I had food and tried to keep an eye out for me, but I was an angry teenager and probably had too much freedom. My grandparents would take me in during the summers, and those months were good." He paused. "You don't really want to hear all this, do you?"

"I do," she said, an almost desperate note in her voice. "Tell me more."

He didn't want to tell her more. He wasn't even sure why he'd told her this much. He wasn't one to overshare, especially when it came to family.

"Did you join the FBI just because it was the family business or because you were trying to find a connection with your dad?" she asked.

He was surprised at how quickly she'd made that leap. "It was actually my grandfather who kept telling me I should make the FBI my career. I wasn't sure. When I went to college, I got a degree in international relations and criminology. I actually thought about joining the CIA, making my own path. I even worked for the State Department for a few years after college, but eventually, I applied to the FBI."

"What did your dad think about it?"

"He was ambivalent. I'm not sure he wouldn't have preferred I do something else."

"Why? He should have been proud to have you follow in his footsteps."

"He was probably afraid I'd embarrass him, screw something up. He was a hard man with high expectations for himself and for his son. It wasn't easy to get a compliment from him." He cleared a throat, wondering again why he was telling her something so personal.

"You don't seem like someone who is a screwup, Jason," she said, giving him a doubtful look. "From what I've seen, you're very good at your job."

"There are times when I could have been better."

"That's true for all of us," she said. "But that's okay. We all need room to grow. And nobody is perfect." She ended her statement with a yawn.

He smiled at her pretty and very tired face. "It appears I've now sufficiently bored you into almost falling asleep."

"I'm sorry." She gave him a guilty look. "It's been a wonderful distraction to think about something else. And your job is so important, Jason. You're a real-life hero."

"So are you. You save people's lives, too."

"I don't think I've ever saved someone's life, but I've helped ease their pain," she said.

"That's important, too. Do you like being a nurse?"

"Most days. Sometimes, I wish I had more power to heal because it's difficult to watch people suffer. But I do everything I can."

"That's all you can do."

"I was planning to go back to work on Monday. Do you think this will be over by then?"

"Let's see what tomorrow brings."

"So, it's day by day, huh?"

He met her gaze. "I think it has to be, don't you?"

"I guess. How do you do this and stay sane? How do you have a life outside of world-changing, life-altering events?"

"I don't have a life outside of my job. It's much easier to do this work and be single. I don't have to worry about someone worrying about me. I don't have to feel bad about missing personal events, like birthdays and anniversaries. I can just focus on what needs to be done."

She frowned. "That sounds incredibly lonely."

He shrugged. "I don't have time to be lonely. I'm busy."

"What about when you're not busy, when you come home

after work, and there's no one there?"

"It doesn't happen very often, or I'm so tired, I just want to sleep."

"That doesn't sound like a pace you can keep up forever."

"It works for me," he said, not wanting to admit that he'd been feeling a little stressed by the constant flow of cases one after the other, feeling like he was on a treadmill that he couldn't get off. But getting off this treadmill wasn't an option. He had to stop Novikov. This might be the only chance he would have. So he decided to change the subject. "What about you, Alisa? What do you do when you're not working? You said you don't have a boyfriend, but are you dating?"

"I was seeing someone for a few weeks until my mom got sick. It turned out he was great with a casual, fun relationship, but terrible with anything serious. He couldn't stand going to the hospital. The smells made him sick. After showing up once for me, I never saw him there again."

"Sounds like a loser. You deserve better than that."

"I think so, too. I texted him after I almost got kidnapped, and his response was so dismissive and uncaring that I told him we were done. I can't be with someone who is that selfish."

"I agree."

"I've always wanted a love story like the one my parents have. They've always been so happy together." Her voice faltered. "At least, I thought they were. Maybe everything was a lie."

He was sorry to see her mood turn. "That part of your father's life might not have been a lie. Your parents have been together for thirty years. That's something."

"I always thought so, but now I don't know." She yawned again. "I know I should go to bed. I just feel like once I'm alone in the quiet, everything is going to come back to me."

"I can't do anything about the nightmares, but I want you to know that you're safe here. I'm not going to let anything happen to you."

She gave him an emotion-filled look that made his gut

clench. They were treading into dangerous territory, and he couldn't let them go there. He cleared his throat and got to his feet. "Do you want me to walk you upstairs?"

"No. I can make it on my own," she said as she stood up. "Thank you, Jason. For everything you've done and are doing for me. I really appreciate it. You're a good guy, and I have to say, I think you might be a little too hard on yourself." She paused, giving him a look that heated the air between them. "I wish we'd met under other circumstances," she murmured. "But I probably never would have met someone like you if all this craziness wasn't happening to me."

"Probably not," he said, feeling once again pummeled by an intense desire to pull her into his arms and drive all the potential nightmares out of her head. "You really need to go upstairs, Alisa."

"So, it's not just me?"

He knew exactly what she was asking. "No. It's not just you. But I'm here to protect you, nothing else."

Her gaze filled with conflicting emotions, and he found himself holding his breath, wondering if she would push back against the wall he'd just put between them.

After a long moment, she said, "Goodnight, Jason." And then she turned and walked up the stairs.

He couldn't stop watching her until she was finally out of sight. Then he blew out a breath. This wasn't good. He couldn't let himself get caught up in her, in feelings that had no place in an investigation, in his search for Novikov. That had to be his focus, his only focus.

Which was why he was going to stay downstairs and review the investigation. He needed to think about work and not about Alisa.

But even as he pulled out his computer and sat down at the dining room table, his mind kept drifting to the smart, beautiful, sweet, and sexy woman upstairs.

He'd made the right decision; he just wasn't happy about it.

CHAPTER TEN

Alisa woke up at seven on Friday morning. The sun was shining through the shutters and when she got up to open them, she saw a blue sky, hopefully a good sign of what was to come. She'd taken a shower before bed, but she took another one now, the hot water soothing her stiff and aching muscles. And when she got dressed in some clean jeans and a pullover long-sleeve knit shirt, she felt a lot better. She'd also found an extensive first aid kit in the bathroom, which had allowed her to clean her wounds and reapply a bandage to cover the stitches on her palm and the long cut on the back. The fact that there were so many supplies reminded her she wasn't in a hotel, she was in a safe house. There had probably been people who had stayed here who had been worse off than her. That fact did not make her feel better, so she hastily tucked the kit away and made her way downstairs.

Jason was in the kitchen. He was standing at the stove, scrambling eggs, and looking very sexy in jeans and a black polo shirt, his dark-brown hair still damp from a recent shower.

He turned his head, giving her a smile, and she felt a jolt of attraction run through her. His eyes were so blue, his face so handsome, she had trouble looking away, especially since he didn't look much like a federal agent today. He looked like a guy she might have spent the night with.

But he'd made it clear that wasn't on the table. Logically, she knew he was right. But she still kind of wished it had happened.

"Morning," he said. "Did you sleep?"

"More than I thought I would." She grabbed a mug from the cabinet and filled it with coffee, needing a shot of caffeine to clear her head. "I need to check in with the hospital about my mother. Can I turn on my phone?"

"I already checked. Your mother had a quiet, restful night. Her vital signs are good. Dr. Grayson is going to check on her at ten and would like to meet up with you then. I told the nurse to let him know we'd be there."

"Okay, but how come you can use your phone, but I can't use mine?"

"I used a second phone that we keep here in the house. It can't be traced."

"Oh. Well, thank you for checking. Maybe my mother is going to be all right." She felt more hopeful than she had in a long time.

"The signs are pointing in that direction. I made some eggs. Are you hungry?"

"If there's enough, yes."

"There's plenty. I've got bacon in the oven, too."

"I thought I smelled bacon." She sat down at the island, watching him work. He cooked in an efficient, no-steps-wasted kind of way. He seemed to be extremely organized and time-sensitive, popping in the toast at just the right moment so that it would be ready when the eggs and the bacon were done.

Ten minutes later, she had an enticing plate of food in front of her, and she savored the feeling of normalcy that came along with it. That probably wouldn't last long, but she was going to enjoy it while she had it.

"I wanted to ask you about Henry Cavendish," Jason said. "You mentioned that he visited with your mother on Wednesday night and that he's a longtime family friend. Is it possible your father would have spoken to Henry about where he was going?"

"Over my mother? I don't think so. If he was going to tell anyone, he would have told her."

"Unless he needed her not to know. But he might have asked someone for help. Would you say anyone else is closer to your father than Henry?"

She frowned, barely hearing the second part of his question because she was stuck on the first part. "Why would he need her not to know?" she asked.

"So she couldn't be forced to tell anyone. Nor could you."

"But someone could still think we know more than we do."

"Yes," he said, meeting her gaze. "But you're both under the protection of the FBI, so let's focus on Henry. Unless there's a closer friend we should discuss?"

"My dad has lots of friends, but I'd say he's closest to Henry. They golf a lot on Sundays. If my father isn't with my mom, he is usually with Henry. And even more so since Henry's wife died."

"How did she pass away?"

"Heart attack. It was unexpected. She'd always seemed to be in good health."

"I'd like to speak to Henry. You said he works in the building next to the hospital? Why don't we stop there on our way in?"

"Okay," she said. "But my mom said that Henry asked where my dad had gone, so he may not know any more than we do."

"Only one way to find out."

———

As Jason drove out of the garage twenty minutes later, he felt a mix of emotions. Getting back to work should have felt like relief, but the truth was...he was getting too close to Alisa. He needed to remember they weren't friends. She was his assignment and maybe the key to finding Novikov. He couldn't let anything else get in the way.

"You're quiet," Alisa commented. "Are you worried someone is following us?"

"No. We're good," he said, taking another look in the rearview mirror just to be sure.

"Can I turn on my phone now?"

"Let's wait until we get to the hospital. They'll expect you to be there, but we don't need them to know where you are when you're not there."

"Okay," she agreed, tapping her fingers nervously on her thighs.

He liked her casual jean look, and that she'd left her thick, wavy hair down. It fell around her shoulders in a very pretty way, making him want to run his hands through her hair, capture her face, and steal a kiss from her also very pretty mouth.

He hit the brakes hard at the next intersection, not so much because he was going too fast with the car, but because he was going too fast in his head.

She shot him a quick, worried look.

"Sorry. I was thinking about something else," he muttered, forcing himself to focus. She was just a job, he told himself. He could compartmentalize, and he would. There was no other option. The stakes were too high.

He kept his attention on the road as he drove them the rest of the way to the medical center. When he headed up the hill, he noticed that Alisa focused her gaze on her hands, which she was twisting in her lap. He couldn't blame her. It would take a while to get over that harrowing crash.

When they reached the medical center, he showed the valet his badge and left the car in front of the stand, keeping his keys with him. Then they walked to a five-story building next to the hospital where labs and medical offices were located. Henry Cavendish's lab was on the top floor, and when they walked into the office suite, he saw a small lobby area with two couches, a couple of chairs, and a receptionist sitting behind a desk. She was speaking to an older gentleman about a clinical trial.

As they waited for that conversation to finish, a woman in a lab coat came through the door. She appeared to be in her early forties, her hair a dark red and pulled back in a bun. She stopped in surprise when she saw them. "Alisa, how are you? How is your mother? Henry told me she'd taken a turn for the worse."

"She's doing much better now," Alisa replied. "Is Henry here? I need to talk to him."

"He's in his office, but he's on a call. I'm sure he'll want to speak to you, though. I'll let him know you're here."

"Thanks, Lauren."

"Should I tell him who you're with?" Lauren asked, sending him a curious look.

"Special Agent Jason Colter," he told her, noting her suddenly wary expression.

"Special agent?" Lauren echoed. "As in FBI?"

"That's right. And you are?"

"Lauren Silenski. I'm a senior lab manager." Lauren turned to Alisa. "Is this about your mother? Henry said he couldn't get in to see her yesterday, that she'd been moved, and visitors were restricted. He said he left you a message, but he hadn't heard back."

Jason thought Lauren was a little too interested in Alisa's mother's condition.

Maybe Alisa thought the same thing because she simply said, "It's been busy. I haven't had a chance to return calls. Will you let him know we're here? We have to get to the hospital shortly."

"Of course."

Lauren disappeared through the door and Alisa turned to him. "She's a very nosy person."

"So, her questions weren't unusual?"

"No. Since Henry's wife died, he and Lauren have developed a relationship outside of work. My parents aren't too thrilled about it."

"Why not?"

"Lauren just seems like she has a lot of ambition and likes to spend Henry's money. They go out to dinner a lot, and the fancier the restaurant, the better. My parents are worried she's taking advantage of his loneliness."

"Maybe he's just enjoying the attention of a younger woman."

"I'm sure he is. I will say that she is very smart. She leads one of his research teams. They're working on a nanoparticle delivery system."

"I have no idea what that is," he said dryly.

"It's complicated, and I'm not sure I know exactly how it works, but in cancer treatment, if they can isolate nanoparticles and deliver medications to certain cells without affecting other cells, it could be a game changer. Only the cancerous cells will be affected, not the healthy cells. They've just started clinical trials, so it will take time to know how effective this new system is, but it looks promising. Henry is very excited about it. I only know as much as I know because my dad always asks him a lot of questions. He's a science nerd."

He thought about how much his mother had hated chemotherapy, how it had affected her entire body in such a negative way that she'd become a shadow of herself. "I'm glad they're working on that because cancer sucks."

She gave him a compassionate look. "How long was your mother sick?"

"About nine months start to finish, but all of it was bad."

"I know. I work in oncology at the hospital, so I know what that looks like. It's why I'm excited about what Henry's team is developing. I just wish the research and the trials could go faster, but it takes a long time."

"It does," he agreed. "And people die while they're waiting for a cure."

Alisa reached out, gently squeezing his hand. The gesture was meant to comfort, but the warmth of her touch lingered, stirring something deeper in him. She was such a sweet person, so genuine, so kind. Her touch felt like a balm to his cynical and wounded soul. He'd spent a lot of time on the dark side of life the last few years. He'd almost forgotten what this felt like.

As he held on to her hand, their gazes met, and something inexplicable passed between them, something he didn't want to define, and he didn't think she did, either.

Fortunately, they didn't have time for words because Lauren opened the door and told them Henry would see them now.

Alisa let go of his hand as they followed Lauren down a wide corridor where glass-walled labs were located one next to the other. The doors were closed, many with coded locks and signs prohibiting entry. At the end of the hall was Henry's office, which was spacious and well-decorated with a view of the city from the windows behind his desk.

Henry got up to greet Alisa with a hug, and Jason took a moment to study him. Henry Cavendish was a tall, lean man with pepper-gray hair, glasses, and pale skin that looked like it never saw the sun.

Henry's warm smile faltered the moment Alisa introduced Jason, tension flickering in his eyes. But he came forward to shake his hand and then waved them toward a couch and two chairs, which surrounded a coffee table laden with medical journals.

As they sat down, he was surprised to see Lauren taking a seat as well. And he wasn't the only one.

"Lauren," Henry said. "Would you mind checking on the experiment? It's time-sensitive, and I need you to make sure it runs smoothly. I can take care of things here."

"Oh, of course," Lauren said, not looking happy about being dismissed.

As she exited the office, she left the door open, and Jason couldn't help but wonder if that was deliberate.

"I spoke to Dr. Grayson last night," Henry told Alisa. "He shared his thoughts with me about what is going on with your mother. To say I was shocked is an understatement. I called you, but you didn't answer, and I didn't want to bother you with a message. I figured you were with your mom."

"I was. I'm also stunned her condition is because of a toxic substance. She has apparently been getting dosed for the last ten days, and I can't imagine who would poison her."

"It's impossible to imagine," Henry agreed, turning to him. "I assume you're investigating, Agent Colter."

"I am. And the person I'd really like to speak to is Dan Hunt. I understand you and Alisa's father are very good friends. Do you know where he is?"

"Pamela said he went to visit a friend," Henry returned.

"And you didn't find that strange, considering his wife is fighting for her life?" he challenged.

"I found it quite odd," Henry said. "And rather appalling, to be honest. I never thought Dan would leave Pamela on her own. He's always been a very loyal, loving husband. Has he spoken to you, Alisa?"

"No," she replied. "But I need him to come back and help me deal with all this."

"I called him, but his phone didn't connect," Henry said. "That surprised me, too. I'm sorry you're having to handle all this, Alisa. What can I do to help?"

"You can try to help me find my dad. Who else would know where he is?"

Henry shook his head, giving them a baffled look. "I have no idea. I'm sorry."

"Did you hear what happened to my parents' house?" Alisa asked.

"Something happened?"

"Someone set a fire. The house is basically gone."

Henry's jaw slackened. "That's terrible. Are you saying it was arson?"

"Yes."

"I don't understand what's going on. I hope you can figure this out, Agent Colter."

"Oh, I'll figure it out," Jason returned. "When was the last time you spoke to Dan Hunt?"

"It was on Monday when he took Pamela to the hospital. We spoke in the ER, and I assured him I'd do what I could to help."

"What about before that? Were you in frequent contact with Dan?"

"We spoke a few times a week. But he didn't mention any problems or concerns. Even when Pamela first got sick, he thought she had just caught a bug. He wasn't worried. But that changed when he brought her to the hospital. That's when I saw genuine fear in his eyes." Henry paused. "Now that I know what's been happening with Pamela, I'm also concerned about you, Alisa. What's with the bandage on your hand?"

"I cut myself. It's fine. I'm fine," she said.

He was surprised Alisa didn't launch into more detail about the kidnapping attempt or the car crash. But he was also fine with not getting into all that with Henry. Maybe she felt the same way.

"If your mother was being poisoned, you could also be in danger," Henry said. "Perhaps you should think about getting out of town."

"I can't leave my mom, especially with my father gone. She needs me. She needs an advocate."

As Alisa finished speaking, Lauren returned.

"I'm sorry to interrupt," Lauren said. "But there is an urgent call for you, Henry. Otherwise, I wouldn't bother you."

Henry gave Lauren a questioning look, then nodded. "Very well." He got to his feet and smiled apologetically at Alisa. "I have to go, but I'd like to visit your mother when that's possible."

"She's not having visitors right now," Alisa said as they stood up. "She needs to be in a controlled environment."

"I understand. If there's anything you need, please call me. I'm not your dad, but I'd like to be there for you."

"I appreciate that."

"It was nice to see you again, Alisa," Lauren said as she walked them to the door. "I hope everything will be all right with your mom."

"Thanks."

As they stepped out of the office, Jason paused, his phone vibrating in his pocket. "One second." He took out his phone to check the message, surprised to see a text from his former partner. Not that they didn't occasionally talk, but it had been a few months. The fact she'd reached out now that Novikov was in town made him nervous. He'd answer her later.

As he put his phone into his pocket, he heard Henry speaking to Lauren in a tense tone.

"Did you tell her I can't speak to her now?" Henry asked.

"I did, but Tatiana is very insistent she speak to you and only you. She's worried about not getting in the trial with her recent symptoms."

His pulse jumped at the mention of Tatiana.

Alisa gave him a questioning look. He put up a hand as she started to speak.

"I can't talk to her right now. Tell her I'll call her back," Henry said.

"Henry—"

"Just do it, Lauren. I have other things to take care of right now."

As Jason heard Lauren moving toward the door, he hurried down the hallway, and Alisa quickly followed.

They didn't speak until they left the building. Once outside, Alisa paused, giving him a questioning look. "What was that all about? What was in the text you read, and why did you want to eavesdrop on Henry and Lauren?"

"The text was from my ex-partner, Stephanie Genaro. She wants to meet, which is a problem for me."

"Why?"

"When Novikov shot her three years ago, her injuries prevented her from working as a field agent ever again. She has been very depressed about that, and while she has returned to work as an analyst, it's still difficult for her to be tied to a desk. I want to be there for her, to support her, but I have to keep this investigation tight. If she knows Novikov is in LA, she'll want in, and I can't let her in."

"Why not? It sounds like Novikov cost her a lot."

"He did, and I wouldn't blame her for wanting to take him down, but I can't let someone's personal desire for revenge complicate things. I have to keep this clean."

"But, Jason, you have a personal desire for revenge. He killed your father. Why should you be involved and not her?"

"Because I'm still a field agent. And most importantly, I am not looking for revenge. I want justice."

She gave him a speculative look. "Can you really separate the two? Wanting revenge wouldn't make you a bad person."

"It would make me a bad agent. It would cloud my judgement." He looked around, not wanting to forget that Alisa was a target, there was no one nearby, no one watching them. Still, he wanted to be alert. "We should go inside."

"In a minute. What about my second question? You seemed very interested in what Lauren and Henry were talking about. Why?"

"Because I heard the name Tatiana. Novikov was involved with a woman named Tatiana Guseva. She runs a dance studio in LA."

"Really? Novikov has a girlfriend in LA?"

"Ex-girlfriend. When we interviewed her after the courthouse bombing, she claimed she hadn't seen him in a decade, and we couldn't find any evidence she was lying. But recently, she had communication with a man who is close to Novikov and who has been friends with both of them. She mentioned to him she had cancer and that hearing from an old friend was the best medicine."

"What does that mean?"

"Maybe nothing. But when I heard Henry use her name, it

made a connection I wasn't expecting. Henry is tied to your father. If he's also tied to Tatiana, he could be more important than I thought."

"If this Tatiana has cancer, it makes sense she would want to talk to Henry. He runs clinical trials, and she wants to get in one. That might have nothing to do with my father. There could also be more than one Tatiana in LA."

"Everything you say is true, Alisa. But my gut tells me it's a possible lead, and I'm going to follow it up."

CHAPTER ELEVEN

Alisa was still thinking about Jason's words as he ushered her into the hospital and up to the sixth floor. But seeing Dr. Grayson come out of her mother's room pushed all thoughts of Henry and Tatiana out of her mind.

"Good morning," the doctor said with a cheerful smile. "I just examined your mother. She's doing well. Her lab numbers are still slightly elevated but improving."

A rush of relief ran through her. "That's great news."

"It is. But she's still fragile. Her immune system is weak, and any infection could spiral out of control, so I would like to keep her here for another day, possibly two." He turned to Jason. "I assume you can provide the same security resources for that time period?"

"Yes. We'll take care of that."

"I'll check in on her again this evening and tomorrow morning. If all is well, she should be able to leave on Sunday. But you'll need to make sure she's going into another controlled environment."

"I will," she promised, not at all sure how she could accomplish that, but she had a few days to figure it out.

"Your mother is concerned about her level of fatigue. I reassured her that her body needs the rest to repair itself. Sleep is good. Keeping stress down would also be helpful. Pamela tells me your father is out of town. I hope you'll relay that message to him as well."

She wished she could relay that message. She wanted to have a full-on conversation with her father, maybe even a full-on fight because she had a lot of things to get off her chest.

"I'll let you visit with her now," Dr. Grayson said.

"Thank you for taking such good care of her and sorting this out," she said gratefully.

"So, good news," Jason said as the doctor left.

"I'm very relieved and also happy she can stay here for a few more days. I feel better knowing she's protected, and everything is being carefully controlled going into her room."

The guard opened the door for them, and she was prepared to give her mother a happy smile, but she was asleep again. Dr. Grayson's reassuring words echoed through her head. She was glad he had mentioned not being worried about her mother's extreme fatigue because it would have concerned her.

"I guess I'll just sit with her," she said to Jason. "What are you going to do?"

"I need to check in with my team. You can turn on your phone now. In fact, why don't you do that? We can see if there are any messages from your father."

She took her phone out of her bag and powered it on. She had messages from friends but nothing from her dad. "He didn't reach out again," she murmured, showing him her phone. "I'll let you know if he does."

"Thank you. And stay in this room. It might be boring, but I'll feel better knowing you're here and someone is watching over you."

She was touched by his concern. "I'll stay here," she promised as she walked him to the door.

"I know you don't want to risk your mother's health with stressful questions, Alisa, but if you find an opportunity to ask her about your father, take it. We need all the information we can get. Nothing may have happened in the past twenty-four hours. But make no mistake—this isn't over."

Goose bumps ran down her arms at his words. "I understand."

He stared at her for a long minute.

"Is there something else?" she asked.

He leaned forward and gave her a shockingly sweet and hot kiss. "Stay safe," he said. "And don't ask me why I did that. Because I don't have an answer."

She stared at the door as it closed behind him. She didn't know why he'd kissed her, but she knew why she'd kissed him back, because she was starting to really like him, and that was probably a terrible idea.

———

He couldn't believe he'd kissed Alisa. He'd promised himself he wouldn't do that again. But she'd looked so damned sexy and sweet, he hadn't been able to resist.

It was good they were taking a break from each other because he was getting too tangled up in her. He needed to get some space and get his head together.

When he got into his car, he received another message from Stephanie asking if he could meet her for coffee, that she needed to speak to him. It was urgent. That didn't sound good. As much as he wanted to avoid her, he knew her well, and once she got a thought stuck in her head, she couldn't let go of it. The longer he went without talking to her, the more she would wonder what was going on, so he might as well have a conversation now before she got more worked up.

He sent her a text saying he was free for the next half hour if she wanted to talk now. She came back with an immediate yes and the name of the coffee shop they'd often visited when they were working together.

He started the car and pulled out of his parking spot, calling Savannah as he did so. "I've got a possible new lead," he said. "I just spoke to Henry Cavendish, Dan Hunt's good friend. He runs a medical research lab next to the hospital. As Alisa and I were leaving, he got a phone call from someone named Tatiana."

"Tatiana Guseva?"

"It seems likely. But Henry's lab specializes in oncology research, and they're running several clinical trials, so she could be in contact with him because of that. The fact that he's Dan Hunt's best friend makes it more suspicious, however. And the lab could also be a potential target for someone wanting to steal hazardous toxins."

"I'll start looking into him."

"Check out Lauren Silenski, too. She's a senior lab manager. She seemed to be on a first- name basis with Tatiana, as if they'd exchanged prior phone calls. And Alisa said Lauren has gotten romantically involved with the much-older Henry since his wife died. It could all be innocent, but we might as well check it out."

"It shouldn't be difficult to find more information about them. How's Pamela Hunt doing?"

"Much better. They may discharge her on Sunday if her recovery continues."

"That's good news. And Alisa?"

"She's fine for the moment. All was quiet last night. But I doubt it will last. Novikov doesn't just give up."

"Unless he doesn't need Alisa or her mother anymore," Savannah suggested. "Maybe he already has her father."

He'd wondered that, too. But why would Novikov need Dan Hunt? That was a question he still couldn't answer.

"Are you coming in?" Savannah asked.

"Soon. I have to meet with my ex-partner first."

"Is this the ex-partner who was hurt in the explosion three years ago?"

"Yes."

"I thought you were keeping the circle tight," Savannah said.

"She contacted me, and with Novikov's reappearance, I need to find out if she knows something. I'll be in the office after that." He ended the call, his thoughts turning from Tatiana to Stephanie.

He hoped she wasn't going to ask him about Novikov. Maybe she just needed to vent again. She'd done that a few months ago when she'd been frustrated by the job that kept her tied to a desk. Hopefully, he could just offer support and friendship and not have to discuss Novikov.

Ten minutes later, he arrived at Fiero's coffee shop in Venice Beach. Stephanie was sitting at a table in the back with two coffees in front of her. He smiled, thinking of all the times they'd met here, sometimes coming in together during a break or meeting up in the morning before they headed into work. For eighteen months, they had worked closely together and had become very good friends. But things had changed after she'd been shot, mostly because she'd had a difficult time accepting her limitations.

Despite some lingering physical ailments, she was still an attractive blonde with short, curly hair, but the cane against the wall by her chair reminded him that at thirty-two years old, Stephanie had a long life of disability to deal with.

She was lucky to be alive, and he was grateful for that, but her dream career had come to a crushing end three years ago, and he couldn't shake the guilt of whatever part he might have played in that.

When he got to her table, he leaned down to give her a hug. Then he took the seat across from her. "It's good to see you, Steph. How are you?"

"I'm doing okay," she said, a strain in her gaze that belied her words. "I got you your cold brew."

"Thanks." He took a sip, then set his cup down. "What did you want to talk about? Is Neil still driving you crazy at work?" he asked, referring to her micromanaging boss.

"Always. I can't write a report without him wanting to add a comma. But I want to talk to you about Novikov. I heard he's in LA. Is that true?"

"Who told you that?" he asked, stalling.

"My former CI."

"Which one?"

"That doesn't matter. I have a right to know if he's here, Jason." She grabbed her cane and tapped the ground with it. "He's the reason I need this to walk."

"I don't have confirmation Novikov is here." He chose his words carefully. He was comfortable lying on the job, but not with friends, not with people he cared about.

"But you know something," she persisted. "And whatever you know, you're keeping out of the LA office. Neil told me he heard you're on a special undercover assignment. I think that assignment is Arseni Novikov. He's here, and you don't want anyone in the office to know because you think there's a mole."

"You thought the same thing three years ago," he reminded her.

"And I still do. But you can trust me. I was with your father when he was killed, and I almost died next to him. If Novikov is in town, I want in. Let me help. No one has to know. I work in white-collar crime now. I'm chained to a desk, and no one pays attention to what I'm doing because it isn't very important."

"Everything is important."

"Not as important as Novikov. I need this, Jason. I need to get that man off the street."

Her impassioned plea moved him. If the situation had been reversed, he'd be doing the same thing. In fact, he probably wouldn't have even asked if he could help. He would have investigated on his own. "I understand where you're coming from, Steph."

"I don't think you do. This has been so rough on me, Jason. I fought like hell to get into the FBI. I wasn't like you. I didn't have an automatic entry into Quantico because of my father and grandfather. I didn't have people in high places looking out for me. I had to fight for every opportunity, and I was damn good," she said fiercely. "I'd still be good if it wasn't for Novikov. Being an agent was all I ever wanted to be. It was my life."

"You're still an agent."

"I'm an analyst. And I hate sitting at a desk, but it's all I'm allowed to do. Come on, Jason, let me help. I still have contacts."

"What exactly did your CI tell you?"

"That Novikov is in town, that he's planning something huge."

"That's vague." He picked up his coffee and took another sip. "Does your informant know where Novikov is?"

"No. But he told me that Dominic Ilyin has a room at the Viceroy Hotel in West Hollywood under the name of Constantine Figueroa. I don't believe Novikov is staying there, but if they're both in town, they're going to meet at some point. You need to get eyes on Dominic."

His pulse leapt. Dominic was the person who had been in contact with Tatiana. He was also a sniper and a high-level associate of Novikov.

"If Dominic is in town, they could be planning an assassination attempt at the global tech conference. The vice president is scheduled to speak on Monday, and he won't be the only one of importance there. The CEOs of four of the biggest tech companies in the world will also be there. It's a target-rich field."

"There will also be a ton of security."

"Novikov has proven he can get through security," she reminded him. "What about the old girlfriend—Tatiana? Have you talked to her? Are you monitoring her communications?"

He realized that he'd basically confirmed he was looking for Novikov. "I'm monitoring her," he admitted. "But I don't know where Novikov is, and I can't confirm he's in LA."

"I'm going to see what I can find out."

"You can't be involved in this, Stephanie."

"I'm sorry, Jason, but you can't stop me. I won't get in the way, but I'm going to do some digging."

He realized she wasn't asking; she was telling him, and he couldn't blame her. But he also couldn't let her screw anything up. "Have you spoken to anyone else in the office about this? It sounds like you said something to Neil."

"I didn't mention Novikov to him. I just said I hadn't seen you in a while and wondered if he knew what you were working on. He knows we're friends. I'm not stupid, Jason. I'm not going to blow this. I want Novikov to go to jail." She leaned forward, lowering her voice as she said, "Actually, I want him to die."

"Which is why you can't be involved."

"You want the same thing I do," she said, challenging him with her eyes. "You lost your dad. I'm surprised you were allowed to take on this case."

He ignored that, not wanting to get into an argument with her, because the one thing they had always clashed on was what she perceived to be the favoritism he received because of his father and grandfather. "Whatever you learn, bring it to me. You can't talk to anyone else."

"Fine," she said. "What about Mick Hadley? Have you talked to him? He worked closely with your dad when it came to Novikov. He always seems to know what's going on."

"He doesn't know this time. And I can't answer any more questions. Let me do this, Stephanie. I know that won't be easy, but the bottom line is that we both want Novikov off the most wanted list, right?"

"Right. Will you at least give me an update at some point?"

"I'll try." He got up and leaned over to give her another hug. "Thanks for the tip."

"I hope it's a good one."

CHAPTER TWELVE

Her mom finally woke up around noon on Friday. Alisa was relieved to see her eyes open, as she'd been sleeping for the past two hours, ever since she'd gone into her room. While she'd sat at her bedside, she'd come up with a lot of questions she hoped her mother might be able to answer. But first, she had to make sure her mom was still feeling well.

"Hello, sleepyhead," she said, getting to her feet. "How are you feeling?"

"So tired," her mom said with a little sigh as she blinked her eyes a few times. "Is it morning?"

"It's almost noon."

"Oh. I think when I woke up before, it was about nine. The doctor was here. He's a very kind man."

"He is. He said you're doing much better, and it's understandable that you're tired because your body is recovering from the toxins."

The light in her mother's eyes faded at her words. "I hoped that was a dream."

"I wish it was, Mom. Jason confirmed that a timed-release capsule was planted in the vase of flowers that was delivered to your room on Wednesday evening. It released a toxin into the air, which is why your symptoms recurred during the night. That's why we moved you here yesterday and why we're restricting visitors and keeping everything very sterile. Remember?"

"It's all coming back to me now," she said wearily. "How are you doing? Where did you stay last night?"

"At an FBI safe house. Jason is looking out for me."

"I hope he's doing a good job."

"He is, but he has a lot of questions, Mom. Do you remember me telling you about the fire at your house?"

"That was real, too?" her mother said with despair.

"Yes, and there's a video from the house across the street showing Dad taking things out of the house a few hours before the fire. The FBI thinks he might have set the fire or knew it was going to happen."

"That's impossible."

"Is it?" she challenged.

"Of course it is, Alisa. You're acting like your father is a criminal. He's just out of town."

Her mother's stubborn refusal to question anything her father did grated on her nerves. "He's not just out of town. He sent me a text last night." She pulled out her phone and let her mom read it for herself.

"Well, there you go," her mother said a moment later. "Your dad is doing what he can to protect us and keep us safe."

"By staying away while people try to kill us?"

"I'm sure he's not just staying away; he's trying to figure out what's going on. He loves us. We have to just focus on that."

"I can't just focus on that," she said, anger bubbling up inside of her. "Every day I learn something new about him, and none of it is good."

"I don't know what you're talking about."

"Well, here's one thing. The FBI thinks Dad stole the identity of someone named Dan Hunt: his educational background, his birthday, and his social security number. It would have happened the year before he met you. Do you know anything about that?"

Her mother drew in a sharp breath and licked her lips. "Could I have some water? My mouth is dry."

Her mom was stalling, but she filled her glass with water and helped her take a drink. "Better?" she asked as she set the cup down on the table.

"Yes."

"Good. Now, you need to stop pretending that everything is fine, because it's not. What do you know, Mom? Tell me."

Her mother gave her a long and pained look. "Okay. Here's what I know. Your father told me before we got married that he'd had some trouble in his past and that he'd had to start over with a new identity, a new name. He couldn't tell me more because it would be dangerous."

She sucked in a breath as her mother finally came clean. "Are you saying he was in witness protection?"

"He didn't call it that. And he said little else, only that he couldn't marry me without telling me his past was a secret and could never be spoken about. He knew it was a lot to ask of any woman, but he hoped I could see the man he was and that the past didn't matter. He promised me he'd had to reinvent himself because he was a good person who didn't want to do bad."

"And you believed him?"

"Yes, because I loved him."

She was truly shocked. "How could you marry someone who told you he was living under an assumed name? Why wouldn't you ask a million questions? Why wouldn't you run away?"

"I just told you why. I was crazy about him, Alisa. And every instinct I had told me he was as good as he was saying and that I'd be a fool to let him go. And I wasn't wrong. You know what kind of man your father is. You've seen him for twenty-eight years. He's been there for you and for me every day of his life. He's followed the rules. He doesn't drink, doesn't smoke, doesn't do drugs, doesn't cheat. He's a family man. He's smart and funny and kind."

Her mother's words were so passionately delivered, it made her feel guilty for doubting her father because he was all the things her mother had just said.

But he was also something else, and she had a feeling that the *bad* he had wanted no part of had caught up to him.

"You can't stop loving him now, Alisa. At least wait until he gets back, until he can talk to you himself."

"If he gets back," she said. "If you and I are in danger, then Dad is, too. Whatever happened in his past—it's come back."

"He promised me everything would be okay. He's doing what he needs to do to protect us."

He might be trying, but he wasn't succeeding. She'd nearly been killed twice, and her mother might not have survived another dose of toxin.

"Did Dad say anything about Russia?" she asked her mother.

Her mom's eyes widened. "No. Why would he?"

"I think he grew up somewhere else, maybe in Russia or Eastern Europe."

"I told you he never talked about his life before he met me. I had questions in the beginning. But I got tired of hearing him say he couldn't answer, and that maybe we should break up. I didn't want to end things. I wanted to marry him. So, I took a risk, and I don't regret it. But I am worried about you. I wish I felt stronger. I wish I could get out of this bed and take you away from here. I really want you to leave town, Alisa. Your father wants the same thing. You need to go—today. Now."

"I can't leave, Mom. And it's not just because I want to stay here, but because I'm in danger. I'm safer here where there are people trying to protect me."

"I am sorry about all this, Alisa. Honestly, over the years, I just forgot about your dad's past. It didn't matter. We had a great life together. He loved his job, his friends—us. Everything was wonderful."

"It was good," she agreed. "Do you think Henry knows about Dad's secret life?"

Her mother hesitated. "I would have said no before the last couple of days, but Henry mentioned something to me the other night about how he knew what I knew, and because of that, he was worried about where Dan had gone. I was so tired, I didn't react. I just said I was exhausted, and I had to sleep. I didn't want to talk to him about anything. But when I think about his words now, it seems like he might know something. Dan and Henry have gotten very close, especially since Jill died. Your father spends almost every Sunday with Henry. He says Henry needs the company, and he doesn't want Henry looking to Lauren to fill the emptiness in his life."

"What about Lauren? I spoke to Henry today, and she seems very close to him, very possessive."

"Neither your father nor I care for her, not that she's ever done anything to us, but it seems like she just worked her way into Henry's life very quickly. And he's so lost without Jill; he's a target."

"A target for what? His money?"

"Or his position. She wants to work her way up at the lab by getting close to Henry."

"She's already pretty high. Getting back to Dad, have you told me everything you know? You can't be more loyal to Dad than you are to me. My life is on the line."

"I would never let you get hurt because of my loyalty to your father. *Never.* I love you, Alisa. I don't know anything else."

"I love you, too, Mom." She reached for her mother's hand and gave it a tight squeeze, needing to believe that at least her mother was the person she thought she was.

"Don't give up on your dad, Alisa. I know you don't under-stand why I did what I did, but one day you will. One day, you'll love someone so much that nothing else will matter."

"I'm not sure I want to love someone that much," she

murmured, thinking that her mother's blind love had put her in this hospital bed.

"It's everything," her mom said with no regret in her eyes. "And whatever your father is doing, wherever he is, I know he's trying to get back to us."

She hoped that was true, but he better hurry, because she didn't know how many more near-death experiences either of them could survive.

———

After leaving Stephanie, Jason went to the office and updated the team on the tip he'd gotten from Stephanie. While a part of him wanted to go directly to the hotel, get a key from the manager, and take Constantine Figueroa—AKA Dominic Ilyin—under arrest, he'd learned a lot in the past three years. Novikov was a master manipulator, and any tip could be a trap that could endanger not only his life but other lives at the hotel.

So, instead, he and Savannah were working with two of their best analysts, Kyle and Jessie, hoping to get visual confirmation of Dominic Ilyin. Working backward in time, they were about thirty minutes into their review when he saw a familiar figure leaving the hotel just before five o'clock the previous evening with another man.

"Got him." He froze the image and put it up on the shared monitor so the others could see it. "Dominic is the one in the suit with the slicked-back brown hair and the beard." Dominic looked more like a successful businessman than a terrorist, carrying a leather briefcase in his hand and showing off a Rolex watch on his wrist. "That's who we're looking for."

"He didn't appear in any of the more recent footage, which would have shown him returning to the hotel," Savannah said. "I don't think he came back. But I checked with the hotel, and Constantine Figueroa is still a registered guest."

"Let's keep reviewing the footage to see if we can determine when he first arrived and any other comings and goings between him and anyone else. We also need to identify the man with him."

"That's Pieter Moldev," Kyle said. "He owns a nightclub in Hollywood. His father is Ivan Moldev, a wealthy financier who currently lives in Zurich."

Beck came up as Kyle finished speaking. "I know Moldev. I met him last year when I was working undercover as an arms dealer. My cover is still intact. I can go to the club and check things out tonight. Maybe I'll get lucky, and Ilyin will be there."

"I'll go with you," Savannah said.

As much as he wanted to go to the club himself, he was too well-known to Novikov and his associates.

"This is a good lead," Savannah said as Beck walked away. "We'll dig into Moldev this afternoon and see if we can trace any money exchange between him and Ilyin or others in Novikov's network. You need to focus on Alisa's connection to Novikov."

"I agree. I'll head back to the hospital and see if Alisa has gotten any more information from her mother."

"What about your former partner? Are you looping her in now?"

"No. But I don't think I can stop her from digging into things on her own. Stephanie's hate for Novikov knows no bounds."

"Well, she came up with a good lead, so she might be valuable. Or her CI might be if you can get her to give him up."

"That won't happen. But I'll give her an update and make her feel included, so hopefully, she'll come to me with any other leads versus chasing something down on her own. I'll check in with you later, Savannah." He got up from the computer, happy to take a break from looking at security footage.

When he got into his car, he gave Stephanie a call.

"Did you find Ilyin?" she asked immediately.

"No. But we spotted him coming out of the hotel last night with Pieter Moldev."

"Do you know where they went?"

"Not yet. But we'll find him. This was a good lead, Steph, but you have to stay out of this now."

"You need me, Jason."

"Actually, who I need is your CI."

"I can't give you that name."

"Stephanie, this person might be the only one who can get us to Novikov. The only one who can stop a mass catastrophe."

"My CI doesn't know where Novikov is, but if more information comes in, I will tell you. I won't sit on anything I learn. I'd like to be more involved, but you were right when you said the most important thing is getting Novikov."

"Exactly, and last time around, we moved too fast. We got ahead of ourselves. We can't take any tip at face value. We can't allow ourselves to be manipulated."

"You just said my tip was good. My CI wasn't setting up me or you. He knows what I went through three years ago. That's why he gave me the lead."

"Okay, let me know if you hear anything else."

"As long as you keep me in the loop."

"I will," he said, not sure if that was a promise he could keep, but he'd have to see how things went. Right now, he needed to get back to Alisa.

CHAPTER THIRTEEN

Alisa was going crazy. It was two o'clock on Friday afternoon, and she'd been stuck in her mom's hospital room since ten. After their one illuminating conversation, her mother had mostly been asleep, so she'd paced the room, driving herself mad with unanswerable questions. She was about to let go of her promise to stay under guard when Jason walked through the door.

"What's happening?" she asked. "I thought you were going to text me."

"It's been busy. How's your mom doing?"

"She's stable. Just sleeping a lot. I need to get out of this room."

"Let's go," he said, opening the door for her.

As she stepped into the hallway, she let out a breath of relief. "Can we get out of the hospital for a while? I need to talk to you, and I don't want to do it here."

"It's probably best to stay here, Alisa."

"I can't." She gave a helpless shrug. "Maybe that's what's best, but I need to breathe fresh air and feel the sun. Or I'm going to lose my mind."

He smiled. "Okay. You've convinced me. We'll get out of here."

"Thank you," she said with relief, moving toward the elevators before he could change his mind.

They didn't talk on the way down to the lobby or out to the car, which was once again parked in front of the valet. As he opened the door for her, his jacket opened, and she was startled to see him wearing a gun.

"When did you pick that up?" she asked.

He followed her gaze. "I've had it all along."

"I didn't notice it yesterday when we crashed. Or this morning when we left the safe house."

"Well, you've been a little distracted."

He was right. Or maybe she just hadn't wanted to see the weapon, hadn't wanted to be reminded of the danger she was in. She got into the car and fastened her seatbelt as he went around to the other side and slid behind the wheel.

She thought her tension would ease as soon as they pulled away from the hospital, but the hill of her nightmares immediately brought it back.

She cracked the window open and said, "Did you get any new leads while you were gone? Do you know where my father is?"

"No. We haven't been able to locate him yet. Did you talk to your mother?"

"I did. I'll tell you all about it, but where are we going now?"

"Back to the safe house."

"How about lunch somewhere? If no one is following us, we should be good, right? We can turn off our phones so no one can follow us and just take a break." She could tell he wasn't super thrilled about her idea, but she pressed forward. "There's a great salad and sandwich place called Stella's near the park by the Santa Monica Pier. The food is excellent. It's pretty fast. And there's even a view of the ocean, which would be nice. I've almost forgotten there's an outside world."

"Aren't you used to being in the hospital all day long?" he asked dryly.

"Yes, but that's different, and I usually have my lunch on the rooftop deck. It has a great view of Los Angeles. I'm just a person who needs to be outside for at least part of the day."

"Well, I can relate to that," he said. "Being stuck in an office all day was never my dream. All right. We'll go to Stella's. Do you want to put it in the GPS?"

"I know how to get there," she said, directing him to the nearest entrance for the 405 Freeway.

"So, what did your mother tell you?" he asked.

"She admitted that my dad told her he had a secret past before they married, that he'd changed his name, and he couldn't tell her why. He could never tell her anything except he'd made some positive changes in his life, and he was committed to being a good man for the rest of his days. He said he would understand if she didn't want to move forward with him, knowing he could never answer her questions."

"That's quite a story to tell someone you're dating."

"Isn't it? But what blew me away was her response. She was fine with it. She said she loved him so much she was willing to see what they could have. It makes no sense to me. I couldn't marry someone who told me he had a secret life I could never know about. It would make me crazy."

"Me, too. It's bad enough you never really know who you're marrying until you're in it, but to know going in that there are secrets—that would be a deal-breaker for me."

"My mom said she has no regrets. She reminded me of how great my dad has always been, how he's treated us so well, and how his love has always been there. She said he kept his promise to her to be the best man he could be."

"Until maybe now," Jason muttered. "Obviously, his past caught up to him."

"That has to be what happened, and he's still trying to outrun it. That's why he left. He must have thought that putting distance between us would make us safer."

"He's wrong. You're leverage against him. And there are two of you, which means one of you is..." Jason's voice trailed away.

"Never mind. It doesn't matter what he thinks about keeping you safe. He's not doing a good job of it, and we need to find him."

"What were you going to say?" she asked. "I can fill in the blank, but I'm curious what word you were going to use."

"I was talking out of hand. Sometimes, I forget you're under my protection and not my partner," he admitted.

"Can't I be both?"

"No, you can't be both. You're a civilian and I need to keep you safe."

"You were going to say one of us is expendable, weren't you? And I'm probably the expendable one because yesterday they tried to kill me."

"Maybe only because you were easier to get to," he said.

"I wonder if my dad knows everything that's happened."

"Did your mother have any idea where he is?"

"No, but she said it was possible my dad confided in Henry. When Henry came to visit her on Wednesday night, he said something like, *I know what you know, and I think we need to talk about it.* She was confused and not feeling well, so she just let the comment drop."

"It seems surprising your father would tell anyone after so many years of living a secret life," Jason murmured.

"My mom said they got very close after Henry's wife died. I think we should speak to Henry again, maybe after work when Lauren isn't around. We could go to his house."

"Unless she's living with him."

"I don't think it's gone that far. I'll text him later and tell him I want to speak to him alone." She felt good that they had a plan, even if it might go nowhere. It was one step toward taking back some control over her life.

Shortly before three, Jason pulled into the lot next to Stella's, careful to survey the area before getting out of the car. He'd made several turns and taken many side streets on their way here, and they had both turned off their phones miles back, so hopefully they were untraceable.

Since it was late for lunch and early for dinner, there were plenty of empty tables in the café. He ordered a chicken wrap with a side salad, while Alisa went for a Cobb salad with chicken. They headed for a table by the window, and he took the seat facing the door so he could see anyone coming into the café.

"You look wary," Alisa commented, as they waited for their food. "Are we okay here?"

"Yes. Don't take my wariness for anything more than just wanting to make sure I've covered my bases."

"Okay. That's good to know. I've always been pretty cautious. My dad always warned me to be aware of my surroundings, whether I was at the mall, the beach or even at a party at someone's house. He hammered away at the idea that good people sometimes have hidden motives, and I need to know, really know, someone before I trust them." She paused. "Considering what I've learned about him, those warnings take on a different meaning now. I always thought he was over-the-top protective, but he must have had some lingering fear that one day my life might be in danger because of him." She took a sip of her water. "I just wish he'd told me. Maybe not when I was a kid, but I'm twenty-eight years old. I'm an adult. He should have brought me into the secret."

He could see the pain and also the anger in her gaze. She loved her dad, but she felt betrayed, and he could understand why. "I'm sure he was just terrified that the truth would put a barrier between you, that you might not understand or be able to forgive him," he said, wanting to dissolve some of the heartbreak in her eyes. There was something about Alisa that made him want to make her feel better. Maybe because she was making

such a valiant effort to be strong and brave in the face of terrifying danger.

"I definitely would have asked more questions than my
mother," she said, taking a swig of her water.

"Another reason for him not to tell you, because he couldn't
give you any answers."

"How do you think his life caught up to him?" she asked.
"And if his old life was tied to Novikov, what was he doing with a
Russian terrorist? Was he a terrorist, too? That seems completely
unbelievable to me. He's not a violent person. He never even
raises his voice when he's angry. In fact, he gets quiet when he's
mad. I can't fathom how he could hurt anyone."

"Well, if he left that life, then he definitely didn't want to
hurt people."

"I guess that's something to hang on to." She paused as his
phone vibrated. "I thought you turned off your phone."

"I turned off one of my phones. This is an untrackable
burner. I rerouted my texts to this phone in case anything urgent
came in." He pulled out the phone and read the message,
unhappy to see that despite their efforts to keep the status of
Novikov within a tight circle, suspicions were flying.

"What is it?" Alisa asked.

"A text from my father's longtime friend and partner, Patrick
Hastings. Patrick was also involved in the case three years ago.
He heard Novikov might be in town and wants to talk to me."

"Why do you have a grim look on your face? Do you not like
him?"

"I like him fine. Patrick was a mentor to me and very close to
my dad. They were friends for thirty years. But Patrick was part
of the investigation three years ago. In fact, he was with me
when we got to the house and found my father and Stephanie..."
He drew in a heavy breath. "I told you I believed there was a
leak, and that's why I wanted to keep the circle tight on
Novikov's reappearance now, but Stephanie caught wind of it
and now Patrick. Clearly, the news is out."

"How big of a concern is that?"

"Maybe not that big. The operational details will still be kept within my task force. But I need to be more careful this time. I have to assume Novikov is playing the same strategic game he always plays, and that involves manipulation and set up."

"He sounds like the worst person in the world."

"He is."

"So, are you going to meet Patrick?"

He thought about that. "I probably should, just to find out what he knows. Patrick retired from the bureau six months after that ambush, so I don't think he'll try to insinuate himself into the investigation. He probably just wants to know what's going on. And maybe I owe it to him. He was my father's best friend, and he helped me a lot when I first started at the bureau. I didn't always take his advice, but I was grateful for it." He paused. "Sometimes, I feel a little guilty that I haven't kept in touch with him."

"Why haven't you?" she asked.

"I've just buried myself in work the last few years. And I haven't wanted to share stories about the good times he had with my dad."

"I can see how that would be difficult. Seeing Patrick would remind you of your father and your loss."

"It would. And his stories would remind me that he had a much closer relationship with my dad than I did."

"Really?" she asked with surprise. "But you're his son."

"I didn't have the kind of relationship with my father that you had with your dad. He wasn't warm and fuzzy. He wasn't even around that much. He was ambitious, and his goals were always bigger than the family. I never could get close to him. And sometimes I was a little envious of Patrick's relationship with my dad, how he brought out this fun, more relaxed side of my father. It wasn't a side I saw very much. My dad wasn't a talker. He didn't express emotion, one reason my mother divorced him. He couldn't say I'm proud of you, or I love you. He just couldn't do it."

"I'm sorry. But I'm sure your dad loved you, even if he couldn't say it. And I bet he was proud of you, too."

He smiled at her words. "You're sweet to say that, Alisa."

"I'm not just saying it; I think it's true. And I'm not that sweet, Jason. I know families can be problematic. Believe me, after working in the ER and seeing how people sometimes treat the people closest to them, I know that not every family is good. But hearing the way you've spoken about your dad and getting to know you, I just can't imagine how he couldn't have cared about you or been proud of you. You're a good guy."

"You don't know me that well."

"I know it's only been a few days, but we've been through such intense moments together, it feels like we know each other on a level I don't get to very often, even with people I've spent time with for weeks."

"Like your last boyfriend?"

"Yes." She paused as a server delivered their dishes. "This looks good. I've been craving a salad."

He was hungry, too. Everything else could wait. For now, he was just going to eat. Then he'd decide what to do about Patrick.

Fifteen minutes later, he felt decidedly better than he had in a while. He'd needed food, air, and a break as much as Alisa had. She looked happier, too, her face filled with color, her brown eyes glowing, no stress tightening her mouth, no nerves making her fidget in her seat. She was relaxed, and so was he. Unfortunately, it wasn't going to last.

He got another text from Patrick. It was urgent that they meet. He just needed a few minutes of his time.

"Patrick again?" Alisa asked.

"Yes."

"He sounds desperate to speak to you. Why don't we just go meet him together?" Alisa suggested.

"I can't take you with me."

"Why not? He's a retired FBI agent. He's not working the case. And he's not a bad guy, so what's the problem?"

He frowned. "It's not a good idea."

"I'll stay in the car," she offered. "If what he has to say is important, I don't think you should put him off."

She had a point. Taking her back to the hospital would take too much time. He sent Patrick a text, asking if he could meet him at the park across the street.

The answer came flying back. Patrick could be there in twenty minutes.

"Okay, he's coming to the park across the street," he told Alisa. "But you will stay in the car. The car windows have bullet-proof glass, so you should be okay."

She frowned. "Really? You had to mention the bulletproof glass? You couldn't just say I'd be fine."

"Sorry," he said with a smile. "I was thinking out loud."

"Maybe some things should be kept in your head. But I'll be fine. It's just a few minutes, right?"

"I'll make it as fast as possible, and hopefully, Patrick has something worth sharing."

CHAPTER FOURTEEN

As Jason parked the car, his eyes scanned the park. Kids played on the playground to the right, and a community garden spread to the left. Tall trees provided shade for picnic benches and people lounging on the grass.

His trained gaze swept over the scene: homeless men by the bathrooms, families near the swings, joggers on shaded paths. Nothing set off alarm bells, but with Alisa in the car, he stayed cautious.

"What's wrong?" Alisa asked, her tone sharp. "Do you see someone?"

"No," he replied, still watching. "Just being careful."

"Because of me?"

"Because it's my job."

"Where are you supposed to meet Patrick?"

"By the community garden. It's right there. You'll be able to see me the whole time."

"Okay, good. I'll be fine, Jason."

He had a feeling she was trying to convince herself as much as him, and he impulsively put a hand on her leg. "You *will* be fine," he said, drawing her gaze to his.

She nodded. "Thanks. You always seem to know what I need to hear. You're very insightful."

He had to grin at that comment. "You might be the first woman who ever thought I told her what she needed to hear."

Her lips curved into a smile. "So, you're not that perceptive?"

"Not when it comes to women. Danger, yes. Women, no."

"Well, I think you're doing a pretty good job handling both right now. Maybe you don't give yourself enough credit."

"You might be giving me too much. I get tunnel vision when I'm working. I put my job before everything and everyone else. That never works in a relationship. That's why I stay single."

"Maybe you've just never met anyone you wanted to put ahead of your job. When two people really connect, they want to be together. They want to give the other person what they need. If the feelings aren't strong enough to distract you from work, then it's not the right relationship."

He was thinking about that when he saw Patrick get out of a car down the block. "That's him," he said, relieved to get back into work mode because the conversation was getting too personal. "I'll be back soon. Here are the keys. Lock the doors when I get out. Can you climb behind the wheel?"

"I think so, but do I need to?"

"If anything happens, I need you to drive away. I'll be fine on my own. I want you to be safe. If you punch in the first number on the phone screen, you'll be connected to my team, and they'll help you. But first, get the hell away from here."

"You're scaring me again," she said, giving him a worried look.

"I'm sure nothing will happen, and I won't be far away, but you have to do what I say, Alisa. Under no circumstances will you get out of this car. Promise me."

"I promise," she said. "Good luck with Patrick."

He didn't know if he needed luck to deal with his father's best friend, but he would probably need some mental fortitude to keep Patrick out of the investigation. Like Stephanie, he was going to want revenge, too.

Jason stepped out of the car, hearing the lock click behind him as he headed toward the garden. Patrick, tall and thin, standing under a tree, phone in hand, his sharp gaze sweeping the park like the seasoned FBI agent he had been for thirty years. Dressed in casual slacks and a polo, Patrick looked more ready for golf than a stakeout.

"Jason," Patrick greeted him, relief in his voice. "Glad you came."

"You sounded worried. What's going on?"

"It's Novikov. I heard he's in LA."

"Where did you hear that?"

Patrick hesitated, then said, "It doesn't matter. You need to step out of the investigation. With your last name, you'll have Novikov's target on your back. He hated your father, and he would be more than happy to take you out, too."

"That won't happen. I'm going to catch him this time."

"You have the same glint in your eyes that your father used to get when he thought he had a chance to bring Novikov in. That made him reckless."

"He wasn't reckless; he was set up. There's a difference."

"I know." Patrick ran a hand through his hair. "I understand where you're coming from. I want to see Novikov get what he deserves as much as you do, but you're too close to the situation. It's too personal. I'm surprised Damon is allowing it."

"He trusts me to get the job done."

"And you're going to do that job with Flynn MacKenzie's team?"

He stiffened. "Do we really need to talk, Patrick, because you seem to know everything already?"

"I have a lot of friends in law enforcement. You can't believe Novikov's appearance on US soil is a secret."

"I figured the news would leak, but we're keeping the operational details within a tight circle. And you should understand why."

"Because someone set your father up," he said with a sigh. "I still rack my brain, wondering who the hell betrayed our team. It makes me angry that I haven't been able to figure it out. I've let down my best friend, my brother. Your father saved my life on more than one occasion, and he was my conscience. If I got a little too close to a line I shouldn't cross, he would yank me back. He would tell me we have to do it the right way."

"That sounds like my father."

"I still can't believe he's gone. At random times, I'll hear his voice in my head. It always surprises me how clear it is. I'm sure you're going through the same thing."

He missed his father, but he didn't hear his voice in his head. What he remembered most was his father's hard profile. He was always looking away, looking at someone else, never looking back at him. That was, sadly, what he remembered the most. But when that image ran through his mind, he reminded himself that there had been some good times.

They had shared beers after work as he got older and more involved in his father's world. Having something in common had brought them closer together, but even then, there had been a distance between them. But he wasn't going to share his thoughts with Patrick. It would sound like he was bashing his father, and he wasn't.

Drew Colter had been a hero. He'd saved many lives in his career. He just hadn't been the best dad. But now that he was an agent, he understood it was difficult to serve country and family. His father had made his choice. The same one he was making now. Not that he had a family anymore. In some ways, that gave him freedom because he no longer had to worry about disappointing anyone, or that one day they'd get the worst call of their lives, that he was gone. There was no one to get that call now.

He frowned, realizing he was losing his focus, which tended

to happen when he got caught up in Patrick's stories about his dad.

Clearing his throat, he said, "Did you have something else to tell me? Because you could have mentioned this concern in a text."

"It's about Mick. He doesn't want to capture Novikov; he wants to kill him."

"Okay. I can't say a lot of other people don't feel the same way. I'm sure you wouldn't mind putting a bullet in him. Nor would Stephanie. But I'm determined to get justice, not vengeance."

Patrick smiled. "Your father would be proud to hear you say that. And I won't deny I wouldn't mind if justice was served with a bullet, but that's not my call. I just wanted to warn you that Mick often has his own agenda. He and your father worked together in Eastern Europe and in the Soviet Union when they were both young, determined-to-be-great agents for their respective agencies. I heard a story that at one point, they had a chance to take Novikov into custody, but their agencies thought he would have more value as an asset, so they were ordered to turn him and then let him go."

"No way. I never heard this," he said in disbelief.

"This was over thirty years ago. Novikov was not the master terrorist he is now. He was twenty-five years old at the time and had just left the KGB and was working for the Bratva. It wasn't unusual to try to get eyes into operations happening in that part of the world, but Novikov conned them. He wasn't turned. Six months later, he blew up a train station in Berlin, and that's when your father and Mick became obsessed with bringing him in. For three decades, they chased him. I think your father's obsession made him act too impulsively three years ago. He was desperate to get the man who had always eluded him."

He'd seen his father's obsession, but he'd never heard the story Patrick had just told him. "My father and I talked about Novikov a lot, especially three years ago when we knew he was in LA. My dad never mentioned having him in custody and letting him go. When did he tell you this? And why wouldn't he have told me when we were working the case together?"

"He told me a very long time ago, probably a year after it happened. As for why me and not you? It's easier to tell your partner a secret that makes you look bad than your son. He wanted your respect."

He didn't know what to make of the story. "All right. Let's say that's all true. Why are you telling me now?"

"I'm afraid Mick might use you to lure Novikov out of hiding, to tempt him to take out another FBI agent named Colter."

"That won't happen. I'm too smart and I'm too careful. I learned a lot the last time we went after Novikov."

"You can be as careful as you want. Mick has connections everywhere. And he's sneaky."

Patrick's words reminded him that Mick had been the one to send him the video from the plane. He could have gone to anyone, but he'd given him the information. "I know who Mick is," he said. "I don't trust him, but I will use him if I have to."

"He'll use you, too."

"I thought you, Mick, and my father were all friends," he said.

"We had to work together at times, but we were always working for competing agencies. There was always a line we didn't cross. I'm afraid that Mick's obsession will now take him over that line. And I don't want you to pay the price."

The blare of a car horn snapped his attention to the fountain, where a man pulled out a gun. Jason shoved Patrick behind the bushes just as the first shots rang out, a bullet whizzing past his ear.

Jason drew his weapon as screams echoed through the park and as people scattered. Peering over the bush, he glimpsed the shooter jumping into a van before it sped away.

"He's gone," he said to Patrick, whose eyes were filled with fury.

"Who the fuck was that?" Patrick said. "Did you see him?"

"The back of him. Male, probably in his twenties or thirties, wearing jeans, a blue windbreaker, and a navy-blue cap on his head," he said as they both stood up. Sirens blared as police cars pulled up in the lot and began running through the park. He tucked his weapon under his jacket and pulled out his badge.

As one officer neared them, he showed him his badge and told him what he'd seen.

Many more questions followed as he and Patrick spoke to the police.

He kept an eye on the car, where Alisa was sitting behind the wheel with a concerned expression on her face. He'd told her to drive away at the first sign of trouble, which, of course, she hadn't done. Instead, she'd hit the car horn and quite possibly saved his life.

That puzzled him. The gunman hadn't tried to shoot the car with Alisa in it. They'd been after him—or Patrick. But Patrick was retired and an unlikely target.

As if reading his mind, Patrick leaned in and murmured, "They were aiming for you, Jason. No one cares about me anymore. I'm retired." Patrick paused. "Who's the woman in the car? The one you keep staring at. She with you?"

"Yes, she's with me. You ever hear of a man named Daniel Hunt?"

There was a blank look on Patrick's face. "No. Who is he?"

"I'm not sure. But he's important to Novikov, and I have to figure out why."

"I could do some digging. I have contacts."

"No. You need to stay out of this. I told Stephanie the same thing. I don't know who set us up before, but it could be someone we all knew and trusted. We need to leave our former contacts out of this, or the same thing could happen."

"I just want to help."

"You can help by standing down. Like you said, you're retired. Go play some golf or something."

Annoyance ran through Patrick's eyes. "I can do more than play golf."

"You can, but you've earned the time off. You've served your country well." He paused. "I appreciate your concern, but now I'm worried you're going to be a target because you're talking to me. I can't let that happen. I need you and Stephanie to stay safe. Please, just let me handle this."

"All right. I'll let you handle it because I know you can. You're your father's son."

He didn't like the comparison, but getting Patrick to back off was the main goal, so he just nodded and said thank you. Then he sighed as another police officer motioned him over. He had more questions that he would have to answer before he could get back to doing what he needed to do—catch Novikov.

———

Jason was taking forever, Alisa thought as she sat in the car, her hands tightly clasped together. But he was all right. He was alive, and that was what mattered.

She still couldn't believe someone had taken a shot at him in broad daylight in a busy, crowded park. When she'd seen the man step behind the fountain and pull out a gun, she'd wanted to jump out of the car and scream Jason's name. But the horn had been faster and louder. It had given Jason a split second to see what was happening. She'd still screamed when the shots rang out and Jason and Patrick had disappeared behind a bush, holding her breath until she saw the gunman run to a car and speed out of the parking lot. She'd made a mental note of the license plate, hoping that would provide Jason with a much-needed clue.

It was another fifteen minutes before Jason made his way

back to the vehicle. She opened the locks to let him in, then crawled over the console to the passenger seat.

"Are you okay?" she asked, as he slid behind the wheel.

"Thanks to you."

"I couldn't believe it when I saw that man pull out a gun. And he was looking at you. I thought I was the target."

"It looks like you have company."

She frowned at his light tone. "He could have killed you."

"But he didn't. Thanks to your quick thinking. Did you get a look at him?"

"He was too far away to see his face. But I got his license plate number."

"Seriously?" he asked in surprise.

She rattled off the letters and numbers. "I'm pretty sure that was it."

He pulled out his phone and made a note of what she'd told him. "I'll send this to my team. You're amazing, Alisa."

"I just looked at his car; I wasn't that amazing." She paused. I don't think I could have handled seeing you get hit. Seeing you on the ground..."

Jason cupped her face, his blue eyes locking onto hers. "I'm fine, Alisa. I'm here."

"You almost weren't," she murmured.

"But I am."

She licked her lips, her nerves still raw. "I'm still numb."

His voice dropped. "Then feel this." And he kissed her.

She closed her eyes, leaning into his kiss, savoring the heat that seared right through the icy fear that had gripped her heart when she'd thought she might lose him, too.

But this kiss was real. It was hot and sexy. It gave her a lot more to think about than just relief because her whole body was tingling.

The rest of the world fell away. She wasn't aware of anything going on outside of the warm, feel-good bubble they were suddenly in. But then Jason's phone buzzed, and he pulled away from her with a muttered swear. She felt the same way about the interruption, the reminder that their momentary escape from reality was already over.

"What is it?" she asked as he checked his phone.

"Just confirmation that they're tracing the plate and checking traffic cameras around this area to see if they can find the shooter."

"Cameras," she echoed, suddenly wondering if a camera might have caught their kiss.

He smiled. "Traffic cameras at intersections. Nothing right here."

"That's good and bad. That means the shooting probably wasn't caught on camera. I should have taken a video."

"You did better than that by warning me."

"I was almost too late. I should have honked earlier when I first saw him."

He shook his head. "No. I wouldn't have wanted you to draw attention to yourself."

"Why are they trying to kill you now? Or was that about Patrick?"

"I believe I was the target. Patrick is retired. And he's not working this case." He paused, frowning. "But..."

"But what?" she asked, seeing an odd gleam in his eyes.

"I know someone didn't follow us to the restaurant. Which means someone followed Patrick."

"Who? Novikov?"

"I'm not sure," he said slowly. "Patrick wanted to warn me that a CIA agent who is involved in the investigation might have a personal vendetta against Novikov. That agent also worked with my father for years. In fact, Patrick told me an odd story I hadn't heard before about how my father and this agent caught Novikov thirty years ago, but at the time he wasn't deemed to be a threat. Their agencies told them to turn him and use him as an asset. He conned them and blew up a train station six months later, the first of many attacks he's taken credit for. That apparently was what drove my father's obsession to get Novikov. And perhaps this CIA agent shares that obsession."

"What does that mean? Are you suggesting this CIA agent might have said something to Patrick, which led Patrick to ask you for a meeting, and then the agent followed you to the park and took a shot at you?"

"When you say it like that, it sounds ridiculous," he said. "It's more likely Patrick started digging into Novikov's reappearance, and someone caught wind of that and didn't like it. They had someone follow Patrick to the park and find an opportunity to take him out. Luckily, they missed. This is why the circle has to be tight. I told Patrick to stay out of it. I hope he listens."

"What about the CIA agent? Are you going to trust him now?"

"I wasn't going to trust him before Patrick told me the story. But I don't care if he has a hidden agenda. If he's useful in bringing down Novikov, that's all that matters." He paused. "I'm just glad I left you in the car."

"I'm happy you weren't the target, although we can't be too sure that they didn't want to kill both of you."

He met her gaze. "No, we can't. But it doesn't matter, because it didn't work."

"What are you going to do now?"

"Find Novikov and arrest him before he can kill anyone else, including me."

She wanted to believe him, but it was feeling like this Novikov had all the power, and now, she was afraid for both of them.

CHAPTER FIFTEEN

After Alisa checked in with the hospital and found out her mother's condition was still stable and she was resting comfortably, Jason drove them to the safe house. They would speak to Henry after the lab closed, and he went home. Until then, Alisa could take a break, and he would check in with the team.

Alisa disappeared upstairs as soon as they entered the house, which was probably just as well. Things had gotten a little too heated between them in the car, and that was happening more and more frequently. While he probably should make another promise to himself to leave her alone, he didn't seem to be able keep that promise, so why waste the time? Plus, he had bigger problems.

With Alisa taking a break upstairs, he went into the den and used his burner phone to call Savannah. "I'm at the safe house now. Any updates?"

"We found the shooter's van a few miles from the park. It was clean, no prints. The van is registered to Nolan Hawthorne, who has an address in El Segundo. Unfortunately, Nolan is an eighty-six-year-old man who moved into an assisted living facility last week. Apparently, a grandson has been living with him, but the manager didn't have information on him. How are you doing?"

"I'm fine. I wasn't hurt. Luckily, no one else was, either."

"Were you the target or was it Hastings?"

"I don't know."

"Why were you meeting with Patrick Hastings, anyway? I thought you were keeping the LA agents out of this, but they keep popping up."

"Like Stephanie, he reached out to me, and I needed to know why. He heard Novikov was in town from one of his contacts, who he declined to name. Our tight bubble of information has sprung more than a few leaks."

"What did he want?"

"To help. I told him to enjoy his retirement and play some golf. This wasn't his job anymore."

"I'm sure that went over well," she said dryly.

"I probably could have used better words," he admitted. "I understand why both Patrick and my former partner, Stephanie, want to help. Patrick lost his best friend, and Stephanie lost her ability to be a field agent. They want Novikov to pay. But I hope they now understand it's important to keep this investigation tight. I can't prevent who they talk to or what they do, but they certainly won't be getting any operational details from me. I've made that clear." He paused. "Are you and Beck set up to check out Moldev's club tonight?"

"Yes. We're going around eight. I'll let you know what we find out. We also have someone watching Tatiana's dance studio. She's been there all day. They'll follow her home. We're monitoring her communications, and she hasn't talked to anyone from her past. What about you?"

"I'm going to follow up with Henry Cavendish. Alisa's mother alluded to the possibility that Henry might know something about Dan's whereabouts. I'll touch base with you later."

Setting down the phone, he opened the computer, checking his email first. There was nothing of note. Then he moved into the open case file, reviewing the notes Flynn's team had made on various points of the investigation.

An hour later, Alisa came down the stairs around five forty-five. She looked like she'd thrown some water on her face, brushed her hair, and applied some makeup. But he could still see the dark circles under her eyes, and while the minor cuts from the car crash were still visible, they were less swollen, less red.

"Did you take a nap?" he asked.

"I tried, but as soon as I closed my eyes, all the images from the park came back to me, followed by other terrible memories. I pretty much just tossed and turned and then decided what was the point?"

"You could try thinking of something good to replace the bad."

The gold in her eyes glittered as she said, "I tried that, too, but that just made things more confusing."

He didn't want to ask what was confusing her because he knew, and he had no answers. Thankfully, she didn't seem to want to talk about it.

"What are you doing?" she asked. "Have you talked to anyone on your team?"

"Yes. They found the shooter's van, still trying to track him down. Beyond that, there's no news."

She pulled up a chair and sat next to him. "Can I use your phone to text Henry and see if he's home?"

"Sure. Do you know the number? Because I think we have his personal number in the file."

"You do? Why?"

"Because he's a potential person of interest."

"I know his number. I memorized it a long time ago, and numbers stick in my head."

He handed her the phone, and she sent the text. A moment later, she got a reply.

"He's home now, and he said he's alone. He wants to know

what I want to talk to him about and why I'm calling him from this number."

"Don't answer. Just tell him we'll see him soon.

"Okay." She sent the text and handed him back the phone. "I was thinking that we could drive by my parents' house on the way to Henry's. He only lives about four blocks away. I'd like to see the damage."

"I've seen photos of the house. There's nothing to salvage. If there was, I would have told you earlier."

She slowly nodded. "Okay. But I still want to drive by."

"It will just make you sad."

"Then I'll be sad," she said with a shrug. "Even if I don't see it, I'm going to feel that way. My mom took a lot of pride in the house. She loved to decorate. We never had much money, but she was great at finding interesting items at thrift stores or flea markets. She loved furniture that had a story, which is odd now that I think about it since she never had any curiosity about my dad's story. But an old teapot made her want to know everything about it."

"The teapot was safer. It wasn't going to upend her life."

"True. Anyway, I guess she'll have to start over. I just don't know if she'll be starting over alone."

He felt a wave of sympathy for how her life had turned upside down. "She'll have you, so she'll never be alone."

"You're right." She took a deep breath. "Shall we go?"

"I'm ready," he said as they stood up.

"I have to admit I hate to leave this place. It's like an oasis of peace and security in a very chaotic world."

"We'll be back soon. We'll stop by Henry's and then the hospital to check on your mom. If all is well, we'll pick up a pizza and come back here."

"That sounds like a plan. But I have this gut feeling that it's not going to go that smoothly."

His gut was saying the same thing. He just hoped he wasn't leading her into another dangerous situation. But Henry had been good friends with her parents for over ten years, and he needed her to get information out of Henry. Otherwise, he'd take the meeting himself. It was a risk, but a calculated one. Hopefully, his calculation wasn't wrong.

———

Jason was right. The three-bedroom, two-bath home that had been filled with love, laughter, and the memories of a lifetime were completely gone. The rubble was a blight on the neighborhood now, with cautionary tape around the perimeter, and the lot would eventually have to be completely cleared.

"We moved in here when I was sixteen years old," she murmured as she gazed at the ashes of her life. My father had gotten a new job, and he said it was too good to pass up, so we moved from San Diego to here, and I had to start my junior year of high school in a new school—his school. That was the only thing that made it more bearable, although it was strange when I had to take his class. The kids were always trying to get me to ask him for inside info on what would be on the tests. But he just laughed and said I'd find out when everyone else did." She paused. "My mother used to have a garden in the back. That's probably gone, too, huh?"

"I think so," Jason said, giving her time to process what was in front of her.

"Even though I moved most of my stuff out of here when I got my place, my parents still had some of my childhood memorabilia, all the family photo albums, things we'll never be able to replace."

"It's possible your father removed some of those things when he left the house."

She turned her head to give him a hopeful look. "Do you think so?"

"He definitely took more than just clothes out of the house."

"I hope that's true, but at the end of the day, I just really want him back. I want my family together again. I don't believe he poisoned my mom. He couldn't have done that. What do you think?"

His blue eyes gave nothing away. She was getting used to his guarded look, which only became less guarded when they found themselves in each other's arms. That's when he showed his feelings in his eyes and in his kiss. Otherwise, he was a tough nut to crack. But he'd give her an honest answer, even if she didn't want one.

"We don't have enough information to know what your father did or why," he said. "But the truth will come out."

"Will it? It seems like my father has been living with his secrets for thirty years. That's a long time, more than my whole life. Why did his past catch up to him now?"

"I don't know, but he was probably taken by surprise."

"My mom wants me to have faith in him. I want to do that, too. I just don't want to be stupid."

"You are not stupid, Alisa. And as much as the past is on our minds, we need to look forward. Are you ready to talk to Henry?"

"Yes, but that forward step is going to take us right back to the past," she said with a sigh.

"If it does, hopefully, it will also bring us some answers."

Henry's house was only a few blocks away. When they turned the corner, a vehicle came racing around the corner so fast that Jason had to swerve not to hit them.

"What was that?" she asked breathlessly, glancing over her shoulder. The car was gone now.

"Nothing good," Jason muttered as he continued down the street.

"What does that mean?"

"I don't know. But I'm going to check out Henry's house before I take you inside." He pulled up in front of the home.

Henry's car was in the driveway and there were lights on in

the house, but even from the street, she could see that the front door was wide open.

Jason jumped out of the car and ran toward the door, removing his weapon from under his jacket as he did so. Then he disappeared into the house.

Her heart was beating fast as she waited for him to come back, to call for her, to tell her everything was okay. She cracked the window and heard a man's voice cry out in distress.

Throwing caution to the wind, she jumped out of the car and ran up the path. If Jason or Henry were in trouble, she wasn't going to sit in the car. When she stepped into the house, she heard someone howl in pain.

"Jason?" she yelled as she moved through the entry. She stopped abruptly at the archway to the living room, seeing Henry bleeding on the floor by the fireplace and Jason calling 911.

She ran toward Henry, dropping to her knees beside him. There was blood coming out of his chest, a massive amount of blood. She ripped off her sweater and pressed it against his wounds. "It's going to be okay, Henry," she said, looking into his face, which was barely recognizable from the bruising on his face. He'd been beaten badly. "What happened? Who did this to you?"

"I tried not to tell them, but the pain was too much," he said weakly.

"Tell them what?"

"Your father's location."

"My father? Where is he?"

"The Sparks Motel in Brentwood," Henry said, gasping out the words. "You need to help him."

"Who did you tell?" Jason asked, squatting down beside them.

"I don't know their names, but they work for...Arseni Novikov," he said, struggling to breathe. "He's wanted to get your father back for a long time."

"Why? Why would he want my father?" she asked in confusion.

"Your dad betrayed him...a long time ago...want to finish what..."

"What?" Jason demanded. "Finish what? Who was Dan Hunt before he changed his name?"

"Alexei Bruno," Henry said. "Brilliant chemist...they wanted him to...to..."

"Henry, stay with me," she said, pressing harder on his wound as his eyes closed. "Dammit! Where is the ambulance? We're losing him."

Henry struggled once more to stay conscious. "I'm sorry, Alisa. Tell him...your mom...so sorry...best friend...ever...had."

Henry's eyes closed again.

"No!" she yelled. "You can't die. You can't die." But her instincts told her that was exactly what was happening.

Jason got up as the EMTs arrived, along with the fire department and two cops. The EMTs took over for her, and within seconds, Henry was loaded onto a gurney and whisked away in the ambulance. She hoped they would get him to surgery in time, but she was afraid they might not.

As Jason spoke to the officers, she gazed down at the blood on her hands, trying to process what had happened. Two men had beaten Henry so badly, he'd been forced to give up her dad's location. Which meant her father was in danger. And her mind flashed on the memory of the speeding car they'd passed. Had it belonged to the men who'd done this?

They had to get out of here. They had to go find her father.

Jason came over and handed her a towel.

"We have to go to the motel," she said as she dried her hands. "We need to save my dad."

"'I'm going there now. The police will take you to my office."

"No. I'm going to find my father."

"You can't. Look what happened to Henry. I'm not taking you anywhere else."

"Then I'll go on my own. There is no way I'm spending time with some random cop who could be working for Novikov."

His gaze narrowed. "The cops aren't working for Novikov."

"You don't know that, Jason," she said fiercely, striding past him.

He bit off a curse as she left the house. She heard him say something to the police officer in charge of the scene, but she didn't stop until she got to the locked car.

At her fierce look, he simply flipped the locks open and got behind the wheel.

"I'll take you to the motel," he said. "But this time, you have to stay in the car until I tell you that you can get out. If you can't promise you'll do that, then I'll take you to the safe house, and I'll stay there until someone comes to wait with you."

"I'll stay in the car. Just go. We might not have much time." Her voice broke as she silently prayed that they wouldn't find her father in the same condition as Henry. Or possibly worse...

CHAPTER SIXTEEN

"Do you think he's dead?" Alisa asked as Jason sped down the dark streets toward West Hollywood, weaving his way in and out of traffic as quickly as he could.

"He was still alive when they put him in the ambulance."

"I'm not talking about Henry, although, I hope he makes it."

He flung her a grim look. "I don't know, Alisa. That's why I need to go into the motel first. I've already called my team. They're on their way. They will probably get there before us."

"That car that almost hit us...it could have belonged to Novikov."

"I know. We'll look into it."

She stared out the window for several long minutes, then looked back at him. "I'm scared, Jason."

He stopped at a light, his expression softening as he gazed at her. "I know. Maybe this is no consolation, but Henry said that Novikov needs your father for something. That suggests he's still alive."

She grabbed the lifeline he was throwing her. "That's true. They won't kill him, at least not yet. But how long does he have? If Henry had only given us the address yesterday. If my dad dies, Henry is partly responsible."

"He was being loyal to his friend, Alisa, and he didn't give up your dad easily. You saw what they did to him. Frankly, I'm surprised they left him alive. That rarely happens."

"Maybe they thought he wasn't going to make it. And he might not." She blew out a breath. "He said my father was a brilliant chemist. What would Novikov need a chemist for?" As soon as the question left her mouth, she shook her head and said, "Never mind. I don't want you to answer that."

Jason continued through the intersection without a word.

"Chemical weapons, right?" she asked a moment later.

"That would be my guess."

She shook her head in disbelief. "I want to say my father would never do something related to chemical weapons. But then, I didn't even know he was a chemist, that he was once involved with a terrorist on the FBI's most wanted list." Her voice rose with every word until she was almost shrieking.

To his credit, Jason let her ramble without commenting or telling her to calm down. Maybe that's because he was smart enough to know she didn't want to calm down. She was terrified and angry, and every emotion in between those two was rocketing through her so fast she felt like she was being battered by feelings she couldn't even define. She felt enormously overwhelmed, and as much as she wanted to go to the motel and find out if her father was there, she also wasn't sure she could handle it if he wasn't.

"Keep breathing," Jason told her. "Breathe in for five and blow out for ten—slowly."

She followed his instructions, finding that the counting of breaths did help to distract her brain from trying to race in a dozen different directions at the same time.

Ten minutes later, Jason pulled into the motel parking lot, which was already crowded with black SUVs and two police cars.

Jason got out to talk to two men who were standing by the front door of a first-floor guestroom. She rolled down the window so she could hear their conversation.

"He's not in the room," one man said.

Her heart jumped at his words, and she instinctively got out of the car to join them, ignoring Jason's pointed look. There was a heavy police presence; she couldn't believe she was in any danger. "My dad isn't inside?" she asked.

"This is Alisa Hunt," Jason told the men. "Agents Flynn MacKenzie and Nick Caruso."

The blond-haired Flynn gave her a quick nod. "Your father is not in the room. The manager said a van went racing out of here about ten minutes before we arrived."

"If he's not there, can I go inside?" she asked. "I need to see the room, to see where he's been staying."

"We're waiting for forensics," Flynn said. "But if you want to take her in..."

She stepped into the room, her gaze sweeping the interior of the very modest motel room. There was one king bed that wasn't made. Several suitcases and boxes were in one corner of the room. One suitcase was open, with clothes spilling out. There were more clothes on the floor. There was also a chair that had been turned over and broken. The old TV monitor was shattered. The coffee pot looked like it had been flung against the wall, leaving coffee dripping down the tired wallpaper.

Worst of all were the spots of red on the bedspread and the floor. Not as much blood as she'd seen pooling under Henry's body, but enough to make her feel sick at the thought of that being her dad's blood, that he'd been beaten like Henry had, that he was in pain and in trouble. She turned around, walking straight into Jason's chest.

He caught her around the waist and held her there as she buried her face in his shirt, needing his solid strength to keep her on her feet.

"Let's get out of here," he said quietly. "There's nothing to see, Alisa."

His words lifted her head. She looked into his compassionate blue eyes and felt his gaze steady her. Then she glanced back at the boxes in the corner, the things her father had taken out of his house before the fire.

"One second," she said, feeling a new energy. She moved toward the boxes. The top one was open, and inside she could see photo frames. "He brought the pictures from the house," she said, wanting to look through them but mindful of her promise not to touch anything. "Maybe not everything is lost."

"Once it's all itemized and documented, you'll be able to get it back," Jason told her.

"I guess that's something." As she looked away from the box, her gaze caught on the desk where there were local magazines flung across the top. That's when she saw a handwritten letter peeking out from under a magazine. She reached for it before she could stop herself, seeing her name and her mother's name at the top of the letter.

"Alisa," Jason said. "You weren't supposed to—"

"He wrote me and my mother a letter," she said, the letters of her name blurring with the sudden tears in her eyes. She wanted to read the letter, but she also didn't want to read it because she was afraid of what he was going to tell her. She was terrified this was a goodbye note.

"What does it say?" Jason asked.

"I'm not sure I can read it. Would you?"

He took the letter out of her hand, then read her father's words aloud:

"*Pamela and Alisa. This is the most difficult letter I've ever had to write. It has been my incredible privilege to love both of you and to be loved in return. Many years ago, Pamela, I asked you to take a leap with me, to trust I was a good person, that I would be a good husband, and to my shocking surprise, you agreed. Your faith in me was inspiring. And then you gave me a beautiful daughter.*"

"Oh, God," she murmured.

Jason looked at her. "Do you want me to go on?"

She gave him a tight nod, her heart pounding against her

chest, her emotions threatening to spill out in angry, sad tears. She wrapped her arms around her waist as he continued.

"*Alisa, I know you won't understand. You're probably furious at being left out of such a big secret, but it was bad enough that I burdened your mother. I didn't want you to ever have to wonder about me. I couldn't stand to think of how you might look at me if you knew who I was, how you would see me so differently. After so many years, I believed I was safe, that I was worlds away from the life I once led, and that no one would ever find me. That's why I let down my guard.*"

Jason paused for a moment and then went on.

"*A long time ago, I was a chemist in the Soviet Union, and I was forced to work for the dark side. With the help of a friend, I found my way out and came to the US, where I got a new identity and started over. It was all worth it, especially when I met you, Pamela, when we fell in love and built our family together. I thought I had everything I could want, but then I met Henry.*"

"Henry?" Alisa echoed, then motioned for Jason to keep reading.

"*Henry told me about his research and how close he was to a break-through, but he couldn't figure something out. I tried to resist the call of science, but his work was so important and could save so many people that I told him I could help him, but he had to keep my secret. He swore he would. And did. Then one day, by chance, I crossed paths with Tatiana Guseva, someone who knew me from my other life. She had come to the lab to sign up for a clinical trial. I wasn't sure she recognized me. But two weeks later, I thought someone was watching me, watching the house. And then you got ill, Pamela, and someone left me a voicemail that you would get sicker if I didn't meet with them. That's why I left. I'm so sorry, my love. I hope you are well now. I never wanted you or Alisa to get hurt. I thought by putting distance between us I could protect you, but Henry told me they went after Alisa. I'm trying to get help from my contact, but if I don't come back, please know I'm sorry. Please know I love both of you more than life itself. And if my existence brings you pain, then I will end it.*"

She sucked in a breath. "Oh, my God! It sounds like a suicide note now. What else does it say?"

"*I'm still hoping to find a way out.*"

"And?"

"That's it," Jason said, looking at her. "It's not a suicide note, Alisa."

She felt a minimal amount of relief. "No. It's an in-case-I-don't-make-it-back note, which is kind of the same thing."

"There's still hope. Your father had it. You need to hang on to it."

"I thought you were the pessimistic one."

"I'm a realist. This isn't over. Until it is, think positively." He paused as Nick walked in with a forensics team. "We'll take this with us," he said, motioning her outside.

She followed him through the door, taking several deep breaths of air as Jason stopped to speak to Flynn. They had taken a few steps away from her, so she couldn't hear what they were saying, but she saw Jason show him the letter from her father. Flynn took a photo of the letter and handed it back to him. And then they conversed in low tones for another minute.

Digging her hands in the pockets of her jeans, she looked up at the starry sky, thinking of how many nights she and her dad had sat out on the back deck, and he'd tell her about the constellations.

She'd wondered how he knew so much about the sky, but he'd told her that when he was young, the night sky had felt like a ticket out of his life, a future he could dream about. She had a feeling he could have never imagined his actual future.

"Let's get out of here," Jason said, waving her toward the car.

As they got in, he said, "Do you want to go to the hospital and talk to your mom now?"

"I know I should, but it feels like too much. I can't get into all this with her now. But I haven't been there since this afternoon. She's probably wondering where I am."

"Why don't we just call her? The nurse can get her phone to

her. You can find out how she's feeling. You don't have to tell her about the letter."

"Doesn't she deserve to know everything? Am I wrong to keep it from her?"

"There's so much we don't know, Alisa, and there's nothing your mother can do. It's your call, but I think you should focus on her condition and assure her you're all right. Then she can rest, knowing you're safe."

"I agree," she said as he took out his phone.

He called the hospital and asked for the nurse's station on the sixth floor. Several moments later, he handed her the phone.

She heard the nurse talking to her mom, and then her mother's voice came on the line. The familiarity almost made her want to cry, but she had to hold it together.

"Hi, Mom," she said, forcing a cheerful note into her voice. "How are you feeling?"

"I'm doing better. I even watched a game show tonight. It reminded me how your father knew all the answers before we did."

"Before they even finished the question," she said, feeling pain at the memory.

"Have you heard anything from him?"

"I haven't talked to him," she said carefully, wording the lie so it would be partly true. "I'm glad you're feeling better."

"Where are you?" her mother asked.

"I'm with Jason."

"Is he keeping you safe? Is he making sure you eat?"

"He's doing all that. In fact, we were thinking of getting dinner now. Are you okay tonight if I don't come by until tomorrow?"

"Of course. You do not need to spend any more time watching me sleep."

"Then I'll come in the morning." She felt guilty at the wave of relief that swept through her.

"That's perfect, Alisa. Have a good night."

"You, too. I love you, Mom."

"I love you, too. I'll see you tomorrow."

She let out a breath as she set the phone on the console. "We can just go to the safe house."

As he pulled out of the lot, she glanced back at the motel where her father had spent the last few days. Hopefully, those days wouldn't be his last.

CHAPTER SEVENTEEN

Jason didn't know how Alisa was still on her feet. But as they entered the safe house, he was once again impressed by her emotional strength. She'd bloodied her hands trying to save Henry's life and had then seen more blood in the motel room where her father had been staying. She'd heard what could have been his goodbye letter, and she hadn't fallen apart, although she looked shell-shocked.

"Do you want a drink?" he asked as they moved through the kitchen and into the dining room.

"Right now, I just need a break. I'm going upstairs."

Not wanting to push her into a conversation she didn't want to have, he let her go. He needed to work, anyway. He went into the den and got on his computer, eager to see what he could learn about Dan Hunt—AKA Alexei Bruno. He finally had the connection between Novikov and the Hunt family, and it was seriously disturbing. If Novikov needed a chemist to carry out his plan, then that pointed to a chemical or bioweapon attack, which could be catastrophic.

After several minutes of searching through the FBI databases, he'd found absolutely nothing on Alexei Bruno, which seemed a little unusual. It almost made him wonder if Alexei's past had been scrubbed from every channel, even the official ones. Tapping his fingers restlessly on the desk, he debated his options, and one jumped out at him. Dan had said he had a friend he was trying to reach. And that friend must have been the person who helped him reinvent himself. Since he hadn't been a part of witness protection, and there was nothing he could find in the FBI files, there was only one other person to ask.

Picking up his phone again, he texted Mick Hadley: *What do you know about Alexei Bruno?*

The reply came within a minute, but it wasn't an answer. It was a question: *Do you have him in custody?*

No. Do you know where he is?

Call me.

He debated for another second, then punched in Mick's number. "Why didn't you tell me Dan Hunt was a former chemist named Alexei Bruno?"

"You didn't have a need to know," Mick returned, using one of the CIA's most popular phrases.

"The hell I didn't. I'm trying to protect Hunt's wife and daughter and find Novikov. This was critical information you were sitting on."

"I didn't know Hunt had been outed until yesterday when he called me, desperate to get security for his wife and daughter. I assured him they were being taken care of. I told him I would help him, too, but I needed to know where he was. He declined to tell me."

"Why wouldn't he tell you if he wanted your help?"

"He said he couldn't trust anyone. He hung up, and I've been looking for him ever since. Where is he?"

"Novikov has him."

"Are you sure?"

"Yes. Hunt's friend, Henry Cavendish, was beaten and shot by Novikov's men. He gave them Hunt's location at a motel in Brentwood. When we arrived at the motel, Hunt was gone.

There was blood and signs of a struggle."

"Is Cavendish dead?"

"He's in surgery. His condition is critical. Hunt is with Novikov. A lot of this could have been avoided if you'd shared the information you were sitting on, Mick. What the hell were you thinking, keeping it to yourself?"

"I didn't believe Novikov knew Dan was in LA," Mick replied, not a trace of guilt in his voice. "Novikov was here three years ago, and there was no connection between him and Hunt then. After the courthouse explosion, I told Dan he should leave LA, but Dan thought LA was probably the safest place because Novikov never hits the same city twice."

"Until now. How long have you known Daniel Hunt?"

"Since he was Alexei Bruno, and I helped him get out of the Soviet Union."

"Why did you do that?"

"He helped us stop Novikov from launching a chemical weapon. While we weren't able to capture Novikov, several members of his gang were killed, including his brother, and we arrested several other members of the organization, some of whom were already setting up smaller cells in the US. Because of Alexei's efforts, Novikov's organization was considerably weakened. It took Novikov another ten, almost fifteen, years to get back to anything close to the power he once had. Alexei was given asylum in the US, and we created a new identity for him."

"All right. Let's focus on what's happening now. If Novikov has Daniel, what's he planning?"

"A dirty bomb would be my guess. When I spoke to Daniel yesterday, he told me he'd been working at the lab with Cavendish. This went explicitly against the agreement we made thirty years ago that he would never, ever work as a chemist again. Apparently, he was trying to find a cure for cancer, and he couldn't resist using his big brain one more time." Mick paused. "Does his daughter know about his past?"

He wasn't going to talk about Alisa with Mick. "She only knows enough to be confused."

"That's probably best. I'm aware you have a guard on her mother's room. I hope you're keeping Alisa safe as well. She and her mother are both leverage for Novikov. He'll threaten their lives to force Daniel to work for him."

"I figured that out days ago. But it would have been nice to have your help."

"As I told you, I didn't believe Daniel Hunt was involved in this until yesterday."

"You always have an answer, Mick, but somehow, I never like it."

"What can I do for you now?"

"Where is this dirty bomb going to go off?"

"If I knew that, I would tell you."

"I hope that's true. By the way, I heard an interesting story about you and my father from Patrick," he said, not sure why he was bringing it up, but since he had Mick on the phone, he might as well ask. "He said you and my father captured Novikov when he was a young man and that you tried to turn him into an asset at the request of your agencies, but it didn't work. Is that true? Did you have him in custody at one point?"

"We did. Novikov was twenty-five years old at the time, and we weren't much older. We didn't want to let him go, but the higher-ups at both our agencies had another plan. We tried to turn him, but it didn't work. He said what we wanted to hear in order for him to become an asset, and then he blew up a train station six months later and sent us both a mocking text. Drew and I would have never let him go if we'd had the choice, but we were young agents then. Your father was doing his first stint overseas with the international team. I was also green. Things would have been different if the same events had occurred later in all our lives."

"I can't believe my father didn't tell me this," he muttered.

"It wasn't his proudest moment, or mine. Which is why I

would like nothing more than for you to take Novikov down."

"I want to believe that, but you sat on the Daniel Hunt information for too long."

"It wasn't my secret to share, not until I had a reason to think his cover was blown."

"Which happened yesterday. What did you do today?"

"I've been looking for him. Where was Hunt staying?" Mick asked. "He could have left a clue behind."

"If he did, my team will find it."

"We're on the same side. Give me the name of the motel."

"I don't think you have a need to know," he said and then hung up the phone. They might be working toward the same goal, but he didn't trust Mick, and he wasn't even sure he believed the story Mick had just told him. But that was something he'd worry about later. He got back on his computer. He had a lot of loose threads now, and he needed to tie some of them up.

As if on cue, his phone vibrated with a text from Savannah. She and Beck were at the nightclub. Pieter Moldev has been there when they first arrived. Beck had spoken briefly to him, but he'd been in a hurry to leave. They'd waited another half hour, but there was no sign of Dominic Ilyin, so they were going to leave.

He thanked her for the update, wishing their trip hadn't been a complete waste of time, but it had been worth a shot. There was still a chance Moldev and Ilyin would reconnect at some point. They just needed to keep on it. Tomorrow, they'd regroup and figure out if there was another approach they could take.

———

Alisa heard Jason working in the den when she went downstairs and decided to leave him be while she went into the kitchen to see what she could find for food. She'd taken a shower and put on her leggings and one of her favorite T-shirts, which had been in the bag Jason had packed for her. She was still scared and confused, but she was also hungry.

She checked the freezer first, excited to see a large frozen pizza with mushrooms and sausage. She pulled it out and set it on the counter. Then she turned on the oven to preheat while she opened the refrigerator, happy to find a bag of salad as well as cucumbers, tomatoes, and salad dressing. As she pulled dinner together, she felt a sense of normalcy that was very soothing. It was nice to focus on something besides her racing and terrified thoughts.

At the sound of footsteps, she turned around, happy to see Jason coming into the kitchen.

"I thought you were upstairs sleeping." His gaze swept her face with a concern she was fast becoming addicted to.

Maybe caring about her safety and well-being was just his job, but it felt more personal than that, especially when they kept ending up in each other's arms. "I took a shower instead. I needed to clear my head. Thanks for packing my favorite T-shirt."

"It looked like something you wore a lot. I can go by your place tomorrow and get you more clothes."

"Tomorrow," she echoed, taking a sip of her wine. "I think I'm going to stop planning for tomorrow. It seems pointless."

"That might be true. What are you cooking?"

"Pizza. It's almost done. Do you want wine?"

"Sounds good," he said, pouring himself a glass.

"Did I hear you talking to someone earlier?"

"My CIA contact, Mick Hadley. While we don't know where your father was born, I'm guessing it was somewhere in Russia or Eastern Europe, which meant his asylum had the CIA written all over it."

"Were you right?"

"Yes. Mick said your father helped them avert a chemical weapon attack thirty years ago and, as a thank-you, they got him away from Novikov and out of the country. The CIA created your father's new identity as Daniel Hunt. He was told at the time he could never work as a chemist again. Your father abided by that until this year, when he decided to help Henry with his new therapy."

"He risked his secrets to help Henry cure cancer. There's nobility in that, right?"

"I think so. I'm sure your father thought he could work in the background with Henry, and no one would ever know. That might have been the case if he hadn't run into Tatiana at the lab. She was probably the only person in LA who would have recognized him."

"So Tatiana told Novikov that my dad was in LA. And that's why he came here to launch an attack? Because of my dad?"

"It's possible that he was already coming here but your father was an added incentive. Novikov's brother was killed during the aborted bombing that your father was responsible for thirty years ago. Novikova may not have just needed a chemist, he may have also want revenge."

"Great," she said dully. "This gets worse and worse."

"Poisoning your mother was his first shot. He wanted your father to know his cover was blown, and he was coming for him."

"It's so cruel to hurt an innocent woman."

"That's who Novikov is. He doesn't have a conscience. He's a cold-blooded killer."

"And now he has my father," she said, a lump growing in her throat.

"Your dad is still alive. Novikov needs him to complete his mission."

"You should be with your team and not with me, Jason."

"I'm working from here. And right now, I'm hungry."

As he finished speaking, the timer went off.

"Well, you're in luck because the pizza is ready."

Their conversation had soured her appetite, but she would force herself to eat. She needed to keep up her strength for whatever was coming next.

CHAPTER EIGHTEEN

"Thanks for putting this together, Alisa."

She smiled. "Frozen pizza is one of my go-to meals. I don't have a lot of time to cook, and it's not exciting to cook for one person."

"I hear you. I can't remember the last time I made anything besides breakfast."

"Your eggs were good, so clearly you have some cooking skills. Did your mother teach you?" She paused, wondering if his mother was a touchy subject. "Sorry, I probably shouldn't have asked that. I know you lost your mom when you were young."

"She taught me how to make breakfast: eggs, bacon, pancakes. That was the meal we always had together. For dinner, she'd usually feed me, and then wait for my dad to come home to share the meal with him. Sometimes, she ended up eating alone after I went to bed. I didn't realize how lonely she was until after they got divorced."

"Did she work?"

"Part-time as a stager for a realty company. She loved getting a house ready to sell. She was very creative and artistic. At one time, she wanted to be a designer, but my dad needed her to be at home, taking care of me. He traveled so much that she didn't want to leave me with a babysitter all the time, so she compromised. After they split, and I was a teenager, she worked longer hours." He paused, shadows filling his gaze. "She was just getting her life back together when she got sick. It felt very unfair."

"It sounds like it," she said quietly, thinking that Jason had lived a far lonelier life than she had.

"I never really thought about whether she was happy until she was gone. I just took her for granted," he murmured.

"We all do that. I took my family for granted until all this started. I used to tell my parents how boring they were, and how I was going to have a far more exciting life. I never expected it to go like this. Now I think about my dad sitting there listening to me question him about why he hadn't wanted more for his life, why he hadn't wanted to travel or see the world. He just kept saying he had everything he wanted: a wife, a daughter, and a home." She shook her head. "I wonder if he ever was tempted to tell me his story."

"He knew he couldn't. And he wasn't lying, Alisa. He had everything he'd wanted. And he knew how important it was to hang on to it."

"But he was living a lie, Jason. It was all fake." That thought still made her angry.

"His life with you and your mother was real."

"Was it? Can something based on a lie be real?"

"That sounds like a question no one can answer, like if a tree falls in the forest, does it make a sound?"

"It does make a sound because it's a tree falling in a forest," she said.

"But if no one is there to hear it..."

"We're not talking about a tree," she grumbled. "We're talking about someone becoming someone else."

"It's still a philosophical question. What do you believe?"

His questioning gaze caught hers. "I don't know what I believe, but I'm pretty sure that when my mother hears about my dad's past, she'll probably think he's even more of a hero than she thought before."

"But you don't think he's a hero?"

"It sounds like he did something heroic way back when, but I don't know about now. He still left my mom and me to fend for ourselves."

"That's true."

She blew out a frustrated breath. "Okay. What about Henry? Do you know anything about his condition?"

"He's out of surgery, but he's been placed in a medically induced coma. He's lost a lot of blood, and there's swelling in his brain. Henry fought hard to protect your dad's secret."

"A secret he should have never known, and now he might die because of it." She paused, thinking about Lauren. "I wonder if Henry told Lauren my dad's secret."

"That's a good question," Jason said. "She said Tatiana's name with a sense of familiarity. I'd like to find out more about that relationship. But that's on the back burner. The priority is tracking the vehicle that took your father from the motel."

"Is that what you're working on?"

"Along with many other people," he said.

"You should get back to it. I'll just watch a movie or something. Although it feels like I should be doing something more important."

"It's been a long day. You could go to bed."

"I'm not ready to sleep yet."

He gave her a conflicted look. "Well, I should work. That's what I do best, you know. I work. My life is my job—there's no room for anything else."

"You've said that before." She met his gaze. "I get it, Jason. Message received."

"I wasn't trying to send you a message," he denied.

"Yes, you were. You think I want something from you that you can't give me, but you're wrong."

"I'm wrong?" He gave her a doubtful look. "I don't think I am, Alisa."

"You have no idea what I want from you, because I have no idea. I'll admit that I'm attracted to you. I like you. But everything in my life is completely messed up, and acting on that attraction wouldn't be smart. But..."

"But?" he asked.

His blue eyes glittered with a question she probably shouldn't answer, but she couldn't help herself.

"But...I don't feel like being smart," she admitted, feeling reckless and impulsive. "Or doing the right thing. Or worrying about tomorrow, because tomorrow might not come. I've been a planner all my life. Thinking I could control everything by looking ahead, but I never saw any of this coming." She swallowed hard. "But you should do what you want to do, and if that's work, that's fine. I respect that. I appreciate it. I shouldn't even be tempting you to do anything else." She got to her feet and took her plate to the sink. As she turned around to clear the table, she ran right into him, and he pulled her into his arms.

"I've changed my mind," he said, his voice husky and filled with desire. "Can I do that?"

"You can do anything you want."

"I want you, Alisa. But all I can offer you is tonight, and you have to be sure you don't want more. Because I don't want to hurt you."

"I want tonight," she said with a certainty that took her by surprise. Because that really was all she wanted.

"Then let's start with this," he said, crushing her mouth under his.

The sparks that had been simmering between them since they'd first met caught fire with their kiss, and everything else fell away.

Kissing Jason was nothing but pure pleasure, a heady mix of excitement and comfort, danger and security. The trust they'd built and the bond they'd forged through fire and fear, created an emotional connection as well as a physical one.

She'd wanted to feel swept away, and that's exactly how she felt now. There was nothing but the two of them: kissing, touching, and taking off their clothes on the way out of the kitchen and up the stairs.

Jason stopped in the bathroom to grab a condom out of the drawer while she stripped off the rest of her clothes.

When he came back to her, she said, "Should I turn out the lights?"

"No. I like looking at you," he said in a way that made her heart jump against her chest and her body flood with desire. His arms wrapped around her as he kissed her lips, her neck, the valley between her breasts, sending more fire shooting through her.

She groaned with delight as every taste and touch sent her nerves tingling. And when they finally made it to the bed, she was more than happy with the light because she enjoyed looking at him, too, at his beautiful, muscled, fit body, at the dark hair that spread across his broad chest.

He was strength and power, and she wanted all of it, all of him. He was eager to give her that and more as they made love with a passionate abandon she'd never experienced before.

Not thinking about the future was more freeing than she would have ever imagined. There was no darkness here, not with Jason, not with how good they were together. It was all light, and it was all amazing, and she would never forget it.

———

Jason laid back against the pillows with a satisfied breath as Alisa settled into his arms, her head on his chest, her heart pounding against his. He hadn't planned on going where they'd gone, but he was damn glad he had. A small voice told him he might not feel that way later, but he pushed that voice out of his head, not wanting anything to mar the moment.

Closing his eyes, he drew in another breath and slowly let it out, feeling nothing but pure satisfaction and a strange feeling of contentment. It probably wouldn't last long, but he had it now, and it was something he rarely experienced.

It felt a little terrifying to be that content, that happy, in the middle of so much drama and danger. But they were in their own bubble right now, safe in each other's arms, not just physically safe, but mentally and emotionally. She wasn't thinking about her family, and he wasn't thinking about his. He wasn't even thinking about the job.

He frowned as the word job came into his mind, because now he was thinking about it, and he didn't want to.

Alisa lifted her head and gave him a sweet and sexy smile that drove away all thoughts of work. He brushed her dark-brown hair away from her face so he could see her better.

"Beautiful," he murmured as his fingers caressed the side of her face.

"If that's my new name, I'm good with it," she said with a smile.

"It's what I've been calling you in my head since we first met."

"I was calling you *Blue Eyes* because you have the most striking pair of eyes I've ever seen. Sometimes they're a light blue, sometimes they're dark, but they always hold my gaze. I have a hard time looking away from you."

"Same here."

"Do you get those eyes from your mother or your father, or both?"

"My mother," he said. "But we don't need to talk about family."

"You're right. Family is not the best subject. Let's talk about how amazing that was. I mean, wow. We're good together."

"Yes, we are," he said, feeling a sense of bittersweet emotion at the thought. Because it had been good. But now it was over.

"Oh, no, not that tone..." She shook her head and gave him a look that told him not to go where he was going. "It's not even eleven yet. We have lots of time before tomorrow, before reality comes back, right?"

"Right," he agreed.

"So, we have time to be good together again."

"Definitely. We have all night."

"And I want to take all night, Jason."

He laughed. "You have some high expectations."

She gave him a playful punch. "I wasn't just talking about that, although, I do want to do that again. But I was thinking we could do something else."

"Like talk?"

"Well, maybe not talk. I have a feeling if we talk, we'll start talking about things we don't want to think about right now."

She rolled off him and grabbed the TV remote from the nightstand. "Let's find an old movie on TV, something funny, something we can laugh about."

"Okay," he said as she turned on the TV and then cuddled up against him in a way that did not make him want to let go of her. "You pick."

She flipped through the channels, pausing now and then.

"What are you looking for?" he asked

"Something silly."

"Like a romantic comedy?"

"Maybe. I was thinking more like something old and funny." She paused. "Here we go. This is a good one."

"*Meet The Parents?*" he said with a laugh.

"Are you good with my choice?" she asked, planting a kiss on his chest.

"I'm good, but if you keep doing that, you're not going to see much of the movie," he teased.

She gave him a wicked smile. "We have all night, Jason. There are lots of things we can do."

Sleep should probably be one of those things, but that was his rational, put-the-job-first kind of thinking, and tonight he didn't want any part of that, not with Alisa curled up next to him, her soft body already stirring him back into action. But it was also nice to watch the movie with her, to hear her laugh, to see her with no fear in her eyes. It was a good break for both of them...

He just wished the break didn't have to end.

CHAPTER NINETEEN

They'd laughed and talked and made love and then did it all again as the night eventually moved toward morning, and when Alisa woke up to the sunshine streaming through the blinds and an empty spot in the bed next to her, she felt deliciously exhausted, and her only regret was that Jason had gotten up before her. But it was almost nine o'clock on Saturday morning, and it was time to face the day, something Jason had already gotten up to do.

She took a quick shower and dressed in jeans and a sweater, throwing on a pair of comfortable shoes, and then made her way downstairs. Jason was in the den, and he was on the phone. She moved into the open doorway, not sure if she should eavesdrop, but he gave her a smile and waved her into the room.

"She'll be there soon," he promised.

"Are you talking about me? I'll be where soon?" she asked as soon as he put down the phone.

"The hospital. Your mother is fine," he added quickly. "I was just checking in. The nurse said your mom is hoping to see you this morning, and I assured her you'd be in shortly." He stepped forward and put his arms around her. "Get rid of that guilty look on your face. Everything is fine. Your mother is good."

She looked into his eyes and saw nothing but honest sincerity. "You'll always tell me the truth, right, Jason? You won't pretend or try to make things sound better than they are."

"I have a difficult time doing that, so I will always tell you the truth," he said solemnly.

"Good. Because I'm living in a world where it's hard to trust anyone, but I do trust you."

"I trust you, too," he said.

Their gazes met for a long second, memories of the night they'd shared flowing between them. And then he leaned down and kissed her, setting off an explosion of feeling inside of her. This man had really gotten under her skin, and she lingered in his arms, in his kiss, hating to break the connection between them because this was where she felt the best, this was where she felt like herself.

It was strange to think a man she hadn't known a week ago had become so deeply entangled in her life, but it also felt right, like they were two halves of a whole that had suddenly found their way back together.

She didn't know if he felt the same way. He liked her, obviously. But she was probably more emotionally invested than he was. He'd certainly tried to warn her that he wasn't looking for a relationship, so she needed to keep things light.

The sound of the phone vibrating on the desk disrupted the moment.

Jason grabbed the phone and said, "It's Flynn. I need to take this."

"Okay, I'm going to grab some coffee."

As she walked out of the den, she heard him say, "Flynn, what's up?"

Whatever Flynn had to say was long because she didn't hear anything come out of Jason's mouth. Hopefully, it was nothing horrible, but she had a feeling her dream night was over.

———

Jason walked into the kitchen after getting off the phone with Flynn, more eager to see Alisa than he should be. He'd gotten out of bed early, thinking that was the best way to start off the day. Get his walls up and keep them up. But as soon as she'd walked into the den, he'd wanted to take her in his arms, and that's what he'd done. It was probably good Flynn had called, or they might have ended up back in the bedroom, and there was too much at stake to let that happen. Their momentary escape was over—at least for now.

Alisa was drinking coffee and buttering a waffle that had just popped out of the toaster. She gave him a wary and worried look. "Is there news about my dad?"

"They're still looking for him. And Henry Cavendish's condition is still critical but stable. He's hanging in there."

"That's good."

"My team also picked up Tatiana Guseva. She asked for a lawyer, but we're going to hold her as long as we can and put pressure on her to give up any information she has, if not on Novikov, perhaps others in his circle."

"It doesn't sound like anyone in Novikov's circle will ever speak against him. Why would they? They'll just end up dead, like Victor Kashin." She paused, giving him a thoughtful look. "Do you think Tatiana would speak to me, Jason? If she knew my father, maybe if she heard from me, she'd think of him as a human being again, maybe she'd care that it wasn't just the FBI looking for him but also his daughter, a daughter who loves him."

He could see how badly she wanted to help, but he knew it wouldn't work. "The fact she gave your father's location to Novikov doesn't suggest that she would care you're looking for him. Like Novikov, she probably thinks your father is a traitor and deserves whatever he gets."

"Well, I could still try."

"I'm not saying no, but I need to talk to her first, see where her head's at. If she's truly worried about dying of cancer, maybe she'll have a different perspective on the rest of her life."

"Like maybe she doesn't want to spend it in jail," Alisa suggested.

"Exactly. The other piece of news was that there was a break-in at Henry's lab last night. A janitor reported it to hospital security early this morning. Someone from my team went to the lab, and there are several canisters of hazardous materials missing."

Her jaw dropped. "Are you serious?"

"Yes. And Lauren Silenski is not at home. Her phone is also dead."

Alisa gave him a confused look. "I don't understand what part she has played in any of this. I never liked her, but what did she actually do?"

"I don't know, but maybe Tatiana or one of her friends saw potential in the lab when Tatiana was looking into clinical trials. They could have tried to buy someone off to get their hands on hazardous materials."

"Someone like Lauren?"

"Possibly. She also could have just disappeared after what happened to Henry. She might have been afraid they'd come after her."

"Maybe you can leverage the clinical trial to get Tatiana to talk," Alisa suggested. "If she doesn't tell you what she knows, she's out of the trial."

"That's pretty ruthless for a nurse."

"Well, we're dealing with ruthless people," she said without apology. "And if she's the one who outed my dad and put him in danger, I don't care what happens to her."

"I understand. I'll talk to her about everything, but I'm also concerned about what's missing from the lab. Whatever was taken is probably in Novikov's hands."

"And my father's," she said with a sigh.

"You should eat that waffle before it gets cold," he said, seeing her entire demeanor shift into the exhausted, terrified, overwhelmed woman he'd brought back from the motel last night. Their escape from reality was over. "Is there another waffle?"

"Yes, take this one. I'll pop another one in," she said, handing him the plate as she reached for the box of frozen waffles.

"Thanks." He was happy to put something in his stomach before they started what was probably going to be a grueling day.

"You're welcome." She gave him a wary look as she waited for the toaster to heat her waffle. "I know we agreed on no morning-after conversations."

"We should stick to that," he said quickly.

"I was just going to say it was really good." She gave a help-less shrug. "But I feel a little guilty that I spent the night enjoying myself and you and not..."

"Not what? There was nothing you could do last night to find your father or anything else. You know that, Alisa."

"It just feels a little wrong, but you were wonderful, and I don't regret it."

"Good, because I don't regret it either." How could he feel bad about what happened? The passion between them was off the charts, but it was also the conversation they'd shared, the laughs, and the feeling of being completely in sync that had been more than he'd expected. The only thing he was sorry about was that the night was over. "You didn't betray your love for your dad by sleeping with me or laughing at a silly movie. I know how much you love him and how worried you are about him. There was nothing you could do last night to affect anything."

"I don't know what I can do today. I feel helpless, Jason. And I'm really scared about what's coming next."

"I'm worried, too. But all we can do is keep moving on. Today is a new day. We start again."

"You always tell me what I need to hear, thank you."

Her words gave him another reason to be wary of the connection developing between them because he had never really thought that much about wanting to make someone feel better. But he always felt that way with her.

However, he couldn't let his feelings for Alisa distract him from finding the man who had killed his father and would kill hers, too, if he didn't stop him. It was time to get back to work.

———

Jason dropped her off at her mother's room around ten, and while she waited for her mother to wake up, Alisa re-read the letter her father had left behind in the motel room. She needed to share it, along with everything else she'd learned, and she hoped her mom would be well-rested for the conversation because she was going to need some strength to get through it.

Her mother opened her eyes and stretched, giving her a happy smile. "It's good to see your face. You look better today, Alisa. You must have gotten a good night's sleep."

She really hadn't slept more than an hour or two, but she wasn't going to tell her mom about that. "How are you feeling today?" she asked as she got to her feet and walked over to the bed, leaving the letter on the chair. She wasn't quite ready to get into that.

"Much better. I woke up around six, and the nurse took more blood from me. But I was able to stay awake for two hours. I had breakfast, and I watched a movie on the television. I was going to look at my phone, but I don't seem to have it."

"It's with the nurse so she can bring it to you when we need to talk to you."

"Oh, well, I'll have to get that back at some point. Have you heard from your father?"

"In a way."

Her mother's brows narrowed with worry. "What does that mean? Please tell me he's all right, Alisa."

Her mother's anxiety was suddenly very, very real, and she had to stop it from escalating. "I think he's all right for now," she said carefully. "Jason and I found the motel where he was staying, and he had started a letter to you and me. I have it." She turned around and picked up the letter.

"Let me see it," her mom said, pushing herself into a sitting position.

She didn't immediately hand over the letter. "Before you read this, I have to tell you I know Dad's secret. I know who he used to be, and I need to tell you about that because then the letter will make more sense."

"Then tell me."

"Dad grew up in Eastern Europe, maybe the Soviet Union, I'm not entirely sure, but I do know he wasn't a teacher. He was a chemist. At some point, a terrorist tried to use him to advance a chemical weapons attack. Dad was able to stop it, and in doing so, the US gave him asylum. He was given a new identity and was told he could never work as a chemist again, so he became a teacher. From that point on, he lived a normal life with us as Dan Hunt."

Her mother stared at her in shock. "That sounds crazy, Alisa. Your father isn't Russian."

"I think he is, Mom. The terrorist he worked for, and the people he used to know, they're all Russian. But when he told you he was changing his life for the better, he wasn't lying. He was telling the truth."

"I always knew that. Where is he now?"

"I don't know. But during the last year, Dad confided in Henry. Henry was having trouble with his therapies, and Dad wanted to help him. He wanted to use his brilliant mind to further the cure for cancer, so he told Henry who he was, and he started helping him on the weekends."

"They weren't playing golf or going fishing? He was working in Henry's lab?"

"Yes. Which probably would have been fine except that, by some random coincidence, someone from Dad's past saw him there and told the people he ran away from where he was. Now, Dad is on the run from the same terrorist he was forced to work with in Russia, and the FBI thinks there's an attack in the making. They're working hard to find Dad and to stop whatever is being planned."

Her mother's face had now lost all of its color. "Is your father all right?"

"The FBI is convinced he's alive."

"Because this terrorist needs him?"

"Yes."

"I want to read the letter." Her mother put out her hand. "Give it to me."

She handed her mom the letter and sat back in her chair, giving her mother time and space to absorb her father's words, the last words he might ever say to them.

———

Jason sat down across the table from Tatiana Guseva, a very thin, frail-looking woman whose brown hair had turned white and whose weary, dark eyes were unreadable. She was in her fifties, but she appeared much older than she had three years ago when he'd interviewed her after the courthouse bombing.

"Hello, Tatiana, we meet again."

"I'm not surprised. You swore you would get revenge for your father's death, even though that had nothing to do with me, just as whatever is happening now has nothing to do with me."

"Except that it does. You told your boyfriend that his former associate, Alexei Bruno, was in LA working under another name."

"I don't know who you're talking about."

"Sure, you do. You met Arseni Novikov when you were sixteen years old and started dating him seriously in your twenties. You were a ballerina. He was in the KGB. But then he went into the Bratva, and you moved to Paris. Some say you were the only woman he ever loved, if such a man is capable of love. Alexei Bruno was working for Novikov during the years you were together. You knew him, whether or not you care to admit it."

Tatiana stared back at him without saying a word. She'd spent enough time in Novikov's world to understand how important it was to keep her mouth shut.

"Did you know that the lab where you want to do your clinical trial was broken into last night? That the man who might be able to save your life was beaten up and shot and is in critical condition?"

Her gaze flickered slightly at his words.

"Did you realize that telling Novikov that Alexei Bruno was in LA might backfire on you? That the drug treatment you desperately need might no longer be available if the doctor is dead? If the canisters from the lab that are now missing might be vital to the clinical trial?" He let his words sink in, then said, "You need to help us find Novikov. It's time to decide how badly you want to live, Tatiana."

"I haven't spoken to Arseni in years," she said.

"But you've talked to Dominic Ilyin, and he's in LA, too. Did you tell Dominic you saw Alexei?"

"I asked for my lawyer several hours ago. It doesn't take that long to get here. Where is he?"

He ignored her question. "You're in serious trouble, Tatiana. We couldn't link you to the courthouse bombing, but we can connect you to the lab, to Cavendish, to the missing canister, to Dominic Ilyin. Is Novikov's life worth more than yours? How can you want to protect a man you haven't seen or spoken to a decade? You've built your life here in Los Angeles. You teach little girls how to dance ballet. They could all be dead in a matter of days. How can you live with yourself?"

"I don't know anything," she said, her lips tight, but he could see the crack in her walls, and he pressed harder.

"You know something. Do you really want to let the treatment that could save your life be destroyed by your ex-boyfriend's terrorist attack?"

She swallowed hard. "I don't know what's going to happen."

"What do you know?"

"If I talk to you, I want immunity. And I want to be in that clinical trial. Otherwise, there's no point in me speaking."

"Done," he said.

"I want it in writing."

"Not until I decide if your information is worth making a deal for. If it is, you'll get your immunity and the clinical trial, if it can still go on."

"I didn't tell Arseni about Alexei. I didn't tell anyone."

"We already know that you saw him."

"I saw him when I was in the lab talking to one of the lab technicians about the trial. He was walking down the hall, and he went into Henry's office. I wasn't completely sure it was him. I only met him a few times, many years ago."

"If you didn't tell Novikov about Alexei, who did?"

"Dominic had driven me to the lab. He occasionally visited me when he came to Los Angeles. Dominic and I were childhood friends. He's the one who introduced me to Arseni. I never imagined what the two of them would eventually become. But when I realized their activities were beyond anything I could handle, I left Moscow. I moved to Paris, and I haven't seen Arseni in at least fifteen years."

"But you have seen Dominic. Did he also see Alexei in the lab?"

"He didn't come to the lab with me. He was waiting for me in the downstairs lobby. He was going to give me a ride home. He saw Alexei come into the building, but Alexei didn't see him. When I eventually went down to the lobby, Dominic was agitated and already on the phone. He paused long enough to ask me if I'd seen Alexei upstairs. I lied and said I hadn't. I expressed disbelief that Alexei could be in LA. But Dominic was sure, and he told me he had a friend in the lab. He was going to get her to confirm that Alexei was working there."

"Who was the friend?"

"Lauren Silenski. She's the reason I went there. Dominic got me an appointment months ahead of when I was unable to get in on my own. He said he'd worked with Lauren's brother at some point."

"Where is Dominic now?"

She hesitated.

He leaned forward, holding her gaze. "You need to tell us, Tatiana. That's the deal. You know that if Dominic and Alexei are working for Novikov, something terrible is going to happen."

She gave him a long look, then said, "Dominic is staying at a condo in a high-rise that's under construction. He knows the contractor, and they gave him access to the model unit that was already completed. It's called the Elliott Tower. It's in Century City. I don't know the address."

"Is Arseni staying with Dominic?"

"I didn't ask, and he didn't say. But if either of them learns I betrayed them, they'll kill me. And it won't be fast, it will be slow and painful because I pledged them my silence years ago. I don't want to die. I want that clinical trial. I want to survive this. I am not part of their lives. I don't want to hurt people."

She might not want to hurt people now that her life was also on the line, but she'd been happy to look the other way for a very long time. "What's Dominic's number? How do you communicate with him?"

"He calls or texts from different numbers. We don't communicate that often. I hadn't heard from him in a long time until a few months ago. He reached out to me, and I had a weak moment when I told him I was sick. I thought back to a time when we were kids, when we were friends. He wanted to help me, and I wanted him to help me." She shrugged. "I didn't know Dominic was coming to LA until he showed up a few weeks ago. He doesn't tell me about his plans, and I don't ask. If I knew what was going on, I would tell you." She paused. "Now, I want that deal in writing."

He got to his feet. "We'll check out the Elliott Tower, and then we'll get you the paperwork."

After leaving the interrogation room, he stepped into the room next door where Flynn and Savannah had been watching his interview.

"Hell of a job," Flynn said, with approval in his eyes. "I didn't think she'd crack."

"You pushed the right buttons," Savannah said.

"We'll see. We need to check out the Elliott Tower."

"Already assembling a team," Flynn said. "We'll leave in ten minutes."

He hoped that wasn't ten minutes too long.

CHAPTER TWENTY

As the team prepared to move, Jason made a quick call to Alisa, who had turned on her phone after settling in her mother's hospital room.

"I only have a minute," he said. "We're chasing a solid lead."

"That's great," she replied. "Anything you can share?"

"I can't share details yet, but I'll update you soon. The info came from Tatiana, and it looks solid."

"Is it about my dad?"

"No, another of Novikov's associates. I'll let you know when I have more."

"Be careful, Jason."

Her concern reassured him, but it also unsettled him. He wasn't used to having someone who worried about him—but it felt surprisingly good.

Clearing his throat, he asked, "Everything okay with you?"

"Yes, my mom and I had a long talk. She's napping now, and I'm going to listen to something light and funny on my phone."

"Good. I'll talk to you later."

He stared at the phone, unsettled by the nagging feeling that he should have said more. But it was too late. Hopefully, the next time they spoke, he'd have good news.

They drove to the Elliott Tower in two vehicles, parking around the corner to keep out of sight. Wearing tactical gear, Jason, Beck, Flynn, and Savannah, along with four members of FBI SWAT, moved silently in teams of two. A drone had spotted at least three people in an eighth-floor apartment. Agents covered both front and back entrances as they entered the lobby.

Flynn had obtained keys from the management company, and any resistance to the search warrant had been firmly dealt with. Now, they just had to make it upstairs without walking into an ambush.

His gut twisted, the memories of three years ago playing through his mind. Stephanie and his father had gone to a motel where they thought Novikov was hiding. They hadn't waited for backup, and that decision had cost his father his life and taken away his partner's ability to go into the field. He hoped they weren't walking into another trap. His gut churned, and he started to sweat inside the thick gear he was wearing.

When they reached the floor where several condo models were completed and ready for sale, they set up on either side of the door, and then one of the SWAT team members kicked it in. He and Savannah were the first ones through the door.

They went into the apartment, guns drawn, calling out their presence.

The shooting started immediately. He took out a man to his left, while Savannah shot another man coming down the hallway. Flynn picked up a third shooter as he made his way further into the apartment. Within minutes, the three people inside the unit were dead or injured. Unfortunately, they hadn't found Novikov, Ilyin, or Alisa's father.

A huge, crushing wave of disappointment ran through him.

His fellow agents looked just as grim.

One of the men they'd shot moved. As Flynn tried to talk to

him, Jason walked into the kitchen, seeing papers on the island. His heart jumped as he realized he was looking at blueprints.

Savannah entered the kitchen. "What did you find?"

"Schematic drawings," he muttered as he flipped through the pages.

"Of this development?"

His gut tightened. "No, the Figueroa Center," he said, referring to the new convention center where the global tech conference would kick off tomorrow afternoon, with a welcoming speech by the vice president of the United States. "This is confirmation of the target. We don't have Novikov, but at least we know where he's planning to attack."

"Hopefully, we'll get more information about where he is right now from that guy," she said, tipping her head to the man who was crying to Flynn about the pain he was in.

"The ambulances are pretty busy right now," Flynn said. "Why don't you tell us where Novikov is, and we'll see if we can get one here faster?"

"You can't let me die," the man begged.

"I'm not letting you die. If you want help, talk."

"I don't know where he went," the man said. "I haven't seen him since yesterday."

"What about Dominic Ilyin?" Jason interjected. "Was he here?"

"He left an hour ago. He didn't say where he was going. Get me help. I think I'm dying."

"What's the plan? Are they setting off a bomb at the Figueroa Center?" he pressed.

Flynn gave him a surprised look as they both waited for the man to reply.

"I don't know. I'm just a driver. I drive people around and I pick people up."

"Did you pick up a man at the Sparks Motel in Brentwood yesterday?"

"No," the man said. "That wasn't me. Them," he said

nodding his head to the two dead men on the floor across from him. "I don't know where they went." He howled in agony at the end of his sentence. "But they didn't come here."

"An ambulance is on the way," Beck said, coming into the apartment. "The rest of the building is clear."

"Were you just guessing on the Figueroa Center?" Flynn asked quietly, pulling him away from the man on the floor.

"Blueprints," he said, leading him and Beck into the kitchen while Savannah stood watch. "This has to be the target."

"We knew it was the most likely one," Flynn said. "We've already tripled the security. It will be difficult for them to get in."

"They must have an inside track, a way into the convention that will get them past security. Maybe they're entering through a company."

"Or they've infiltrated security," Beck suggested.

"Or they could be part of the janitorial service, the catering..." Flynn's mouth drew into a tight line. "I suggested to Damon and the director that we cancel the conference, but the vice president was unwilling to go that far. So, we need to cover every base. Let's get to work."

While he knew securing the Figueroa Center was a priority, finding Novikov and Alisa's father before that would be a far easier way of shutting down the attack. "We have to find him before he gets to the center. He has to be somewhere else putting these bombs together with Alexei Bruno's help."

"Dominic Ilyin was here," Flynn said. "We can track him from this building to wherever he went."

"I'm sure he covered his tracks," he said, feeling a deep sense of frustration. "We're always one step behind."

"Until we're not," Beck said positively. "That's why we keep going."

He nodded. "I'm not giving up, just saying we need to get on offense."

Savannah joined them as the EMTs attended to the injured man. She had her phone in her hand. "I just spoke to Nick.

Dominic Ilyin was grabbed and thrown into the back of a van just three miles from here. He'd parked in front of a liquor store and appeared to be heading across the street when a van came screaming up. He disappeared into the back of it."

"Was he grabbed, or did he get in willingly?" he asked, shocked by her words.

"That's the question. We need to get back to the office." Savannah's phone buzzed. "Nick. Did you find something else?" She put the phone on speaker.

"In looking at footage from the scene where Ilyin disappeared, I got a hit on a license plate, a vehicle registered to former Special Agent Patrick Hastings."

His jaw dropped. "Seriously? Patrick Hastings? My father's best friend? He was at the scene?"

"Yes. He followed the van down the street. Both disappeared from view, and we haven't been able to find either of them again."

"I'll call Patrick and get a meeting with him," he said.

"Take the car," Savannah said as she tossed him the keys. "I'll ride back with Flynn and Beck."

He jogged through the apartment and took the elevator to the bottom floor. His mind was racing as fast as he was. He jumped in the vehicle and called Patrick on the phone. He wanted to see him face-to-face, but he didn't know where he was at the moment. That might be a revealing answer, too.

Patrick answered a moment later. "Jason," he said. "I'm glad you called. I need to talk to you."

"I need to talk to you. Where are you?"

"I'm in Hollywood."

"Meet me at Jack's," he said, naming a famous burger place. "Twenty minutes."

"I'll be there in fifteen," Patrick said.

As he ended the call, he started the engine. Before he could pull away, he saw Steph's name flashing across his phone with an urgent request to meet. He sent her a quick reply that he couldn't talk now but would call her as soon as he could. And then he sped down the street.

———

Alisa was going crazy wondering what had happened with Jason and the lead he'd gotten. He'd promised to get in touch with her as soon as he knew anything, so she had to be patient, but that wasn't easy. She was tired of sitting in a chair next to her mom's bed. She was tired of this room. She needed to be outside. She wanted to be with Jason. She wanted to be searching for her father. She wanted to be doing anything but this.

"You're worried," her mother said, muting the television that had been distracting them both for a while. "Do you know something you haven't told me?"

"No. I'm just wishing I could be more helpful. Jason said he'd keep me updated, and I know he'll try. He's just busy. He's doing everything he can to find Dad. And I'm sure he'll succeed. Jason is good. He's great at his job, and he's obsessed with finding this terrorist, so I know he won't stop until he does." She paused, seeing her mother's speculative look. "What?"

"You seem like you've gotten very close to Jason."

"Well, he's saved my life twice, and he's been protecting me."

"Is there more to it than that?"

She shrugged, avoiding the gleam in her mother's eyes. "I don't know."

"Well, that isn't a no."

"This whole situation is complicated."

"That's true. But I haven't ever heard you talk about a man the way you talk about him."

"Well, he's different than everyone else."

"In what way?"

"Pretty much every way."

"Do you think it's possible you have a little hero worship going on?" her mother asked tentatively.

"It's more than that. I really like him. He's very blunt and calls it like it is, and that's refreshing. There aren't any games. I feel like he's someone I can trust. Like he means what he says. He is who he is."

"You're talking about your father now."

"Maybe a little. I think what he did was wrong, Mom. He should have filled us in on his life a long time ago."

"I understand why he didn't."

"I know you do, but maybe we could have prevented what's happening now if we had been better prepared."

"Or maybe our lives wouldn't have been so wonderful if we'd known what darkness might come after us."

"You'll never be angry at him, will you?" she asked with a sigh.

"I wouldn't go that far," her mother said. "He's made me angry plenty of times. But it's never diminished the love I have for him or his love for me. We have a connection that is strong and steady and will never go away."

She had to admire her mother's unwavering belief in her dad. "I've always wanted a love like you and Dad have."

"It's real. Even if the foundation is built on something false, what we have together is pure. He's not perfect and neither am I. But we've built a good life together, and I really hope..." For the first time, her mother's voice broke.

She moved to the bed to hug her mother. "He's going to be all right," she said as they embraced each other.

"He will be," her mother said, infusing strength into her voice. "He said he'd make things right, so I'm going to keep believing until I can't."

She pulled away from her mom, her eyes filled with the same moisture she saw in her mother's. "I'm going to try to do that, too."

"He's a good man, Alisa."

"I think you're right." She blew out a breath. "Maybe we should unmute the TV and try not to think about everything."

"Why don't you take a break?" her mother suggested. "You've been here all day."

"I promised Jason I wouldn't leave."

"You don't have to leave the hospital. You can go to the nurse's lounge, talk to some of your friends, or go to the cafeteria and get lunch. It might do you good."

She thought about that. She really needed to get out of this room. "Do you want me to bring you something?"

"Maybe something sweet out of the vending machine. That would be safe. But don't come back too soon. Catch your breath. This could be a long day."

"All right. Call the nurse if you need anything."

"I'm feeling very close to normal, Alisa. You don't need to worry about me anymore."

"Okay, I'll be back soon."

As she entered the hallway, she saw a woman with a cane walking slowly down the hall. She offered her a brief smile, surprised when the woman stopped.

"Are you Alisa Hunt?" the woman asked.

She was surprised by the question and a little put off. "Who are you?" she asked, glancing at the security guard who was watching their exchange and had taken a step closer to her.

"I'm Special Agent Stephanie Genaro." She pulled out an FBI badge and showed it to her, and then to the guard.

He took it, gave it a long look, and then handed it back to Agent Genaro with a nod.

The agent gave her a smile. "I'm looking for Jason Colter. I heard he might be here with you. I'm his former partner."

At her words, she realized where she'd heard the name before. This was the woman who had almost lost her life along with Jason's dad. "Oh, right. Jason mentioned you. But he isn't here."

"Oh." Disappointment filled her gaze. "I've been trying to reach him, but he hasn't picked up. I need to talk to him about the case he's working on, the case involving your father."

She stiffened, surprised Stephanie knew about her dad, since Jason had said he was keeping his former colleagues out of the investigation. "What do you know about my dad?"

"Quite a bit, actually. That's what I want to talk to Jason about. One of my informants just gave me some valuable information, and I need to pass it on. I already went to Jason's office, but they didn't want to tell me anything. I guess I'll just have to wait."

"What kind of information?" she asked.

Stephanie hesitated. "I can't share it with you. I'm sorry."

"If it's about my father, you can tell me. I'm in the middle of this."

Stephanie looked around. "This isn't the place. And I'm sure Jason wouldn't want me to talk to you."

"I was on my way to the cafeteria. Do you want to get coffee with me?"

Stephanie hesitated. "I don't know."

"We don't have to talk about my dad. You can tell me what it was like to work with Jason."

"I guess I could do that. I have to wait for him to call me back, anyway."

"Let's go." She led the way to the elevator, walking at a slower pace so that Stephanie could keep up her. "Jason told me you were injured in an ambush."

"Yes. By the man he's now chasing," Stephanie replied. "He has tried to keep me out of the investigation, but I have my sources, and I can't just do nothing."

"It is hard to do nothing," she agreed. "I'm going a little crazy myself."

"Me, too," Stephanie said with a sigh. "That man took everything from me, and I want to put him behind bars."

"Hopefully, Jason will make that happen," she said.

The elevator doors opened, and they stepped inside. Two orderlies stood next to an empty gurney, which struck her as slightly odd. She turned her back to them to push the button for the lobby and heard Stephanie say, "What the hell?"

Before she could turn around, she felt a sharp jab in the back of her arm.

Suddenly, she couldn't move, and the world faded away...

CHAPTER TWENTY-ONE

Jason spotted Patrick sitting in the corner as soon as he walked into Jack's. Patrick had ordered two coffees and a plate of fries.

He pulled out the chair across from him and sat down. "What were you doing at the scene of an incident involving Dominic Ilyin getting pulled into the back of a van?" he asked.

Patrick's gaze widened. "That's what you wanted to talk to me about? How do you know I was there?"

"Your car was caught on camera."

"Then you must have seen what happened."

"What were you doing there?"

"I picked him up at the Elliott Tower and followed him. He parked in front of a liquor store and waited for the traffic to clear so he could cross the street. A van pulled up next to him, and then he was gone. I was stunned. I tried to keep up with the van, but I lost it in traffic."

His story matched what Nick had said, but Patrick was leaving out some important information.

"How did you know Ilyin was at the Elliott Tower?" he asked.

"Stephanie called me. I was surprised because there was tension between us after what happened three years ago. She said you were keeping her out of the investigation, and she had a good lead that she couldn't chase herself. Her CI told her Ilyin might be staying at the Elliott Tower, so I went to check it out. I wasn't there more than ten minutes when I saw him leave the building, so I followed him. Once I had better intel, I was going to call you, Jason."

"You should have called me right away. What's your game, Patrick?"

"There's no game," Patrick denied, giving him a look of surprise.

"You're acting shady. So is Stephanie. She has some CI who seems to know where Ilyin is, but she can't tell me who her CI is."

"I don't know who he is, either. Stephanie wouldn't say. Look, we're just trying to help. I may be retired, but I want Novikov behind bars. Stephanie feels the same way. We can both be assets. Use us."

He shook his head. "I can't use you. You don't work for the FBI anymore, and Stephanie is part of the LA office, which is excluded from the investigation, on orders of the director. If you have information, you have to give it to me. That's it. That's the bottom line. Stop chasing leads yourself."

"Got it," Patrick said, with irritation in his voice. "But you're being shortsighted, Jason. I was an agent for thirty years. I know a lot about Novikov and his organization."

"Believe me, so do I. Is there anything you can tell me about who picked Ilyin up?"

"I didn't see the driver. The van came up fast, slammed on its brakes, and drove off just as quickly. Unfortunately, I was on the wrong side to see how Ilyin got in, if he was willing or if he was grabbed. Maybe you can get footage from a camera in the area."

"We're trying." He paused as his phone vibrated. It was Savannah. "I need to get this."

"Go ahead," Patrick said.

"Jason," Savannah said. "I have bad news."

"What's happened?"

"Alisa has been kidnapped."

"What? How?" he demanded, fear rocketing through him.

"She left her mother's room to take a break and ran into your former partner, Stephanie Genaro. The guard said Stephanie showed him her ID. He had no reason to think she was a threat, and she likely wasn't the threat."

"What does that mean?"

"Alisa said she was heading to the cafeteria to get lunch, and Stephanie went with her. They got in the elevator where they were attacked, although the camera was covered, so we don't know exactly what happened. When the elevator doors opened, two men moved a patient on a gurney out of the elevator. The doors closed. When they reopened, Stephanie was found unconscious on the floor. She wasn't visible at first, but she was in the elevator when the attack occurred. Alisa was taken away in the back of a private ambulance."

He swore as he hit the table with his hand. Patrick gave him a startled and concerned look.

"Stephanie is regaining consciousness," Savannah continued. "I'm on my way to the hospital to talk to her."

"I'll meet you there."

"What happened?" Patrick asked.

"Alisa Hunt was kidnapped by Novikov."

"Can I help?"

"No. You and Stephanie need to stay the hell away from this investigation before you get someone killed." It wasn't Patrick's fault that Alisa was missing, but he was the nearest person he could yell at. Stephanie would be next. But ripping them apart wouldn't get Alisa back, and fear ran through him as he jogged to his car. He had to find her. He had to save her, but he had no idea how he was going to do that.

———

When Jason arrived at the hospital, Savannah, Flynn, and Stephanie were in a conference room in the security offices. Stephanie's face was a mix of apology and guilt, but he didn't care about her apology. He was ready to rip someone apart, and she was at the top of the list.

"Why were you here, and why were you talking to Alisa?" he demanded.

"I was looking for you. I left you a message. You didn't answer. I needed to talk to you, Jason. I thought you might be here."

"How do you know anything about Alisa? Why would you assume I was here?"

"Because I heard about Alisa's father and what was happening with her family from my CI. But I didn't ask her to go anywhere. She wanted to have coffee with me. We weren't going to leave the hospital."

"That's bullshit."

"It's not," she said hotly. "It's the truth."

"The guard confirmed that Alisa asked Stephanie to go to the cafeteria with her," Flynn interjected.

He shot Flynn a dark look, then turned back to Stephanie. "Why would she ask you to go with her?"

"She wanted to know what I knew, and I was curious about what she might tell me. There was no plan. All we did was get in the elevator. The next thing I knew, I woke up on the floor and there was security around me."

Her story made sense. It was backed up by the guard, but he still didn't like it. "I told you to stay out of this."

"Well, I'm in it now," Stephanie shot back. "And I should have been from the beginning."

"Jason, step outside with me," Flynn said.

He followed Flynn out of the conference room. "There's something off with her."

"Her story checks out. I not only spoke to the guard; I also talked to Alisa's mother. She encouraged her daughter to go to the cafeteria, and now she is feeling tremendously guilty about that. She said Alisa needed a break." He paused. "I know you're feeling all kinds of rage right now, but Stephanie isn't our problem."

"You're right. Novikov has Alisa," he said tightly. "Her father must have been balking. He needed to give him incentive."

"Then we find Novikov, we find her. Let's go back to the office and regroup."

"I want to speak to her mother first. I'll meet you there." He jogged down the hall and took the elevator to the sixth floor. When he entered Pamela Hunt's room, he was shocked to see her standing by the edge of her bed, hanging onto the railing. As she swayed, he rushed forward.

"Hang on," he said. "I've got you."

She leaned against him. "I thought I would be stronger. I need to get out of here. I need to find my daughter. Alisa is gone, Jason."

He saw the fear in her eyes. "I'm going to find her."

"It's my fault."

"You need to sit down," he said, helping her onto the bed.

"I told her to go," Pamela said, wringing her hands together. "Alisa was pacing around this room, and she was so frustrated and tired; I made her leave. I sent her into danger. Please, tell me she's going to be all right."

He wanted to tell her what she wanted to hear, but he couldn't. "I will do everything I can to find her and bring her back. I promise you that. I care about your daughter."

"She cares about you, too. I don't know what's been going on, but she trusts you. Don't let her down."

A chill ran through him. "I won't," he said, but he was afraid he already had.

———

"You must wake up, Alisa," her father said. "Before they come back."

"Before who comes back?" she murmured, her eyes feeling so heavy she didn't think she could open them.

"Everyone."

His voice sounded close but also far away.

"I'm so sorry," he added. "I never should have let this happen to you. I never should have even had you. I was selfish to want a family."

She frowned as a wave of nausea ran through her along with a metallic taste in her mouth that made her want to gag.

"Alisa," he said sharply, urgently. "Please, wake up."

She finally got her eyes open, first one then the other. It was difficult to focus. Everything was dim. But as her vision cleared, she realized her dad was standing about ten feet from her. There was a table filled with lab equipment in front of him.

Her gaze moved past him and around the room. They were in some sort of a warehouse with high windows. The room was filled with boxes and very little furniture, an old couch, a couple of chairs, and a cot in the corner.

"Alisa, are you feeling okay?"

"Where—where are we?"

"I don't know. I was blindfolded when they brought me here."

She lifted her hand to wipe the sleep from her eyes when she realized she was tied to a chair. "Can you untie me?"

"I'm sorry, baby, I can't." He held up his wrist, and she saw a cuff attached to a chain. "I can only make my way around this table."

"What are you doing?"

"Something I don't want to do," he returned heavily.

"Oh, my God! Are you building a bomb?" she asked, coming fully awake at that thought.

"I'm supposed to be. I've been trying to stall, but now I can't."

"Because I'm here." She could see the truth in his eyes. "You look tired, Dad." He didn't just look tired; he looked like he'd been beaten. There were bruises on his face, and his brown hair had become grayer in the last few days. "They hurt you, didn't they?"

"It doesn't matter what they do to me." He bit down on his lip as he shook his head. "It's you I'm worried about. I never imagined this could happen to you."

"I found out your secret. You were a chemist in Russia, right?"

"I was."

"You stopped some attack, and the US gave you asylum. And you married Mom without telling her any of this."

"Does she know now?"

"Yes."

"She must hate me."

"She loves you. I mean, she really loves you. There is no doubt in her mind about the man she married. I have to admit I've had more than a few doubts, wondering why you left her in the hospital, why you didn't warn me."

"I was going to. I tried to tell you in my text."

"That was already too late. They tried to kidnap me Wednesday night, and then they cut the brakes on my car on Thursday."

He blew out a breath. "I knew about what happened in the garage, but I heard you were all right, that the FBI was protecting you. I didn't know about the car. But you're right to be angry with me."

"I don't want to be angry. I love you, Dad. But how are we going to get out of here?" The situation seemed overwhelmingly hopeless.

"I just have to do what they want, and then they'll let you go."

"No, they won't. Don't lie to me. I can't take any more of your lies. As soon as you do what they want, they'll kill me.

And you, too, probably. Unless they need you to build more bombs."

"I won't ever work for them again." He looked over his shoulder to make sure they were alone. "I've implanted a secondary timer in the two devices. They'll think the bombs will go off at eight-thirty, but I can trigger them with the remote in my pocket. I'll wait until we're in the van on the way to the venue. I'll try to do it where there will be the least amount of collateral damage. The van will blow up with them in it."

"Them? Will they leave you here?"

He didn't answer her question, and she knew the answer. "Oh, my God! You're going on a suicide mission."

"It's the only way to stop them. They need me to go with them. I've made them believe only I can set off the toxin within the device. If it was an ordinary explosive, they could do it themselves, but they want the maximum damage, and that requires my assistance. That will work in my favor. They'll have to take me along."

"There has to be another way. The FBI will find us. Jason will find us."

"Jason?"

"Jason Colter. He's an FBI agent; he's been protecting me. I know he'll come. He hates Novikov. The man killed his father."

"Colter?" her father echoed. "Is he related to Drew Colter?"

"If that was his father's name, yes," she said. "Did you know him?"

"Drew Colter helped get me out of Russia, along with someone from the CIA."

Her stomach flipped over. What were the odds that Jason's dad had helped her father reinvent his life? It was as if the two of them had been connected a very long time ago.

"I hope the FBI will find us," her father continued. "But Novikov has already moved me twice. He doesn't stay in one place for long, and he always covers his tracks."

"How did you get involved with him?"

"I knew him when I was young. I knew them all. Arseni Novikov, Dominic Ilyin, Tatiana Guseva. We were unformed teenagers. We had dreams that would take us in very different directions. I always knew Arseni was cold, but never that he was as cruel as he turned out to be. Unfortunately, by the time I found out, I was in his clutches. He forced me to work with him."

"How did he force you?"

"He threatened my mother. I couldn't let him hurt her."

"I have a grandmother?" she asked in wonder. "Is she still alive?"

"No. She died many years ago. Long after I disappeared from her life. She believed I was dead. Everyone in my family was told that. The CIA faked my death when I defected. I thought I was safe, especially after so many years had passed. But I made a mistake. I wanted to help Henry with his cancer treatment. I took a gamble and told him about my past. It was a poor decision."

"Even worse for Henry. Novikov's men tortured your location out of him. He's in critical condition."

"God! Poor Henry. He didn't deserve that. He's trying to do good things. He wants so badly to cure people. He inspired me. I wanted to help him achieve his goals. But I put him in danger."

"What happened at the lab? How did Novikov know you were in LA?"

"I ran into someone who had known me in Russia. I wasn't sure she'd recognized me; it had been many years. Then a week later, your mother got sick, and I got a call from someone who called me by my former name. That's when I took your mother to the hospital. I thought she would be safe there, and if I disappeared, you would be safe, too."

"What about the house? Did you burn it down?"

"No." He shook his head. "But I was afraid that something might happen at the house, so I moved some of our things with me when I left. I don't know if they're still at the motel."

"They appeared to be," she told him. "So, you knew the house burned down?"

"I went by there, and I saw the destruction. I'm so sorry, Alisa. I made a lot of mistakes."

She drew in a shaky breath. "You did make mistakes, and I don't need apologies; I need an action plan. You're brilliant, right? You have a plan for the bombs, but what about now? Is there any way out of here?" She yanked on her arms, but she could barely move them, and already her shoulders were cramping.

"No, there isn't," he said, stiffening as they heard voices. "Pretend you're still unconscious."

As the door opened, she shut her eyes, hearing a spate of words in a language she didn't recognize, but it was probably Russian. There were also heavy footsteps, and then someone kicked her leg. She couldn't help but flinch.

"Leave her alone," her dad said. "She's not part of this."

"Oh, but she is," a man with a thick accent said as he slapped her hard across the face.

Her eyes flew open, tearing up from the sting of the slap. She gazed into cold gray eyes. The man with the silver hair, the man Jason had been hunting for years, was suddenly right in front of her. He was tall and dressed all in black and appeared fit for a man in his mid to late fifties.

Cruel amusement lifted his lips. "Ah, so you are awake, the child of Alexei Bruno."

"I don't know who that is."

"Of course, you do. He's standing right over there. My once very good friend, Alexei."

"If he's your friend, why are you doing this?"

"Because he betrayed me. Now he must pay. Sadly, you will pay, too."

"I don't believe you're at all sad," she said, drawing another evil smile.

"You're right. I have no feelings whatsoever about you or

him. I have a mission, and I need you both to complete it." He looked back at her father. "You will finish the job you started by six-thirty. If you are not done, your daughter will be punished for every minute you are late."

She had no idea what time it was now because she couldn't see her watch, but it sounded like she might be safe for an hour or two. After that...

She shuddered at what they might do to her, terrified she wouldn't be able to survive it, that her mother would be left alone, that her father might be forced to watch her die, or she might be forced to watch him die.

She had never in her life imagined she could end up in a situation like this, trapped in a dirty, dark warehouse with an insanely evil man whose only intent was to hurt and kill as many people as possible. Of course, he wouldn't have mercy on her. He had no soul. No conscience.

Her only chance for survival was probably in Jason's hands. But knowing how few leads he probably had, that would take a miracle. And the clock was ticking...

CHAPTER TWENTY-TWO

He didn't know what it would take to find Alisa, but some divine intervention might be required, Jason thought, as he and the rest of his team spent the next three hours studying security footage around the city in a desperate attempt to find a clue to Alisa, her father, and Novikov.

His eyes were blurring, his gut churning, and it took every ounce of energy he had not to scream from the insane amount of pain that ripped through him every few minutes when he thought about what Alisa might be going through. It was almost five, and she'd been gone too long. But it was unproductive to focus on the worst possible scenario because fear wouldn't get him to her any faster. It would only slow him down. But he kept seeing her face in his head, her eyes pleading with him to save her, and he didn't know how to do that.

The thought of losing someone who was becoming very important to him was almost paralyzing. But he couldn't afford to be paralyzed. He had to think, to act...

Stephanie suddenly showed up, taking a seat next to him as she put her cane against the desk. She'd come back to the office with the team, desperate to help, and Flynn had decided she was more valuable working for them than getting in the way. He had seen little of her since he'd returned, which had been fine with him. He still had mixed feelings about her going to see Alisa.

"Still pissed at me?" she asked, giving him a wary look.

"I'm too busy to be pissed," he returned, keeping his gaze on the security footage playing across his computer monitor.

"I just wanted to talk to you, Jason, and I thought I could find you at the hospital. I couldn't have predicted what was going to happen. If she hadn't been in the hallway, I wouldn't have even run into her."

"I've already heard this. Right now, I'm focused on finding Alisa, her father, and Novikov. That's all that matters."

"I agree, and I have a new lead from my CI."

He looked up from his screen. "What is it?"

"Pieter Moldev, an associate of Dominic Ilyin, owns three buildings in LA: a nightclub, a gym, and an automotive shop. The auto shop was closed last year. But my CI drove by and saw lights on in the back. I think it's worth checking out. Dominic or Novikov could be using the shop as a base for their operations."

"What's the address?" he asked, his gut tightening. Steph's CI had given them a lead on Dominic before, and it had been accurate. Maybe this one would be, too.

She rattled off the address, and he jotted it down on a notepad by his computer.

"What's going on?" Savannah asked, popping up from the cubicle across from him.

"Potential lead," he replied.

"Let's go," she said immediately.

"I'd like to come, too." Stephanie got to her feet, a little unsteady until she grabbed her cane.

"No. You stay here," he said with a firm shake of his head.

"Jason, I can help. At the very least, I can watch the door when you go inside."

"Thanks, but I can't involve you in this." He saw her frustration and felt some empathy for her. "You're helping by giving us the lead. That's going to have to be enough."

She gave him a long look. "I really want to nail that bastard."

"So do I."

She let out a sigh of resignation. "Good luck."

By the time, he left the building, he had Savannah, Nick, and Beck at his side. They took two cars across town, with an FBI HDU, otherwise known as Hazardous Devices Unit, set to meet them at the address. With Novikov and Dominic's love of explosives, they couldn't discount the possibility that the building could be rigged.

It took them about twenty minutes to locate the address in an industrial area near the airport. It was a little past six now and dark on a block with few streetlights. The front door of the shop was boarded up, as were the windows, but there appeared to be a light on in the back of the building, just as Stephanie's CI had described. There were no vehicles in front or back, but it was possible a vehicle could have been driven inside through one of the two large garage doors.

He parked on the street, with Beck and Flynn pulling in behind him.

They met on the sidewalk.

"HDU is five minutes out," Flynn said. "We need to wait."

He didn't want to wait five seconds, much less five minutes, but he forced himself to rein that feeling in. "I agree," he said heavily. "Three years ago, my father died chasing a lead like this, a lead so tantalizing he couldn't slow down for a second. He couldn't wait for backup. And neither could Stephanie. And if Patrick Hastings and I hadn't gotten delayed by a train, we'd probably be dead, too."

The other three agents stared at him in somber silence.

"Sorry. It all just came back to me." He paused as an HDU team of two men arrived.

Within minutes, they sent a robot around the perimeter of the building to check for heat signatures, vibrations, and other acoustic disturbances that might indicate the ticking of an explosive device. The robot was outfitted with numerous cameras and sent the photos back to them on a computer they had open in the back of the SUV.

"No heat signatures apparent," one of the officers said.

"Are you sure? There's no one inside?" he asked, disappointed by that comment.

"Doesn't appear to be. But depending on variables, we can't be one hundred percent sure," the officer replied. "We can have the robot breach the back door on your order," he added to Flynn.

"Do it," Flynn said. "Jason and Savannah, why don't you go around the back? Beck and I will watch the front door."

He nodded, following Savannah to the rear of the property, staying in the shadows of the adjacent building as they did so. When they got to a good vantage point, they watched as the robot moved toward the back door, its mechanical hand placing several small, focused explosive devices around the lock on the back door. Then the robot backed away as one of the HDU officers used a remote device to blow open the door.

It fell off with a dusty thud. The robot moved over the debris field and into the building. He and Savannah waited on either side of the building with their guns drawn.

No one came out of the building. It could be empty. This could be a dead end.

He took a few steps forward, wanting to at least take a look inside, but a second later, he was knocked off his feet by a series of thunderous explosions that sent a heavy spray of rubble all over him, and fires lit up the building.

A moment later, Beck and Flynn came running around the back, helping him up, and pulling him away from the fire.

Savannah had been further away and had some pieces of plaster in her hair, as did he, but otherwise, they were fine.

Breathless, he stared at the inferno, knowing if they hadn't gotten the HDU team to the site and sent the robot inside the building first, none of them would be alive.

But the real question was whether there had been anyone else in that building.

The robot hadn't picked up any heat signatures, but what if someone inside was already deceased?

His body clenched with the thought that Alisa might have been in that building. Maybe her father, too.

But his gut told him this entire scene was just another ambush, a way to kill him and maybe his team. The real threat still loomed ahead.

Which meant that Alisa and her father were hopefully still alive.

———

The clock was ticking, and every minute heightened Alisa's fear. Novikov had promised to punish her if her father wasn't done by six-thirty, and it was minutes to that now. "Dad," she said, knowing he was doing his best. He'd been working nonstop for the last few hours, barely speaking to her except to say he had to get this done. There would be time to talk later.

"Almost there," he replied.

She tried to breathe through the panic that threatened to overwhelm her. Aside from being allowed to use the bathroom once, she'd been tied to the chair, with various guards coming in and out of the makeshift lab to check on her father's progress.

Novikov had not reappeared since his first visit, but she'd heard voices outside the room where they were being kept, and she suspected he was out there with at least three other men.

She had so many questions she wanted to ask her dad, but it had been difficult to have a private conversation, and her father had been focused on his task. It had been strange to watch him making a bomb. For her entire life, she had thought he was a science teacher and just a very ordinary, normal man. She'd certainly never imagined he was a brilliant Russian chemist who had defected to the US so that he wouldn't be forced to build chemical weapons.

A man came into the room, barking at her dad in Russian.

"Five minutes," her father said in reply to whatever question he'd been asked.

The man left the room, probably to give Novikov an update.

"Alisa, listen to me," her father said quickly. "I've set timers on these explosives, but they can also be stopped manually by putting in a code."

"Why are you telling me this?"

"In case you need to know. This is what will happen. Arseni will take me to the venue to plant the bombs. As I mentioned before, I have a remote in my pocket, and if I can find a way to detonate the explosives in a location that will only take out me and whoever else is with me, I will do it."

"No, Dad. You can't."

"I have to. I can't let him kill thousands of people."

"There has to be another way."

"There's not. Not unless we get a miracle."

She was starting to lose faith in a miracle. Jason would be looking for her and Novikov. Everyone on his team would be doing the same and probably every other agency they worked with. But how would they know where they were?

"There's something else you need to know," her father said. "I don't believe Arseni will take you with us. He'll keep you here alive until everything is complete. You must try to escape. If you see any opportunity, you must take it."

His words chilled her to the core. "I will."

"Hopefully, you will be rescued, and you will have a chance to tell someone how to disarm the devices before they go off at eight-thirty. I have created a code. It's your mother's birthdate followed by your birthdate, plus star, pound, ampersand." He rattled off the code, then said it again.

"I don't know if I can remember," she said, panic swamping her brain. "Is it pound and then star?"

He repeated it once more. "This is only if I can't stop everything myself. You're just a backup."

"Where are the explosives going to be set? Is it the convention center? They're amping up security for the conference tomorrow. How will you even get in?"

"It's the Kensington Hotel, which is attached to the new Wilshire Mall and two other office buildings. The complex is connected by ventilation systems, and when the bombs go off, the toxins will go everywhere, killing many people. I also believe the vice president is staying at the hotel tonight."

"It's happening tonight?" she asked in surprised. "I'm pretty sure the FBI thinks it's all happening tomorrow at the convention center."

"They would have been made to think that. Novikov likes to be unpredictable."

"But there will be Secret Service and other agencies at the hotel, too, right? How will you be able to get bombs into the hotel without anyone seeing you?"

"He will have someone on the inside helping. And there will be many rooms and many places to hide the devices."

"This is so sick."

"It is. Science should not be used to destroy mankind. This is why I left, so I could do good in the world, not evil. But here I am again, being forced to do an evil man's bidding."

"Because of me and Mom. You shouldn't do it." She paused as an inescapable fact hit her hard. "They're going to kill me anyway. Hopefully, Mom will be okay. But I'm not getting out of this, and neither are you. You should just let them kill us."

"You *are* getting out of this," he said fiercely. "By playing along and going with them, I will buy you as much time as I can for someone to save you. If I can't detonate them early, I will try to leave some clues at the venue to show where the bombs are located. Whatever happens with me, don't blame yourself. I love you, Alisa." He gave her a sorrowful look. "And if you have a chance to tell your mother I love her, too, please let her know how sorry I am. And tell her that being with her, our family, was the best time of my life. I only wish I hadn't been selfish enough to take a love that has now ended like this."

She could hear the break in his voice. He really did love her mother and her. That part of him was very real. "You'll tell her yourself," she said defiantly, but inwardly, she was losing hope.

The door opened, and Novikov strode in, flanked by his guards and someone else.

Her heart stopped. "Oh, my God," she breathed. "You?"

CHAPTER TWENTY-THREE

Jason had only been in the office a few minutes and barely had time to wash the dust from the explosion off his hands and face when he got a call from Mick Hadley.

"I found the van that took Dominic Ilyin," Mick said shortly.

"What? How do you even know about that?"

"It doesn't matter. I'm behind a container store at Howard and Davis Street in Hollywood. Ilyin is dead."

"And the kidnapper?"

"There's no one else here," Mick said. "I'm sending you a photo."

He checked his messages as a photo appeared of a man bloodied and beaten lying in the back of a van. "It looks like Ilyin," he muttered.

"He gave me an address before he died. I need you to get a team together and meet me there."

"Wait a second. He was alive and gave you an address? I thought you said he was deceased."

"He talked before he took his last breath. You're wasting time, Jason. I'd do this myself, but it's your turf."

"We almost got killed chasing a lead. How do I know this one is better?"

"Because it is," Mick said. "You're going to have to trust me."

He would never trust Mick, but he had to go. What choice did he have?

"I'm sending you the address," Mick said. "I'll be there in fifteen minutes. Don't stall on this, Jason. I don't think Novikov will be there much longer."

"I'm on my way." He ended the call and walked into Flynn's office where Flynn and Beck were talking. "Hadley found Ilyin dying in a van in Hollywood. Before he passed away, he gave Mick the location of where we can allegedly find Novikov." He handed his phone to Flynn so he could see the photo of Ilyin.

Beck moved around the desk to take a look as well.

"It looks like someone tortured that information out of him," Beck commented. "Is this Hadley's work?"

"I don't know. But I have an address. Mick is meeting me there. I realize this could be a distraction or another setup, but it could also be real."

"I'll go with you," Beck said immediately. "We'll grab whoever else is still here."

"I have a meeting with Homeland Security, so you two run this," Flynn said, picking up his phone. "I'll give the HDU team the address as well."

He appreciated the fact his new team was willing to do whatever needed to be done, even though his last lead had not panned out. "Thanks," he told Beck as they left Flynn's office.

"No thanks required. This is what we do, Jason." Beck paused. "Did you tell your former partner about this lead?"

"I haven't seen her since we got back. I'm sure she heard about the explosion and knew she wouldn't be my favorite person to talk to right now."

"She could have been set up."

"Which is why I wanted her out of this from the beginning," he said. "But she's the least of my concerns right now."

"You're working with him?" Alisa asked in shock, staring at the woman in front of her. "But you're an FBI agent. You said you were Jason's partner. You were there when his father was killed. And you were in the hospital for weeks. I don't understand. How did you go from being Novikov's victim to being his accomplice?"

Stephanie gave her a look that was impossible to decipher. She didn't seem apologetic or trapped. She wasn't trying to explain or make excuses. She was just there, as if she belonged there. "You don't need to understand," Stephanie said coldly.

"You were the one who orchestrated my kidnapping, weren't you? What if I hadn't asked you to go to the cafeteria with me? What were you going to do?"

"It doesn't matter," Stephanie replied, stepping forward, her limp no longer as pronounced as it had been. "You made it too easy for me, Alisa. I prefer a challenge."

"You're a traitor."

"You should be careful what you say. Your life might depend on it."

"Oh, please, I'm not going to make it out of here alive, no matter what I say, so you might as well hear the truth. Jason cares about you. He's been worried about you for years. He thought you were the best agent he'd ever worked with. And you were a fraud, a traitor. You didn't deserve his respect."

Stephanie's face tightened. "He didn't know what I went through. I did what I had to do."

"Silence," Novikov said. "We are done talking." He turned to her father. "Are they ready, Alexei? Or do we need to inspire you by showing your daughter what pain feels like?"

"They're ready," her father said quickly, motioning to the two cylindrical canisters on the table.

Novikov nodded to two of his men.

They walked toward her father, one with a vest in his hand. They forced her father to put on the vest, strapping his arms to his sides, and she suddenly realized his plan of detonating the bombs before they reached the complex had just ended. There was no way he could reach for a remote in his pocket.

Then her stomach flipped over when she saw them put one canister inside the pocket of the vest with the timing device showing through an open slit. Her heart stopped. Her father was going to be a suicide bomber. He would be sacrificed. He would be killed with everyone else, and there wasn't a damn thing she could do about it.

After ensuring the vest was in place, the other man forced her dad to put on a coat that would cover the vest. Now, he would look like any other guest at the hotel.

"No, Dad," she said, tears filling her eyes.

"I love you, Alisa," he said, his voice breaking. "You are the best daughter a man could have."

"I love you, too," she said as he was taken out of the room, leaving her alone with Novikov and Stephanie. "How can you do this? How can you want to hurt so many innocent people? What is wrong with you both?"

"Innocent?" Novikov spat. "Your father was never innocent, and his betrayal cost my brother his life. Did he tell you that?"

"He didn't tell me anything, and I can't stop you. I can't hurt you. Just let me go." It felt wrong to plead for her life when her father was about to be killed, but she had to beg because there was nothing else she could do.

"You will stay here, and you will remain alive until I'm ready to destroy this city."

"How can you want to kill so many people you don't even know: women, children, babies?"

"They are the means to an end," he said with a shrug.

"The end to what?"

"Power," he said simply. "Money. Control. That's all that matters, and it's mine for the taking. It always has been. No one can stop me. I'm invincible."

He was completely insane and without a soul. She could see why he was one of the most wanted men in the world.

"And you're going to help him?" she asked Stephanie in bewilderment.

Stephanie gave her a long look, then said, "A long time ago, I had to choose a side."

"And you chose *his* side?"

Stephanie didn't answer as the two men who had taken her father out of the room returned to carefully remove the other canister and put it in a backpack. They left again, and Novikov nodded to the man remaining in the room. "When it's done, I'll send the order."

Send the order? As Novikov and his associate looked at her, she knew what that order would be. *They would kill her.*

Her breath came fast and furiously as she hyperventilated from anxiety and panic. She might have only a few minutes of her life left.

When Novikov and Stephanie departed, the man gave her an evil smile. "We can have some fun while we're waiting."

She swallowed hard, terrified of what was coming but also determined. She would have to fight. And if she had a chance to kill him before he killed her, she needed to take it.

———

Jason's heart was pounding against his chest as they raced across town. He had Beck in the passenger seat, with Savannah and Nick in the back. The HDU team was en route. Mick had texted one minute earlier that he was waiting for them on the corner of Rossmore and Carville.

He hoped to God this was not another false lead, another setup, another distraction. But he had to follow it. If the intel was good and Alisa and her father, maybe even Novikov, were inside, they had to go for it. Every minute that they waited or debated was another minute Alisa would have to endure, and he had a continual prayer going through his head, begging for her to be okay.

He parked a block away from the designated address and jumped out, with the rest of his team following. Mick came forward, dressed in black jeans and a black T-shirt, a weapon in his hand. It was seven-fifteen, and all the other buildings in the area appeared to be closed. It looked like a good location for Novikov to be holed up, building his bombs. But there were a lot of these areas in the sprawling city of Los Angeles. Hopefully, this was the right one.

"What have we got?" he asked Mick.

"One guard watching the front door, another at the back. Not sure how many are inside," Mick said in a terse tone. "There are two cars in the lot. One is registered to Stephanie Genaro."

Jason sucked in a breath of shock. "And the other vehicle?"

"Carl Hodges. Nothing on him. Could be stolen."

"And you're sure this intel is good?" he asked, still reeling with the thought that Stephanie was inside. Had she gotten another lead? Had she come on her own?

"It's good," Mick replied. "Novikov is either in that building now, or he's been there recently."

"Okay. Let's do this."

With humans guarding the doors, there was little doubt in his mind there was someone or something inside worth securing. The presence of security also implied the building was not rigged to explode.

They'd already geared up and developed a tactical plan in the car. Now they just had to execute. The HDU team would check in with Mick when they arrived and wait to be called in.

The four of them would take out the guards at the front and the back and make their way into the building. While Nick and Beck took the front, he and Savannah once again went around the back.

The guard at the back door was looking at something on his phone.

Savannah feigned a stumble into the light, drawing the guard's attention.

"Who's there?" the man asked, looking in her direction.

"Can you help me? I'm lost," she said.

Jason used her voice for cover, sneaking up behind the man, and using his weapon to knock him out. The guard barely got out half a groan before he slunk to the ground.

The door was unlocked, and as they made their way inside, he heard a shrill and terrified scream. His heart stopped.

Alisa was here, and she was in trouble.

He raced toward the sound of her voice, through a loading area and down a dark hallway, her frantic, panicked cries piercing his heart with each step. She was so close. He could not be late. He could not lose her now.

And then the sound of a gunshot rocketed through him, and there was no more screaming.

CHAPTER TWENTY-FOUR

Jason burst through a door, his anxious gaze searching for Alisa. She was standing in the middle of what looked like a makeshift lab, staring at a man on the floor, a gun shaking in her hand. At the sound of their approach, she suddenly whirled around, pointing the weapon in his direction, her brown eyes wide and panicked.

"It's okay. It's me, Alisa."

She stared at him with shock, as if she couldn't believe he'd just suddenly appeared as if she couldn't trust what she was seeing.

Savannah moved past him to check on the man on the ground.

"Put the gun down, Alisa," he said gently as she still held it pointed toward him.

"I...I shot him. I can't believe I shot him."

"You did good."

"I can't breathe," she gasped. "Is he dead?"

He looked to Savannah for the answer. She gave a negative shake of her head as she cuffed the man who was barely conscious and bleeding from a wound in his abdomen.

Turning back to Alisa, he said, "He's not dead, but he won't hurt you again." His gaze swept her body, noting the bruising on her face, and the ripped sleeve of her sweater. He couldn't imagine what hell she'd been going through or how she'd ended up with the gun and the man on the ground, but clearly, she'd fought for herself.

"Are you sure?" she asked, her breathing still coming too fast.

"Yes." As Savannah communicated with the rest of the team, and he heard Nick and Beck clearing other areas of the building on the radio, he moved forward and took the gun from her hand.

Then he pulled her into his arms, needing to hold her, to know she was okay. She sank into his embrace, burying her face in his chest as he stroked her back, as the terror began to seep out of her.

"I was so scared," she muttered.

"You're safe now."

"It's hard to believe."

Her body shook in his arms, and the last thing he wanted to do was let her go, but he had to find out what she knew. "Was anyone else here but this man and the guards in the front and back of the building?"

"They were all here. My dad was forced to turn the explosives into chemical weapons. If they didn't, they were going to torture me."

His chest tightened. "Who else?"

"Novikov. He slapped me in the face. He looked right into my eyes. He was terrifying. He was so cold." Her expression changed suddenly as if she'd just remembered something. "And Jason, Stephanie was here, too. She's working with Novikov. She's helping him, Jason. She's a traitor."

His lips drew into a hard line. He'd had doubts about Stephanie, but he'd been unwilling to see what was right in front of his face. "Did she set you up to be kidnapped?"

"I think so. Why else did she show up at the hospital? And I went along with her. In fact, I invited her to go to the cafeteria with me. She played me, Jason. I thought she was your friend. She used your trust in her to make me trust her."

Another wave of anger swept through him, but he couldn't get derailed by emotions about Stephanie. "What happened when she showed up here? What did she say?"

"She said she made her choice a long time ago. She's the reason your dad is dead. She's been working for Novikov the whole time. And now she's going to help him set off the bombs. They left together. Novikov, my dad, Stephanie, and some other guy."

His gut churned with intense anger, but he couldn't give in to rage. He'd deal with Steph's betrayal later. Right now, he had to worry that she might use her badge to get Novikov and the bombs through security. He turned his head as Nick and Beck ran into the room.

"You got her," Nick said with relief.

"Yes. What about the rest of the building?"

"It's clear," Beck replied. "The two guards have been tied up. They're not going anywhere. But they're also not talking. What do we know?"

He turned back to Alisa. "Did Novikov go to the convention center? To another location? Do you know what they're planning?"

"They went to the Kensington Hotel where the vice president is staying. I think that's where they are putting the explosives. My dad said the ventilation systems are connected to the mall and another office building. If the bombs go off, the toxins will spread a great distance."

His heart sank. The complex was an even worse location than the convention center.

"And, Jason," she added. "One of the bombs is in a vest strapped to my father's chest."

He saw the terror in her eyes, but there was nothing he could say to diminish it because Novikov's target was a huge multiplex where thousands of people were spending their Saturday night.

"Do you know what time it's happening?" he asked, hearing Beck already on the phone to Flynn.

"Eight-thirty."

Shit! They had less than two hours to evacuate the area and disarm the bombs. "Let's go," he said to the others. The HDU team can wait for law enforcement to pick up these guys."

"They can watch over Alisa, too," Nick suggested.

"No," Alisa said fiercely. "I'm not staying here. I'm not staying with anyone I don't know, Jason. I'm going with you."

It went against protocol to take her with him, but he didn't give a damn. He didn't want to let her out of his sight, either. "Fine," he said as he grabbed her hand, and they ran out of the building and back to the car.

Mick was gone—no surprise. He'd probably been listening in with the HDU team and knew exactly what was going on and was already on his way to the hotel.

Alisa got in the front seat as the other three squeezed into the back, and Jason sped out of the parking spot.

"Do you know how many bombs there are?" he asked her.

"There were two cannisters." Alisa turned slightly in her seat to face him and the others in the back. "They forced my dad to make the bombs. They were going to torture me if he didn't comply. He didn't want to do it. He didn't have a choice, but he did have a plan. He built a remote device to set off the bombs before they could get to the multiplex, but once they strapped him in the vest, he couldn't access his pocket where the device was. He was going to kill Novikov and himself and anyone else in the van, but now he can't." She drew in a breath. "When they left, Novikov told the man with me that he'd text him when it was done. That's when I was going to be killed."

His gut twisted at her words, at what might have happened to her if her father hadn't complied and what might have happened if they hadn't found her. His heartbeat was so fast that he had to forcibly calm himself down. He couldn't think about how close he'd come to losing her. There was still an entire city to save and a madman to stop.

"But when everyone left," she continued. "The guard said he wanted to have some fun."

He drew in another forced breath. Every word coming out of her mouth felt like a knife going through his heart. He never should have allowed any of this to happen.

"When he untied me, I knew I had just one chance..." Her voice faltered. "I can't talk about it."

"You don't have to," he said. "What's important is that you're all right, and we have a chance to stop the attack."

"I want my dad to be all right, too. I want everyone in that complex to be safe," she said desperately.

"Evacuations have already begun," he assured her, not mentioning that it would take a long time to get everyone out of that thirty-story hotel along with the shopping center and office buildings attached to it. It was seven-twenty now. There was a movie theater in the mall. The shops and restaurants would be open. The hotel was probably packed. And they had one hour and ten minutes to find the bombs and dismantle them.

———

They had to make it in time, Alisa thought. There were too many lives at stake, and she couldn't lose her father now. Not after she'd fought so hard to survive back in the warehouse. After he'd released her from her ties, she'd attacked him with a ferocity that had surprised both of them. He'd expected her to be scared and weak; she'd been anything but. He'd hit her several times, and her face and eye felt swollen and painful, but none of that mattered now. She'd found a way to get to the gun he'd set on the table. Seeing him rush toward her had compelled her to pull the trigger, something she had never done in her life. It had felt like they were in slow motion.

For a moment she wasn't sure she'd hit him because he was

still moving forward, and then he'd screamed, or maybe she had; it was blurred in her mind. He'd grabbed his stomach and fallen to the ground, and she'd watched his blood spread across the dirty floor. She'd been mesmerized by the sight, not even hearing Jason and Savannah come into the room, until they were suddenly there.

And thank God they were there because the other guards would have come running in when they heard the shot, and she didn't know how she would have killed all of them.

She'd gotten her miracle. But the miracle couldn't stop there. It just couldn't.

As Jason drove across town, she barely registered the conversation going on around her. There was back and forth on different phones, various plans of attack being discussed, and an air of tension and determination. She knew the four people in this car along with all the other first responders would do everything they could to stop the catastrophic explosions.

Finally, they arrived at the Kensington Hotel. There were dozens of police vehicles lined up outside the hotel and the attached mall. The spinning lights made her feel dizzy, and she looked down at her hands to escape them, which only made her realize that one finger on her right hand was swollen. Her brain hadn't even acknowledged that pain. She had a feeling a lot of things would hurt later.

After parking the car, Jason and his team jumped out, and she followed them over to a command center that had been set up in the parking lot of the hotel. There were two vans fully equipped with monitors and other equipment and techs working on those computers, probably picking up the security feeds from the adjacent buildings.

Flynn MacKenzie, Jason's boss, filled them in. Evacuations were underway, but the vice president had left the penthouse party he was supposed to be attending, and the Secret Service was looking for him, which was complicating the evacuation of the top floor. Homeland Security and the local and state police were focused on the mall and adjacent office building, while his team and the entire LA FBI Field Office would be concentrating on the hotel.

More manpower was on the way, but until they arrived, they needed to focus on finding the explosives, which according to her father should be somewhere in the hotel. She hoped she was right about that information, but it was certainly possible her dad hadn't even known exactly where Novikov wanted to place the bombs. But she couldn't think about the worst possible scenario; she had to focus on the positive. They were here. And they had a chance to stop the attack. They just didn't have much time.

"You'll stay here, Alisa," Jason told her. He turned to one of the men in the van. "This is Alisa. Keep an eye on her, Kyle."

"Will do," Kyle said shortly.

Jason gave her a sharp look. "Don't go anywhere else, Alisa. We will find your father. But I can't do that if I'm worrying about you."

"I'll stay here," she promised, touched that this man who had professed to be an unemotional workaholic dedicated to his job, would be worrying about her during such an important moment. She wanted to tell him to be careful, to be safe, but that caution could play no role in what was happening now.

Jason looked at his team, then checked his watch. "We've got fifty-three minutes. Let's go."

"Why don't you sit in here with us?" Kyle said, motioning to an empty chair in the van.

She took the seat as Jason and his team ran into the hotel. At least, from here she could see some of what was happening inside on the monitors. She knew Jason would do his best to find the explosives and save her father along with everyone else, but he had a monumental task in front of him, and she felt an amazing amount of admiration and respect for him and all the first responders, who were running toward the danger instead of running away. His job was incredibly dangerous and one for which he could lose his life, and she was immensely proud of him. She was also grateful that he was the one searching for her father because he would do whatever it took to bring him back to her. She just didn't want to lose either of them.

Drawing in a deep breath, her gaze moved to the monitors, which showed feeds coming from different parts of the hotel. There were people in every frame, officers going through the hotel, knocking on doors, helping guests out of their rooms, some carrying babies or helping a disabled person down the hall.

It was overwhelming to see how many people were inside, and she was only looking at the hotel and not the other areas in danger.

Her gaze moved to the monitor on the other side of Kyle, which showed the industrial areas of the hotel, the laundry, the loading dock, the food service offices, and the heating and venti-lation systems. Of course, that would be the first place they would look. But it almost seemed too obvious. Novikov liked to be unpredictable. She wondered where he and Stephanie were now. They would have to place the bombs and then get out of the area. Were they even still here now? Another question she couldn't answer.

As the minutes ticked by, her heart raced faster and faster. Despite the massive effort to get everyone out as quickly as possible, there were still steady streams of people pouring out of the hotel, and she kept hearing on the various radio feeds around her that the mall evacuation was complicated by panic and a stampede that had already injured dozens, who now had to be attended to.

She picked up glimpses of Jason, Savannah, and other members of his team racing through the hotel. According to the Secret Service, the vice president had left with a federal agent, for a private meeting, and the officer who had gone with him had been found shot in a hotel stairwell. She had a feeling that the federal agent was Stephanie. Another crime to add to her list of traitorous and evil actions.

Jason was going to have a lot to deal with when it came to her. His respect and concern for his former partner had been evident every time he spoke about her, not to mention the guilt he'd carried thinking he was partly responsible for her getting shot in the first place. Her injuries must have been an accident. She must have gotten caught in the crossfire between Novikov and his father. But even having suffered at Novikov's hands, she'd continued to work for him. She'd probably had no choice after that. He would have killed her if she'd balked at anything he asked, and if she'd come clean about her involvement with him and told the FBI where he was, she would have been sealing her own arrest warrant. She had tied herself to him, and she couldn't untie herself.

She didn't feel an ounce of sympathy for Stephanie, but she did feel bad that Jason would have to detail with her betrayal. But all that would come later, once this was over, and it was going to be over soon, one way or the other.

Twenty-eight minutes...

Her body tightened as the time was called out on the radio, and the sense of urgency turned to complete and utter desperation.

"You should get out of here," Kyle suddenly said, turning in her direction. "There could be radioactive fallout. We don't know what we're dealing with. You should run down the road, get as far away as you can."

"I...I can't," she said.

His lips grew into a tight line, and he turned his attention back to the monitors.

Was she wrong to stay? She did have her mother to consider. But as the minutes ticked by, she didn't think it would matter anyway. It would take her more than twenty-eight minutes to run out of the area, and she probably wouldn't be able to get that far away.

Kyle and his partner continued to direct the agents to clearer hallways and better exit routes, as she sat and watched, her blood pressure rising, her fear increasing, as every minute took them further away from a good resolution.

Fifteen minutes...

She got to her feet, feeling like she couldn't breathe.

She heard one of the incident commanders outside the van call out the time to the brave men and women who were still inside, risking their lives to save others.

No one was running out. The only fear was from the innocent people fleeing to safety. Everyone else was focused on their mission to clear the area and find the bombs.

Looking back at the screen, she watched as the monitor images changed over to a different view. "What are we looking at now?"

"We just got a feed onto the top floor," Kyle said. "Cameras were disabled when the VP was taken away."

As she looked at the new feed, she saw Jason making his way down the corridor. Her heart stopped at the sight of him.

Would this be the last time she saw him?

She couldn't stand that thought. Tears rushed into her eyes, blocking her vision for a second, and she hastily blinked them away, needing to see him for as long as she could.

Twelve minutes...

"He needs to get out," she said aloud. "It will take longer than twelve minutes to get down from that floor."

There was no response from the men next to her, just an air of grim determination because everyone knew that no agents were going to leave until they found the bombs.

She felt a wave of overwhelming despair.

Then she saw a shoe in the hallway, next to a guestroom. It was a man's loafer, like the ones her father always wore. It could have been left by a guest. Or...

Her father had told her he would try to leave a clue.

CHAPTER TWENTY-FIVE

"The shoe," Alisa cried out, pointing to the screen. "That's my father's shoe. Jason needs to get in that room. That's where the bomb is."

Kyle gave her a sharp look, then got on the radio, relaying the message to Jason.

She watched on the monitor as Jason backtracked. Savannah also came into view from the other end of the hallway.

The door was locked.

Jason kicked it open and ran into the room with Savannah behind him.

"What's happening now?" she asked in frustration as they disappeared.

Kyle's hands flew across the keyboard as he picked up the feed from the bodycam on Jason's vest.

"VP is here," Jason said at the same time they saw the vice president strapped in a chair.

The older man was panicked, his face red and blotchy, as he cried out for help.

As Savannah ran forward to cut him loose, Jason's camera turned to the man lying on the ground in a suicide vest.

She clapped a hand to her mouth. "That's my dad. Is he

dead? Is he dead?" she cried out, knowing Jason couldn't hear her.

She watched him put his fingers on her father's neck.

"He's alive, but he's unconscious," Jason said, then carefully unzipped the vest to reveal the timer on the bomb, which was at ten minutes, twelve seconds. "We need to disarm the device fast. I need a tech now."

Commands barked across the radio. The nearest tech was on the second floor. It would take several minutes for him to get there. That was too long.

"The code," she said suddenly, her father's words ringing through her head. He'd told her the code just in case. "I have the code, Kyle. My father gave it to me."

Kyle gave her a sharp look. "What is it?"

Her breath was coming so fast she was struggling to breathe, but she had to pull herself together. She was their only chance. "It's 061764032296*#&."

"I have the code," Kyle said into his microphone. "It's from Alisa."

"Go," Jason said.

Kyle relayed each number slowly and precisely as Jason's confident, calm fingers hit the keypad on the timer. Each number ratcheted up her fear.

What if she was wrong? What if she had given him the numbers and symbols in the incorrect order? Would the bomb go off early? Or would he have to try new combinations as the time ticked down?

When Jason punched in the ampersand, her breath caught in her throat. They waited for something to happen, but the clock kept ticking.

Eight minutes, fifteen seconds...

"I don't think that worked," Jason said. "Should I try it in a different combination? Alisa? Are you there?"

"She's here," Kyle said, looking at her.

"That was right," she said, staring at the timer on the screen. "I'm sorry. I'm so sorry."

The timer hit eight minutes, and then it dinged.

"It stopped," Jason said with excitement. "It stopped. This one is done."

She felt an enormous wave of relief, but it didn't last long because that wasn't the only bomb.

"Mr. Hunt," Jason said, shaking the man on the ground.

She realized her father was waking up. He blinked his eyes open. "The timer," he said.

"It stopped," Jason told him. "Alisa gave me the code. Where's the other bomb?"

"Parking garage."

At her father's words, everyone in the van froze, realizing their command center, which was on the top floor, open-air part of the garage, was now ground zero.

The word *evacuate* flew across the radio channels.

"We have to get out," Kyle told her, jumping to his feet.

Jumping out of the van, she saw new chaos and commotion as people started running away from the garage toward the roads leading out of the complex.

She couldn't follow them. She couldn't leave. The bomb was nearby. It was in the backpack she'd seen them take out of the warehouse. There were agents already going car to car, but there weren't enough people in this immediate area, and she knew the bomb wouldn't be in the open air, it would be downstairs, on the lowest level.

She ran toward the stairwell, flying down the cement stairs, her fight-or-flight reflexes colliding in her brain as one voice told her she was crazy she should run to safety, and the other said this was her chance to be as brave as Jason. He had risked his life to save her father, and even if he was further away than she was, if the bomb went off in this garage, it could still kill him and so many more people.

So, she kept going, even as more recent, post-traumatic memories filled her head. The last time she'd gone to the bottom level of a dark parking garage, she had almost been killed. She hadn't thought she'd ever be able to go into a garage again, but now she was racing to the bottom.

As she hit the last step, her gaze swept the area. There were a half-dozen cars, but no one in sight. When she saw a door to a utility area partially open, she headed in that direction, terrified that Novikov or Stephanie might be waiting inside with the backpack ready to blow. But she told herself they wouldn't be that close to the bomb, not with minutes to spare.

She threw the door open and saw the backpack on the ground. She carefully unzipped it, and the timer flashed in her face.

Three minutes, twenty-one seconds...

Telling the code to Kyle to give to Jason had felt dangerous, but this was worse. She had no one to help her, to coach her. She had to do it herself. And she had to make sure she didn't inadvertently set off a toxic bomb that would kill her.

Her hand shook as she pushed the first number, then the second. She heard heavy footsteps and Jason shouting her name.

"Here," she yelled, but she stayed focused on the keypad as she put in the next two numbers, knowing she needed to speed up because the time was ticking down.

Two minutes, sixteen seconds...

"Alisa!" Jason stopped abruptly when he saw what she was doing.

Her fingers froze.

"You can do it," he told her.

"You need to leave now in case it doesn't work."

"You've got this. Keep going."

She didn't have time to argue so she turned back to the keypad, putting in one number after the next and then the three symbols.

One minute, two seconds...

It was too late to run. If it didn't work, they wouldn't make it.

Jason pulled her up and into his arms as they both watched the clock tick down six more seconds. And then it stopped.

Fifty-four seconds.

The lights on the timer went out.

"Oh, God! Did I do it? Did I stop the bomb from going off?" she asked.

"You did it, Alisa." He flipped on his radio. "The last explosive has been located and disarmed on the bottom level of the parking garage. The threat is over. Repeat: The threat is over."

They could hear cheers from inside the garage and across the radio.

Jason gazed into her eyes with admiration and respect. "You are crazy brave, you know that?"

"I knew if I didn't find the bomb, no one else would know the code unless Kyle remembered the numbers I gave him, but he was trying to move the van, and—"

"You're amazing." He crushed his mouth against hers.

It felt like forever since she'd kissed him, and this kiss was filled with joy, relief, and gratitude. They were alive. It was over. The bombs were not going to explode tonight. Everyone was safe.

But then she had to ask...

"My dad?" she questioned, looking into his blue eyes. "Is he okay?"

"He's on his way to the hospital. He probably has a concussion, but he's fine, Alisa."

"Is he going to be arrested for what he did? He was forced to build the bombs. He was going to try to detonate them before they ever got to the hotel. He gave me the code to disarm them."

"I don't know what's going to happen. I wish I could tell you I did."

"I wish you could, too, but I appreciate the fact that you never lie to me. What about Novikov and Stephanie?"

He shook his head, his expression angry and grim again. "In the wind. No idea where they are."

"So, they get away without consequences—again."

"Well, you foiled this plan, so that's something. A lot of people are alive tonight because of you."

"And you. And my dad. He gave me the code. He's the reason we were able to stop the attack."

He gave her a smile. "Don't worry. I'll go to bat for your father. I'll do whatever I can." He paused as they heard pounding footsteps and raised voices. They moved out of the utility room as Flynn and Beck came running into the garage.

"The bomb is in there," Jason said, tipping his head to the backpack on the ground.

Flynn shook his head in amazement as he looked at the open backpack. "I can't believe you disarmed both bombs in minutes. I didn't know I was getting a superhero when I hired you."

"Alisa did this one," Jason said, giving her a proud look.

All three of them looked at her with an enormous amount of respect.

She shrugged. "I was the closest one, and I knew the code. I was watching on the monitor when Jason did it in the hotel. I also knew the bomb was in a backpack. My hand was shaking so bad, though, I almost messed up."

"I'm sure you didn't come close to messing up," Beck said. "You're very tough under pressure, Alisa."

"I'm just glad it's over, although I guess it's not really over until you find Novikov and Stephanie."

"We have three of his men in custody," Flynn said. "Novikov's right-hand man, Ilyin is dead, along with two others at the Elliott Tower. We're going to pick up Pieter Moldev as soon as possible. Novikov's group has taken a big hit, and someone will talk. We'll get him."

She wasn't so sure, but she didn't want to dim the hopeful mood.

"I want to get Alisa out of here," Jason said.

"Go," Flynn said. "We'll monitor this device until the HDU team gets here." He paused. "Here they are now."

"Come on," Jason said, taking her hand as they went up the

stairs.

When they reached the top-level parking lot, she saw a very different scene than the one she'd left. There was no longer any panic, no screaming, no running in different directions. There were plenty of cops and teams from various agencies roaming around, but now there were clusters of groups conversing without the anxious urgency of just minutes before.

Jason stopped to speak to Savannah, who told him the vice president was shaken but physically okay and was on his way to a secure location. The vice president had confirmed that Agent Stephanie Genaro had taken him out of the party and a man waiting in the stairwell had killed his Secret Service detail.

While they talked about that, Alisa took a minute to compose herself. There was still a lot to do, but it was all good now. She would go to the hospital and check on her dad. Then she would tell her mom that he was alive, that they were both alive. Things could have turned out so differently.

It didn't seem quite real yet, and there was a part of her that still didn't know if she'd ever feel safe until Novikov and Stephanie were caught.

"I can take you to the hospital now," Jason said, returning to her side.

"What about the rest of the team?"

"They'll be working here for a while, and there are plenty of company vehicles to get everyone back to the office and home, but that won't be for a few hours."

He took her hand once again as they walked to the car, and she was more than happy with the connection, the reminder that she hadn't lost him, and he hadn't lost her.

As they got in the car, she said, "I want to be happy, but Novikov and Stephanie are still out there, and who knows what they'll do next?"

"I feel the same way," he admitted. "But we have to take the victories where we get them. No one died tonight. That's what matters. And you got your father back."

She looked into his warm blue gaze and said, "Thank you for working so hard to save him, Jason. I owe you."

"No, you don't. You spotted the shoe in the hallway. You had the code."

"That was all from my dad. He said he'd try to leave a clue if he couldn't detonate the bomb before they got here."

"Well, you still had the presence of mind to recognize the clue and remember the code. Then you disarmed the second bomb. That's a very good night for—what did you once call yourself—an ordinary woman from a rather boring family?"

She smiled. "Well, I was wrong about the boring family part, that's for sure."

"And wrong about yourself. You are nothing close to ordinary. You saved the day, Alisa. Don't you realize that yet?"

"It hasn't sunk in." She paused, looking into his eyes. "I was so scared when you were trying to disarm that bomb. I thought I was going to lose you and my dad, and I couldn't stand that thought."

"I had the same feeling in the garage just now. But I knew you could do it. I had faith in you, Alisa."

"I had faith in you."

They kissed again, a longer kiss than before, one filled with even more emotion, and they didn't stop until they both needed to take a breath. "To be continued," Jason said with a smile. "Let's get out of here."

"Happily," she said as she fastened her seatbelt. It felt strange to take that small measure of precaution when she had come to realize just how much danger there was in the world, how a happy Saturday night out at the mall could have been so many people's last night. That's why she needed to live in the moment because nothing else was guaranteed.

But she had also learned that there were hundreds of people who worked hard every day to make sure tomorrow came, and she would never take them for granted again.

As Jason drove away from the hotel, his phone buzzed with a

series of texts. He paused at the light and picked up his phone, his gaze widening.

"What is it?" she asked.

He drove through the green light, then pulled over. "I just got a photo," he said. "Two, in fact."

Her jaw dropped when he showed her the photograph of a silver-haired man lying on the floor with blood pouring out of his chest and his head. "Oh, my God! That's Novikov."

"Yes." Jason flipped to the next picture.

"And Stephanie," she breathed, seeing Jason's former partner tied to a chair but very much alive.

His phone dinged again, and she leaned forward to see the text coming in.

Novikov didn't kill your father. She did. He was mine. She's yours.

"Who sent this?" Alisa asked.

"I don't recognize the number. It's probably a burner phone." His heart pounded against his chest at the four short sentences.

Another text came in with an address: *Office Suite 2207, 420 Pierce Street.*

"Damn," Jason muttered. "Pierce Street is just around the corner.

She followed his gaze to the skyscraper across the street, less than three blocks from the hotel-mall complex, probably just far enough to be safe from the release of toxins and just tall enough to see everything.

Jason threw the car into drive and sped down the street and around the corner. They parked in front of the commercial building that reached high into the sky.

"You should stay here," Jason said.

"No way," she told him. "Not alone in this car. I'm going with you. Novikov is dead, and it doesn't seem like Stephanie can hurt us anymore."

He hesitated, then said, "Okay, but stay close. This could be a trap."

"Trust me, you do not have to tell me that."

CHAPTER TWENTY-SIX

He should probably call Flynn and get his team over here, but
first, he wanted to see for himself what was going on. Taking
Alisa with him might be a bad idea, but after everything they'd
been through, he couldn't stand to leave her behind, and she had
already proved to be as brave as anyone he'd ever met.

Novikov definitely appeared to be dead in the photo, cour-
tesy of who, he had no idea, but he had a gut feeling. Stephanie
could tell them what had happened.

When they reached the front doors, he found them wide
open. Whoever had taken out Novikov had made it easy for
them to get in. There was no one in the lobby, so they took the
elevator to the twenty-second floor, and the office suite listed in
the text. That door was also conveniently unlocked.

He entered first, with his gun in hand. Stephanie was tied to
a chair with her back to the door, facing the window, and
Novikov was six feet behind her, lying on the ground. He
checked Novikov first, looking down at the man who had evaded
capture for three decades, the man his father had been obsessed
with taking into custody, the man who had taken his father's life
and had almost killed them.

Novikov had once been invincible. Now he was lifeless, his

power destroyed, his evil curtailed. He hoped Novikov had seen the bullet coming and realized he was going to die, that he'd finally lost.

"Who's there?" Stephanie demanded, her voice filled with fear. She tried to twist around to see them, but she was tightly strapped to the chair.

He hated to admit it, but her fear pleased him. He had protected and cared about her from their partnership days to the aftermath of her injuries. He'd always been there for her. And until this past week, he had never had any reason to doubt her patriotism or her integrity. But she was not who she had appeared to be. He had completely misjudged her.

He didn't know exactly what she'd done three years ago, but he did know that earlier today she'd been with Novikov. She'd used her badge to get herself and Alisa's father into the building, onto the restricted floor where the vice president had been staying, and she'd also used that badge to kidnap the vice president, to kill a member of the Secret Service.

It was hard to believe she was the same person he'd partnered with. *How had he never seen this side of her?*

Standing up, he told Alisa to close and lock the door. He took a quick look into an interior office and bathroom. There was no one else in the suite. They were alone.

"Jason?" Stephanie said. "It's not what you think."

As he walked toward the back of her chair, he could see the view from the window in front of her. The hotel and mall complex were supposed to be on fire now, and Novikov had picked a good location to watch and enjoy his personal fireworks.

But the show hadn't happened. He must have been disappointed. It was surprising he hadn't left as soon as he'd realized time had run out on the bombs.

Perhaps Novikov's own time had run out before that.

Finally, he walked around the chair and faced Stephanie. She'd been hit hard across the face. There was blood around her nose and down her chin, and her eyes were worried, but also defiant.

"So, this is where you and Novikov were going to watch the buildings explode," he said. "How excited you must have been to see the fireworks, to know you were safe here in this room, while thousands were going to die or be dosed with a deadly toxin."

"Novikov forced me to help him. I was his victim and then his pawn," she returned.

"I don't believe you."

"I'm telling you the truth. He shot me three years ago. Why would I help him?"

"I have a better question. Why did you kill my father?"

She paled at his words. "I didn't. That was Novikov. He shot us both."

"You're lying, Stephanie. You were working for Novikov. You took my father to that motel alone. That's why you maneuvered Patrick and me into riding together that day. And when you got to the motel, you shot my dad." He saw the truth in her eyes even if she couldn't say it. "How could you do that?" he asked in bewilderment. "We were friends. You were my partner. We had each other's back. I saved your life."

"I saved yours, too," she reminded him.

"Why did you kill my father?" When she didn't answer, he added, "You know, you're not getting out of this, Stephanie. You used your badge to access a restricted floor. You kidnapped the vice president and were at least partly responsible for the death of a Secret Service agent. And you were here with Novikov. The proof is irrefutable, so start talking. I want to know what happened three years ago."

"Novikov forced me to kill your father. I didn't want to, but it was him or me."

Finally, a confession!

"Was Novikov even in the motel room with my dad? Tell me the truth. You owe me that much."

She stared back at him, and then she said, "No, he wasn't at the motel, but two of his men were next door. I shot your father, but your dad got off one shot before he collapsed."

"My father shot you?" he asked in shock. "It wasn't Novikov? But my dad's gun wasn't at the scene."

After the shots were fired, one of Novikov's men came in and took our guns, so no one would know we'd shot each other. Novikov needed me to stay free of suspicion. And he needed your father to die because he had been a thorn in his side for thirty years."

"Did my father know you were working for Novikov?"

"He guessed it when we got to the motel. He looked right at me and said you're the mole. Then I pulled the trigger."

He shuddered at the image of his father knowing the truth and then being killed. He wanted to put his hands around Stephanie's neck and stop her from talking, stop her from breathing.

He paced around in a small circle, trying to get a grip on his emotions. Then he said, "What about Patrick? Was he working with you, too?"

"No. Patrick was getting suspicious, though. Afterward, he asked me a lot of questions. I had to make him look like the possible mole. No one completely bought the rumors I planted, but he became ostracized and siloed, and eventually, he retired. I thought I was done with him until a few days ago when he started poking his nose into what was going on. I was afraid he would get to you and put doubts in your head about me."

Her words made him realize another truth. "It was you who set up the shooting at the park, wasn't it? You sent a gunman to take out Patrick. I wasn't the target, was I?"

"To be honest, it would have been fine if you were both hit, but the money was paid on Patrick. We didn't know you were there until it was over."

"How long were you working for Novikov?"

"I started a few months before we became partners," she admitted.

"You worked for him the entire time we were partners?" That fact blew him away. "I talked to you about Novikov, about my father's longtime quest to bring him in. I shared information with you my father gave me. You betrayed me long before you killed my dad." He'd thought he was too cynical to ever be surprised by someone's criminality, but this one was hard to stomach. He had really misjudged her.

"You never told me anything I could use. I didn't intend to betray you, Jason, but when your father got close to finding Novikov before the courthouse bombing, I was ordered to take him out, and I couldn't say no. Novikov owned me. He had paid off my gambling and credit card debts. He had blackmail that could destroy my career, so we made a deal. I could do my job, but when he needed me, I had to follow his orders."

"It wasn't just my father who died three years ago. Lots of other people in the courthouse died or were injured. How could you live with yourself?"

"People die all the time," she said harshly. "I lost my parents when I was a kid, an aunt when I was sixteen, and my best friend at twenty. Safety is an illusion. You can't worry about other people. You can only worry about yourself. I grew up knowing I had to take care of myself. I had to be a survivor, and that's what I am."

"A survivor who kills people for money."

"Like I said, I do what I have to do, and I made my deal with the devil a long time ago. But I have paid a price, Jason. I'll never be the same physically after your father's shot affected my spine."

"Am I supposed to feel sorry for you? I'm glad he shot you. I'm just sorry he didn't kill you."

She flinched at his harsh words. "Is that what you're going to do now?"

"I don't know. What happened here tonight? Who shot Novikov?"

"There were two men. They were dressed in black track

pants and black jackets, with ski masks covering their hair and their faces, dark glasses over their eyes, and gloves on their hands. One shot Novikov before he could get his gun. The other one grabbed me and tied me up. And then I heard another shot. I think that one was probably just for pleasure. Arseni was already dead."

"Did they say anything?"

"Not a word. They were here for less than ten minutes, and then they were gone. They left me to wait, to wonder what my fate would be." She paused, giving him a questioning look. "Are you going to shoot me, Jason?"

He was tempted. He really wanted to put a bullet in her. The hatred he felt for her was intense and overwhelming. There was no one here but him and Alisa. And she probably wouldn't care all that much if he killed the woman who had gotten her kidnapped.

Or would she?

His gaze moved from Stephanie to Alisa.

She looked back at him with uncertainty in her gaze.

"What do you think?" he asked her. "There's no one else here but us. We can say we found them both dead."

"We could say that," she replied. "I don't think anyone would be sad they were gone, not after what they've done."

"No one would miss them," he agreed, looking back at Stephanie.

"Then do it," Stephanie said. "But you won't be able to live with yourself. I know you, Jason. You can't kill without conscience. It's not who you are."

He raised his gun and pointed it at her head, seeing her flinch, seeing her suddenly realize she might be wrong about him, that he might actually kill her.

As the moment stretched out, he thought how easy it would be to pull the trigger, to not go through the trial, to not have to listen to her make up stories about herself, her actions, and what happened to his father.

But Stephanie was right. He couldn't kill without conscience. He wasn't a criminal. He wasn't evil.

He had told Flynn on the first day he'd joined the team that he wasn't out for revenge; he wanted justice. He'd been talking about Novikov then, but now it was about Stephanie.

"Dying would be too easy for you," he said. "You're going to pay for what you did. You're going to live the rest of your life in prison. You will get to spend every day thinking about the people you hurt and the choices you made. And I will be very happy I'm the one who put you there." He lowered his weapon. "I can't stand to look at you."

He walked around her, and as he gazed at Novikov, lifeless on the floor, he heard Stephanie start to cry. He felt completely unmoved.

The man at his feet was a monster, and the woman in the chair was one, too. Novikov was gone and Stephanie would pay for what she'd done. And this was finally over.

Pulling out his phone, he called Flynn. "I've got Novikov and Stephanie," he said. "I'm texting you the address."

"What do you mean you've got them?" Flynn asked in surprise.

"Novikov is dead. Stephanie is tied up," he replied as he texted the details to Flynn.

Flynn swore in amazement. "How did you make that happen?"

"I had some help. I'll tell you about it when you get here."

"The address is close by."

"They were going to have a great view of the fireworks."

"I'll be there in five minutes," Flynn said.

Jason put his phone in his pocket, took Alisa's hand, and pulled her into the hallway. "I'm sorry, but we need to wait for Flynn to get here before I take you to the hospital. It won't be long."

"You don't have to apologize to me, Jason. I'm so relieved Novikov is dead, and Stephanie is going to jail."

"Me, too." He paused, gazing into her beautiful brown eyes with the golden flecks that were now shimmering with happy relief. "I thought about killing her. It would have been very easy."

"I knew you wouldn't do it," she said. "You have too much honor and integrity for that. But if I'd had the gun, I might have pulled the trigger."

He smiled at the fierce look in her eyes. "I don't think so, Alisa."

"I did it earlier today. I had never shot a gun in my life until this afternoon. I never believed in an eye for an eye, but I feel a little differently now."

"You shot that guy in self-defense. That's different." He paused. "I didn't kill her because I believe in justice and in the law. It's my job. It's what I do. It's who I am."

"I know. And you do your job very well," she said, putting her arms around his waist. "I feel like a huge weight has finally slipped off me. Novikov is dead, Stephanie will go to prison, and my father is free of his mortal enemy. That seems worth at least a small celebration, maybe a minute of your time before everyone arrives..." She gave him a questioning look.

"Maybe four minutes," he said as he cupped her sweet face and kissed her again.

It was a different kiss this time, one that wasn't inspired by the thought that this might be the last time, that tomorrow might not come. This kiss felt like a promise for the future.

But that thought was immediately followed by another, more rational thought, that once this whole situation was over, maybe they would be over, too.

He didn't want to think about any of that now. He just wanted to kiss her...until he couldn't.

———

Alisa and Jason walked into her mother's hospital room at ten-thirty. Her mother was awake and sitting in bed, but she had a robe over her hospital gown, and she'd brushed her hair and looked so much like her old self, it was amazing.

What was even more wonderful was the smile of relief on her face, having already heard from the nurse that her daughter was on her way in to see her. Jason had called the hospital from the car on their way over. She hadn't wanted her mom to spend one more minute worrying about her.

"Alisa," her mother said, opening her arms wide.

She ran across the room and fell into her mother's arms, hugging her tight, knowing how close they'd come to losing each other.

"I'm so glad you're all right," her mother added as Alisa sat down on the bed next to her. "My beautiful girl. I've been so worried."

"I'm fine."

Her mother's gaze moved to Jason. "Thank you for finding her, for saving her. You kept your promise."

"She saved herself," Jason said. "You raised a very strong and determined daughter. You have a lot to be proud of."

Her mother gave her a teary smile. "I am so proud of you, Alisa."

"I get my strength from you, Mom. How are you feeling?"

"I'm completely better. The doctor just kept me here because he wasn't sure where to send me." Her mother paused. "You look exhausted and battered, Alisa. Your face is swollen. Who hurt you?"

She had no intention of going into any of those details with her mother, who had suffered enough stress the last two weeks. "None of that matters now. I'm okay, and Dad is, too."

"The nurse said something about that, but I was afraid to believe her. What happened? Where is he? Can I see him?" She turned to Jason again. "I really need to see him, Jason."

"I understand. I can take you to see him, but it's a complicated situation, Mrs. Hunt."

"Is he hurt badly?" her mother asked.

"No. He has a concussion, but they'll keep him in the
hospital overnight for observation."

"And then?" her mother asked.

Jason looked to her for guidance.

She took her mother's hands, waiting for her mom to look at
her. "There's so much to tell you, and I don't think we should go
into it all tonight. I'm exhausted, and it's late, and it's a complex
situation. But here's what's important. Dad was forced to do
something bad, but he did good in the end, and I think that will
be taken into consideration. There are a lot of facts to come out
and investigation to be done, and we're just going to have to let
it play out."

"I'm confused. Does that mean he's under arrest?"

"He's temporarily in custody, yes," Jason replied. "I'm going
to do what I can to straighten this situation out, but it will take
time."

"Okay. I just want to see him. I want to go down to his room.
Can I do that? Can Alisa and I be with him for a little while
tonight before he's taken away? Please."

"I can take you there. He's just down the hall. Do you need a
wheelchair, Mrs. Hunt?"

"No. I can walk," she said. "I've been standing up a lot today,
pacing around this room. When I realized Alisa was gone, I
knew I had to get better faster, so I've been trying."

"You don't have to push it, Mom," she said as she stood up.
"I can get you a wheelchair."

"I can do it," her mother said, swinging her legs to the side of
the bed. "I need my slippers."

"I've got them." She put the slippers on her mother's feet
and then helped her up.

Her mother was surprisingly steady, and that made her feel
even better. Things were turning around for all of them.

They walked slowly out of the room. The security guard who had been watching her mother's room was no longer there now that the danger was gone. At the end of the corridor, Jason opened the door to her father's room and waved them inside.

Her father was sitting up in bed. He had a bandage on his forehead, and his face was even more bruised than hers, but he was alive and that was a miracle.

Her mother rushed toward him, practically falling into his arms. Her father put one arm around his wife. The other arm was handcuffed to the bed railing.

"Is the cuff necessary?" Alisa asked Jason.

"I would need to get permission from people higher than me to take it off, and that's not happening tonight. I'm sorry."

"It's okay, Alisa," her father said. "I understand I may have to pay for what I did. I am ready to face whatever comes. As long as you and Pamela are safe, it doesn't matter what happens to me."

"Of course, it matters," her mother said, planting a loving kiss on his lips.

Her parents' overt displays of affection had often embarrassed her, but now she found it to be a beautiful thing. Despite everything, all the secrets between them, their love was as intense and pure as it had always been. Her mother had no idea what her father had done, but she loved him unconditionally. Maybe that made her a little foolish, but it was also incredibly sweet.

She glanced at Jason as her parents continued to kiss, giving him a helpless smile. "This is the way they are."

He smiled back at her. "They're lucky."

"I was lucky, too, growing up in the circle of their love."

"Can I stay here and sit with my husband?" her mother asked as she finally let go of her husband for a minute.

"I'm afraid not," Jason said, a regretful look in his eyes. "But you can come back in the morning. He won't be moved before eleven, so I'll make sure the nurse gets you when you're both awake, and you can visit until he's discharged."

"I wish I could stay," she said, giving her husband another loving look. "I will come back as soon as I can."

"And I'll be here, my love," her father replied.

"The doctor said I could go home tomorrow, too," her mom added. "But I don't know where to go. I guess our house is gone."

At her words, her father stiffened. "Pamela and Alisa still need to be protected," he said. "Novikov will come after them."

She realized her father didn't know the latest. "Novikov is dead, Dad. He was killed tonight."

"Are you sure?" he asked in surprise. "He never even entered the complex. He was going to watch from afar."

"Yes, I'm sure. I saw him," she said. "And Stephanie is in custody."

"She's going to jail for a long time," Jason added. "We have also arrested several of Novikov's men, and now that Novikov is dead, as well as Dominic Ilyin, everyone wants to make a deal."

"Ilyin is dead, too? Thank God!" her father said with tremendous relief.

"Novikov's organization is done. He's no longer a danger to you or your family."

"I can't quite believe it. Who killed him? You, Jason?"

"No. I'm not sure who killed him, but his reign of terror is finally over."

"What about Henry? Alisa told me he was badly hurt. Does anyone know his condition?"

"I haven't gotten an update," Jason replied. "I'll do that tomorrow. I'm sorry to break this up, but it's late, and everyone needs to get some sleep."

Her mother gave her father another kiss and then got to her feet. "I'll see you as soon as you wake up tomorrow, Dan."

"I can't wait," her father returned.

They walked her mother back to her room. It felt a little odd to leave her there without a guard at the door. It was going to take a while for her to believe they were all safe.

After helping her mother into bed, she said goodnight and left the room with Jason, casting another anxious look back at the door. "Are you sure?" She couldn't help asking him.

He put his arms around her and gave her a hug. "I am very sure she is safe, and so are you. Let's get out of here."

"Where are we going?" she asked as they got into the elevator. "Are you taking me to my apartment or back to the safe house?"

"Where do you want to go? Either is fine."

She thought for a moment. "I want to go wherever you're going."

His eyes glittered with her words. "That's good because I want to go wherever you're going."

"My stuff is at the safe house. We'll have to go back there and get it at some point. Should we just go there?"

"Perfect."

She thought so, too, because they'd been living in a little bubble, and she wasn't ready for it to break.

A part of her wondered if she would ever be ready because she really cared about Jason. But, tonight, they could be together. She'd worry about tomorrow when the sun came up.

CHAPTER TWENTY-SEVEN

There were so many things he had to do, Jason thought when he woke up Sunday morning, but with Alisa's warm, naked body curled up next to his, he didn't want to do any of them. And it was only eight, so they had some time. Still, it felt a little strange to feel so lazy, so unfocused, so uninterested in what was coming next.

He lived for the job, but even he needed a break. They'd just stopped a potentially catastrophic attack and gotten Novikov off the FBI's most wanted list. That was a huge accomplishment, and he had every right to savor the victory.

He still wondered about the men who had found Novikov and Stephanie. He had some idea about who they might be, but he wasn't sure he even wanted to know. Then, he might have to do something about it.

He'd let that situation sit for a while. There were other issues to deal with, like Stephanie's official interrogation. He was curious about her role in what had happened this week and also three years ago. Her betrayal still felt like a knife to his heart, and he inwardly raged with *what-ifs* about the day his father was killed, knowing he'd probably be tortured by those thoughts for a long time to come.

And then there was Alisa's father. He didn't know what would happen to Dan Hunt. He had helped the US before, which had led to his defection and getting asylum. He had lived an exemplary life for the past thirty years, until he was forcibly kidnapped by Novikov and his daughter's life was threatened unless he cooperated. He'd also given Alisa the code to disarm the bombs and had intended to blow them up before they ever got to the site. But the suicide vest had derailed that plan. Dan had done a lot of things right, but he had also put together two dirty bombs and for that, there might still be a cost.

He would have to see what the higher-ups at the Bureau, Homeland Security, the White House, and the Department of Justice would have to say because they would all be weighing in. He hoped that if there was a punishment, it would be short, and eventually Dan would be able to go home. Alisa and her mother needed him in their lives.

While Dan's actions in running away didn't sit well with him, neither Alisa and nor her mother seemed to blame him. The Hunt family was all about love, forgiveness, and faith in each other.

His family hadn't been like that at all. There had been acrimony, doubts, complaints, and accusations. His parents had barely kissed or touched around him, even before their divorce. They had never been in sync. They had never looked at each other the way Dan and Pamela had looked at each other last night. Their love had truly seemed unconditional. And Alisa's love for them was the same. She'd been angry with her dad, but in the end, she loved him, and she accepted him for his limitations, for his duplicitous life.

Maybe that just made the Hunt women a little too easygoing, or maybe it was something to admire; he wasn't completely sure. He thought Dan had made some big mistakes, but then he'd never been in a situation like Dan. And who was he to talk about trusting the wrong people or not seeing something right in front of his face when he hadn't seen any sign of evil in his former partner?

Stephanie had worked alongside him for eighteen months, but she'd felt no guilt in taking his father's life because hers was the only one that mattered. In fact, she'd probably liked the idea that by taking his dad away, she was also taking away some perceived advantage he'd had over her because of his family background. She'd always pushed the narrative that everything he'd gotten or achieved was because of his connections while she'd had to struggle every step of the way. She definitely had a victim personality. It was never her fault.

Well, she could stew about all that in jail for the rest of her life.

As Alisa began to stretch like a sleepy cat, his body tightened, and he wanted her again. The passion they'd shared last night was reawakening with the daylight. He was becoming addicted to her. And he didn't know what he was going to do about that. Because things between them were coming to an end.

Unless he didn't let them end.

That thought made him uneasy. He was courageous in the face of danger and even the potential loss of his life, but losing his heart was a different story.

Alisa's eyes fluttered open, drawing his gaze to hers.

She gave him a happy smile. "Morning."

"How did you sleep?"

"I don't think I dreamt at all, which was a good thing. What about you?"

"Same." He hadn't had to dream because he'd fallen asleep with her in his arms.

"Do we really have to get up?"

"I was wondering the same thing," he admitted with a smile.

She lifted her head and propped it up on one elbow. "But?"

"I didn't say but."

"I heard it even if you didn't say it."

"There is a lot of follow-up to do, and I need to go into the office."

"I know. But it's Sunday. Can you start a little later?"

He laughed. "Like how much later?"

"However much time you'll give me," she said with a sexy smile.

He wanted to give her all the time in the world. But they were both living in the euphoric afterglow of what they'd survived, what they'd conquered, and this wasn't either of their real lives.

"Jason?" she asked, her smile dimming. "Where did you go?"

"I was just thinking about time. It's been controlling us since the first moment we met."

"I know. Last night, that ticking clock seemed to match the beat of my heart. Watching you disarm that bomb was one of the scariest things I've ever seen. I don't know how you were so calm because every second that ticked away filled me with dread."

"I just had to focus on stopping the timer because there wasn't another option. You did the same minutes later," he reminded her.

"It was easier for me; I'd already watched you succeed."

"You still had to do it and get it done in seconds. In fact, if you had been a little later finding the backpack..."

She put a finger against his mouth. "We're not thinking about that."

"No, we're not," he agreed as he kissed her finger before she moved her hand away from his mouth. "We can finally stop looking back and just focus on the future."

"There's a lot I have to do in my future, too. I have to get another car for one thing."

"At least, you seem to have conquered your fear of garages," he said lightly.

"Yes, but I have a feeling I'll still be thinking about carjackers and bombs every time I go into a garage. I know I won't ever walk to my car again without the keys in my hand."

"Probably a good idea."

"I also have to figure out where my mom is going to go, and what we're going to do about her house. My dad said he wasn't the one who burned it down. You were wrong about that. He just had an idea that Novikov would do something to the house. That's why he took some personal memorabilia when he left."

"I'm glad he wasn't the one to do that. As for figuring out your mother's future living situation, she seems ready to help you with all of that."

"She's doing so much better, but I'm not sure she's fully grasped the idea that her house is completely gone. That will be a shock."

"Having her husband back and knowing you're both safe will absorb that shock."

"I used to think my life was so ordinary, so normal, so boring. I yearned for adventure." She gave him a helpless smile. "I guess it's true that you should be careful what you wish for." She paused. "Are you ready to get back into action, work on another case, dive into another perilous situation?"

"Not right this minute," he admitted. "And there's still a lot to do in this investigation."

"I'm sorry about your father, Jason, about the betrayal of your partner, your friend. I know you must be reeling from that."

"I'm still processing. It's difficult to believe she killed him. But she told me the truth. And I guess I'm a little glad he got a shot off, and her limp is a reminder of what she did to him. Plus, she'll be in prison, and that won't be easy on her."

"I hope it's as hard and as uncomfortable as possible. I know I played right into her hand by going with her. It was stupid. You told me not to leave the room, and I did."

"You weren't stupid. I was the one who wasn't seeing the red flags she was showing me," he said heavily. "But we can't change anything, and I don't want to give her any more of my time or my energy."

"You're right. Enough about her, my family, and Novikov. I have other places I'd like to spend my time and energy," she added, running her fingers down his chest. "I know we have to get to the hospital by eleven, but we have a couple of hours. What do you think?"

He laughed as he captured her hand and brought it to his mouth again for another kiss. "I think I have some other places in mind, too."

"Good," she said, putting her mouth on his lips, and then his neck, his chest, and lower...

———

Jason took Alisa to the hospital a little before eleven. They got to spend about ten minutes with her father before he was taken away. Then it was time to get her mother dressed and released from the hospital. While Alisa was waiting with her mother for the discharge papers, he went to check in on Henry and was relieved to hear his condition had improved. It looked like he would have a long recovery and might have some long-term health issues, but he was going to survive and that was good news. The world needed more men like Henry.

He'd shared the happy update with Alisa and her mother and then drove them to Alisa's apartment, stopping along the way to pick up a few groceries to tide them over until Alisa could get a car and get to the supermarket.

After they were settled in, he said goodbye to Alisa with a far-too-short kiss in the hallway and then got back in his car around one-thirty. He was about to head into the office when his phone vibrated with a call from Mick.

"Hadley," he said. "I assume you're up-to-date."

"You had a good night," Mick said. "Excellent work, Jason."

"You provided a crucial piece of information on where I

could find Alisa. I'm still curious about that. Can we talk? Are you available?"

"I could make myself available," Mick said. "I'm at the Santa Monica Pier about to order a beer at Steelworks Brewery. Want to join me? The beer is on me."

"I'll be there in twenty minutes," he said, making a U-turn at the next light.

On the way to meet Mick, he gave Patrick a call and asked if he could meet him and Mick at the brewery. He wanted to give him an update on Novikov.

Novikov's name got the result he wanted, and Patrick immediately said he was on his way. Mick might not appreciate that he'd invited Patrick to join them, but he didn't want to have the same conversation twice.

He got delayed by Sunday traffic to the beach and arrived at the brewery half an hour later. Patrick was already there, sitting at an outdoor table with Mick. The men didn't seem bothered to be together. But then they'd known each other for a long time.

As he sat down, Patrick poured him a beer from the pitcher on the table and passed it to him. "Mick was just telling me what happened last night," Patrick said. "You did a hell of a good job, Jason."

"It wasn't all me."

"That's not what I heard. You dismantled a dirty bomb, right?"

"I did do that," he admitted. "But I had help. I was given the code by Daniel Hunt's daughter."

"That was helpful," Mick agreed. "I'm glad you found her alive and well."

"Thanks to your tip," he said.

Mick and Patrick looked happier and more relaxed than he'd ever seen them. He didn't know either of them that well, Patrick more than Mick, of course, but his experiences with both of them had been limited to short-term situations that had often been fraught with tension.

"Your father would have been proud," Patrick said, lifting his glass. "We should drink to your dad. Hopefully, his soul is at peace now."

He raised his glass. "To my father," he echoed, clinking glasses with both of them. "So, I'm sure you've both heard Arseni Novikov was shot in an office building across from the mall where he and my former partner Stephanie Genaro were going to watch their deadly fireworks show. Novikov was shot twice, once in the head and once in the heart. Stephanie was left tied to a chair. She'll be going to prison."

"Did she set up that ambush three years ago that took your dad's life?" Patrick asked.

It wasn't an unexpected question, but one he thought Patrick already knew the answer to. "Yes," he said. "And she's the one who shot and killed my father at Novikov's order. The only reason she was hurt was because my father got off a shot before he died. One of Novikov's men removed their guns before we arrived so that Stephanie would look innocent."

"But they left her bleeding on the floor," Patrick commented. "That was cold."

"Novikov never cared who he hurt," Mick interjected.

"Stephanie is also the one who sent the shooter to the park a few days ago, Patrick. You were the target, not me. She was afraid you were going to put doubts in my head about her. I didn't realize you thought she was the mole."

"I had a bad feeling about her, but I could never prove anything," Patrick said. "She seemed to feel the same way about me, spreading gossip that made my job more difficult. I got tired of the sideways looks, so I retired. I must admit I'm surprised she thought she needed to kill me now."

"She wanted me to believe she was helping me so she could keep an eye on the investigation and report back to Novikov. I'm sure that's why she gave me a lead to Ilyin that didn't pan out. It was legit, so I trusted her, but it got me nowhere. It was a win-win for her."

"Makes sense," Patrick said.

"Well, at least the era of Novikov is over," Mick said. "One of the most wanted terrorists in the world is dead, and several of his associates are either dead or on their way to prison. You've done well, Jason. I'm glad I gave you the tip."

"Like I said before, I didn't do anything on my own, and I didn't kill Novikov."

"Then who did?" Mick asked, his gaze questioning.

"Stephanie said there were two men, both wearing black, their faces fully covered by ski masks and dark glasses. According to my team, security cameras in the office building went offline probably minutes before Novikov was shot. There were no prints left at the scene, and no evidence leading to the two masked shooters. They were pros."

Mick shrugged, his expression unreadable. "Does anyone care who did it? I know I don't."

"I don't, either," Patrick said. "If I knew who they were, I'd congratulate them on a job well done."

"Exactly," Mick said.

"We also haven't found out who killed Dominic Ilyin yet, either," he added, watching Mick's face closely. "We don't know who was driving the van that kidnapped him or who killed him. They beat him up before they took him out, so it seems like his last minutes were painful."

Mick didn't flinch. "Dominic Ilyin tortured many people in his life, Jason. He was also responsible for multiple assassinations in Europe. It's good that he's dead. I'm just glad I found him before he expired. I was able to get the information you needed to find Alisa and her father."

"I'm puzzled at how both of you seemed to be nearby when Dominic was taken and then when he was found. Were you working together?"

"Work together?" Patrick echoed with a laugh that was a little too pronounced. "No. I don't work with spooks, no offense, Mick."

"None taken," Mick said easily. "I don't much like working with the feds, either, but sometimes it's necessary."

"That's true. Sometimes it is necessary," Patrick agreed.

"So, hypothetically speaking, if the FBI were to keep digging into Novikov's murder and Stephanie's capture, do you think they'd find anything?"

"You would know that better than us," Mick said. "I work for the CIA. I like to help when I can, but I'm not one of you."

"And I'm retired," Patrick said with a shrug. "I'm out of the loop, Jason."

"I just thought with all your experience, you each might have an opinion."

"I don't think they'll ever be caught," Patrick said, a small smile playing around his lips. "In my opinion."

"And you, Mick?"

"In order to find Novikov and Stephanie Genaro, those two men must have been very smart, very strategic. I doubt they would have left a clue behind. They did what they intended to do, and that's it."

"I wonder how they figured out where Novikov and Stephanie were hiding."

"They obviously weren't closely involved in the operation, so they weren't consumed with the evacuation and the disarming of explosives. They had time to consider where the creators of such mayhem might be positioned to watch the results of their grand plan," Mick said.

"There was a lot going on last night," he agreed.

"I think we should have another toast." Patrick raised his glass. "To the end of an era. The chase that went on for thirty years is over. Now, we can all move on."

He clinked his glass against theirs once more.

He'd found out what he wanted to know. While they hadn't admitted to anything, he had no doubt they had been the shooters in the office building. They'd taken out the man who had taken out his father. And they'd left Stephanie for him because she was the one who had betrayed him.

He also believed that they, or at least Mick, had tortured the information out of Dominic Ilyin that had allowed him to find Alisa.

He didn't believe in personal vengeance, but he had no proof they were guilty, and with a man as dangerous to mankind as Novikov was, he wasn't going to look for evidence. He was just going to move on.

If they were responsible, they would have to live with what they had done. They had both served their countries for decades, and Mick continued to do that. Their choices were theirs, and having lived the lives they'd led, he couldn't help wondering if his father would have done the same thing, if at some point, he would have tried to take justice into his own hands.

He didn't want to get to that point, but he could see how his obsession with work could turn him into someone as jaded and hard as the two men in front of him. They were a mirror to what he could look like in thirty years, and he didn't like the reflection.

CHAPTER TWENTY-EIGHT

Two weeks later...

After a whirlwind week of interviews, meetings, and reports, Jason was ready to wrap up his part in the case. Novikov, Ilyin, Kashin, and two of Novikov's team members from the high-rise assault were deceased. The three men who had been at the warehouse with Alisa and her father were in custody, as well as Pieter Moldev, Ilyin's associate, and the man who Stephanie had hired to take out Patrick Hastings at the park. Tatiana Guseva had gotten her deal and would be starting a clinical trial at Henry's lab the following week.

Henry was slowly recovering, which was good news for everyone. Lauren Silenski had, unfortunately, been found dead, and they'd traced money transfers to her account back to one of Dominic Ilyin's shell companies. Tatiana had told them that Dominic had gotten her in the trial, so they assumed some of the money had been for that and the rest had probably been for access to the lab to obtain some of the chemical materials needed for the bombs.

With Novikov's terrorizing presence gone, all of his lower-level soldiers had been willing to talk in an attempt to make their own deals. With their information, they'd been able to arrest seven more individuals in the Los Angeles area, four in Washington D.C., and six in New York City, all of whom had been responsible for many crimes over the last several decades.

Novikov's organization was completely destroyed, and they were still in the process of seizing some of his assets, and the assets of other members of his team like Dominic Ilyin and Pieter Moldev. Novikov's reign as one of the world's most wanted terrorists was over. And while others around the world were probably already scrambling to take his place, that was something Jason was going to think about much, much later.

Flynn had asked him to get a drink after work, so he was now entering a bar in Santa Monica, just a mile from their office. The bar was on a cliff overlooking the beach, and Flynn was seated at an outdoor table, his blond hair blowing in the breeze. He'd already changed into faded jeans and a T-shirt and looked more like a surfer than the head of a very elite task force.

Flynn pushed out the chair across from him with a welcoming smile. "Glad you could make it. It's nice to be out of the office. It's been a long few weeks."

"It has," he agreed, taking a seat across from him. He ordered a beer from the server who'd immediately come over and then took a look at the view. The deep-blue waves were crashing on the rocks below, providing a soothing ambiance to the afternoon and the sun sinking beyond the horizon had turned the sky into a colorful array of pinks, purples, and blues.

"Nice sunset," Flynn commented, following his gaze. "Sometimes I forget what a beautiful place we live in."

"I can't remember the last time I just watched the sunset." Pausing, he added, "The investigation is wrapping up nicely."

"Due to your excellent work," Flynn said. "I mean that, Jason. I'm not blowing smoke. You've done a tremendous job."

"Thanks, I appreciate that." He gave the server a smile as she set down his beer. Then he picked up the glass and took a long sip. "This hits the spot."

"Nothing like a cold beer on a hot day after too much work," Flynn said.

"Agreed."

"Damon called me today," Flynn continued, referring to the head of the LA Field Office. "He wants you back. I think there's a big promotion coming your way."

"He mentioned something about that to me."

"After taking Novikov off the board, you could probably do whatever you wanted, maybe get your own team, if you leverage the situation correctly."

"I've thought about that. I'd like the freedom you have to move quickly, cut through red tape, make snap decisions."

"It's why we're as good as we are," Flynn replied. "But there are limitations in working for my team. I don't have a hierarchy with field agents. Everyone works at the same level. Some people get tired of that and move on to offices where they can get bigger titles and bigger money. I don't ever blame them for making that choice. As long as they give me what they've got when they're with me, I wish them well."

"Are you going somewhere with this conversation?"

Flynn grinned. "Of course. I want you to stay with the team. I'm making my pitch. It won't be the money or the title you could get somewhere else, but there is freedom and autonomy in decision-making and an unusually high level of trust."

"Your team is fantastic. I've enjoyed getting to know them, and they are very, very good."

"But you're leaning another way?" Flynn asked, giving him a speculative look.

"I've been working nonstop the last six, almost seven, years, Flynn. And since my father died three years ago, my workaholic tendencies went out of control. I didn't have a reason to be home. I didn't have a family who wanted my time, and I was obsessed with finding Novikov and making him pay. Of course, I had to work on a lot of other cases, too, because Novikov stayed safely out of reach for a long time, but he was always on my mind. And when I wasn't thinking about him, it was every other criminal who needed to be stopped. I was just head down all the time. I certainly never took a minute to look at the sunset."

"You can't run at that pace forever. The longer you're in the business of law enforcement, the more you realize there's always going to be another case, another person to stop, another crime to solve. But you also have to have a life."

"Do you have a life?"

"I do," Flynn said. "Maybe not the last few weeks, but I make time for my wife, and now that we have a baby on the way, I'm going to make more time."

"I didn't know. Congratulations. When is the baby due?"

"Three months. Which will give Avery time to figure out who's going to run her restaurant while she's on maternity leave. She also has a job she loves and spends a lot of time at. But we're both ready for the next chapter. Which is why I also want to make sure I have enough team members to make things run smoothly, not just for me, but for everyone. I have a lot of agents now who are married and have kids. I don't want to lose them, but realistically, I know I need to keep bringing in people who also have more of a single-minded focus. It's a balance, but I can find it."

"That would be an achievement," he said, taking another sip of his beer.

"So, what are you thinking, Jason?"

He looked out at the sea again and then back at Flynn. "I had drinks with Mick Hadley and Patrick Hastings right after everything ended. When I looked at them, I saw my future, and I didn't like what I saw. Mick is a hardened man."

"He is. He's been married and divorced twice, and I don't think his kids talk to him. He's an agent who has to be in the field all the time. It's where he feels alive. I don't know Hastings, so I can't comment on him, but I don't think you and Mick are anything alike." Flynn paused. "You had the chance to kill Stephanie Genaro. You didn't take it."

"That would have been revenge, not justice."

Flynn nodded approvingly. "You kept your word to me."

"I did. And I don't know that Mick had anything to do with what happened to Novikov, so maybe we're not that different."

"None of us knows who killed Novikov, and I'm not accusing Mick Hadley, just saying the two of you are very different people."

"I'm not Patrick, either. Or my dad. Or my grandfather. I've had a lot of men to follow in my career, but I need to make my own path." He blew out a breath. "Here's the thing, I don't want to be the single-minded, focused agent you're looking for. I want more in my life than the job."

"I wasn't putting you in that category. Not after seeing you with Alisa."

"She is important to me," he admitted. "I don't know if I can juggle being the agent I want to be with the broader life I now want to have."

"You can, Jason. And you can do that working for me. I told you I was looking for a balance of team members, and I meant it. Everyone has value, and everyone gets to choose what they want to do, not what I want them to do. That's how we operate. How I get the best out of my people." He paused. "Do you really want to quit being an FBI agent? Or do you want to have it all—on your terms?"

He smiled. "You are quite the salesman."

"I hope I am. All you have to do is say yes..."

Things were finally returning to normal, Alisa thought, as she looked around the two-bedroom condo her mother had just moved into. They'd spent a few days looking for the right place for her parents to live in and had finally decided to rent this townhouse for a year and make longer-term decisions later. They didn't know when her dad would eventually be able to get back to his life, so for now, it was just her mom.

After signing the lease, they'd shopped for furniture and kitchenware and had spent the last several days unpacking and getting organized. There was still a ton to buy and to unpack, but her mom had a bed and a dresser, a couch and a TV. There was food in her cupboards and her refrigerator, so all the basics were there for her to start the next chapter of her life. They'd also gotten back the suitcases and boxes of family photos and personal papers that her dad had taken to the motel, so there were some memories that would soon be going up on display.

Since she and her mother had been together nonstop the past two weeks, she'd seen little of Jason. He was busy wrapping up all the details of the case, too, so aside from daily text messages and one evening when they'd shared a pizza with her mother, she'd seen little of him.

And she missed him. She missed him more than she'd thought she would. She'd tried to tell herself their intense relationship had to come to an end along with everything else, but she didn't want it to be the end. She just didn't know how he felt about it.

"This blanket goes perfectly with the couch," her mother said, drawing her gaze to the sofa where her mother had placed a rose-colored fluffy blanket on the gray couch. "It's girly, though. Your father might not love it."

"If you love it, he'll love it," she said dryly. "He adores you. And he feels so guilty about what happened to you that you could probably decorate this entire place in pink and buy him nothing but pink clothes, and he'd be fine with it."

Her mother smiled, looking so much like her old self that Alisa had to send up another silent prayer of thanks for her mom's recovery.

"I really want him home, Alisa. I know some of his decisions might have been wrong, but he didn't know what he was dealing with. By the way, I don't know if I told you this, but your father thinks the toxins that made me sick were probably in a fruit basket that I thought the library sent me for my ten-year anniversary. He didn't eat any of it because he's allergic to kiwi and mango, but I nibbled on it for several days straight."

"So if he'd eaten the fruit, he would have been sick, too."

"Yes, but he said that Novikov might have known he wouldn't touch those fruits."

"I guess we'll never know for sure since the house burned to the ground, but it does make sense that the poison was in the food and not in the air, at least not at your house. We know they used a different tactic at the hospital. Anyway, I want Dad home, too, and his lawyer says it looks good."

"What does Jason say?"

"He says it looks good, too," she said with a smile.

"I thought we might see more of Jason. You two seemed to have made a really strong connection."

"We went through a lot together, but he's busy, and I'm busy. And our lives are our own now. I'm not in danger. He doesn't have to protect me. We don't need to see each other every day." She shook her head at the gleam in her mother's eyes. "Mom, don't start matchmaking."

"I don't think I have to start. The two of you are already falling for each other. You like him, and he likes you. I saw that with my own eyes, not just when you were in danger, but the other night when we had pizza. The air was electric."

She laughed. "I wouldn't go that far." Although she and Jason had exchanged a very steamy goodbye kiss that night. But that had been four days ago, and they hadn't seen each other in person since then.

"Well, I like him, so I'm rooting for you two."

"Jason has been very up-front with me about how much he loves to work. He devotes himself to his job. He doesn't do relationships, and I don't think I could settle for anything less, not with him." She shook her head. "I thought maybe I could, but I can't. I'm too..."

"In love with him?" her mom finished.

"Well, I wasn't going to use that L word. It's too soon for me to be in love with him. Love takes time."

"Love doesn't take time. It's there, or it's not. Relationships —those take time, but if you don't have the feelings from the beginning, I don't think it ever works."

"You might be right," she admitted, glancing down at her phone as it buzzed with a text from Jason.

"Is that him?"

She looked up with a smile. "He wants to get together if I'm free."

"You're free. Go."

"We have so much to do here."

"You have more to do with him. I appreciate everything you've done for me, Alisa. You have helped in so many ways, and I am forever grateful you are my daughter. But it's time for you to get back to your life. And maybe it's time for you to also start a new chapter. You've had a tendency to bury yourself in work, too."

"I love you, Mom," she said, then hugged her mother and headed out the door.

It seemed to take forever to get to her apartment, even though it was only ten minutes away. Her mother had wanted to stay close to her, and tonight, she was very happy about that.

Jason was waiting for her in front of the building, looking as handsome as ever in a pair of jeans and a button-down shirt. His blue eyes sparkled in the moonlight, and his smile was so invitingly sexy that a shiver ran through her.

"You look good," he told her.

"Are you kidding? I've been moving and unpacking all day," she said, wishing she was wearing something sexier than jeans and a T-shirt.

"You look beautiful to me." He pulled her in for a quick kiss, then said, "Let's go upstairs."

She nodded, then unlocked the door, happy that the elevator was already waiting. A few moments later, they entered her apartment, and the door had barely closed before they were in each other's arms again, kissing each other with a hunger that couldn't be denied.

The desire that had been simmering in the background built into a hot, demanding flame, and she wanted to rip off her clothes and his, too.

But Jason was pulling away, putting some distance between them, giving her a ragged, breathless look that she couldn't decipher.

"We're stopping?" she questioned. "Because I thought we were just getting going."

"We need to talk."

Her gut twisted uneasily. "Those words don't usually mean anything good."

"This time they do," he promised.

"Okay. What are we talking about?"

"First, your father will be released tomorrow. There are contingencies and other restrictions, but he's going home to your mother."

A wave of relief ran through her. "I'm so glad. She misses him so much. Thank you for helping to make that happen."

"His actions played a significant role in the results. And what he will do going forward to help stop similar attacks is also part of the deal."

"No more teaching high school, I guess."

"He's going to work for Homeland Security and the FBI and whatever agencies need his expertise."

"That's great. Is that it? Because you said first..."

"There's a second," he said, pulling a piece of paper from his pocket. He handed it to her.

She stared down in confusion, wondering why he'd given her a colorful flyer of a beautiful hotel in Greece. "What's this?"

"The first place I want to go on vacation."

She raised her gaze to his, giving him a questioning look. "But you like to work. You don't take vacations."

"That's going to change. Everything is going to change, Alisa. I don't want to be a workaholic anymore. I don't want to focus only on the job. I want to participate in a relationship with someone I care very much about." He paused. "That's you, by the way."

Her heart skipped a beat. "You want a relationship with me?"

"Yes. You're an amazing woman: courageous, strong, loving, kind, sexy as hell...I can't imagine not being with you, Alisa."

"I've been trying to imagine that for the past two weeks, but it seems unbearable not being able to see you every day. You're an amazing man," she said, echoing his words. "Heroic, honest, and the way you kiss me..."

"That's all you, Alisa. You make me crazy."

"I'm right there with you. I want to go on vacation with you, and I want to have a relationship. I want it all."

"I want it all, too, and Flynn tells me I can have it. He offered me a permanent job with his team. He said his agents can have a work-life balance if they want it. And I want it. But mostly I just want you. I know it's fast. Our connection was forged in fire, in high-stakes drama. I may not seem so exciting in regular life. We can take things as slow as you want. Nothing has to be decided now."

"Are you kidding? I don't want to go slow. I want to go fast. I want to jump because I know you'll jump with me. You'll be there when I need you, and I'll be there when you need me." Happy tears gathered in her eyes as she finally let herself savor the fact that he felt exactly the same way she did. "When do we leave?"

"As soon as you can go. I told Flynn I'm taking a minimum

of six weeks off before I start working again, and he was fine with it. So, it's your call."

"I've been on temporary leave since I've been helping my mom rebuild her life. I'll extend it for six weeks. This is going to be so great. Where shall we go?"

"Wherever you want. It doesn't matter to me as long as we're together. Greece was just an idea."

"It doesn't matter to me, either. But let's start here."

"In Greece?"

"The vacation part, yes. That hotel looks awesome. But for the relationship part, I'm thinking here and now." She pulled off her T-shirt, loving the way his eyes lit up with desire.

"That works for me," he said as he unbuttoned his shirt.

She moved toward him. "We're going to be good together, Jason."

He gave her a loving smile. "We already are."

WHAT TO READ NEXT...

Want more thrilling romantic suspense?

Don't miss SHATTERED TRUTH,
the next book in the OFF THE GRID: FBI Series.

Have you missed any of the books in this series?

ABOUT THE AUTHOR

Barbara Freethy is a #1 New York Times Bestselling Author of 85 novels ranging from mystery thrillers to romantic suspense, contemporary romance, and women's fiction. With over 15 million copies sold, twenty-eight of Barbara's books have appeared on the New York Times and USA Today Bestseller Lists.

Barbara is known for her twisty thrillers and emotionally riveting romance where ordinary people end up having extraordinary adventures.

For further information, visit www.barbarafreethy.com

Printed in the USA
CPSIA information can be obtained
at www.ICGtesting.com
LVHW041547021024
792752LV00009B/144